A Heart's Desire

Solara Gordon

Published by THE EARTH MOVED, LLC, 2020.

A HEART'S DESIRE

First edition. January 23, 2020.

Copyright © 2020 Solara Gordon.

ISBN: 978-1733039451

Written by Solara Gordon.

When you know you've hit upon a story that tugs at your heart and mind, you don't write it. The story writes itself. That is what I experienced writing Parker and Angela's story. I hope you have as much fun reading their story as I did writing it.

Special thank you goes to:

Tom Crepeau, you helped flesh out parts of the story. Your insights and catches add depth and character.

Laura Hughes, your editing services and proofreading are awesome. Thank you for your assistance.

Da Bear, My heart and Life Partner, thank you for believing in me and taking the time to discuss, muse and hear about the adventures of writing this book.

And to my readers and Street Team (Solara's Glamourous Stars), this is the one you've been waiting for. Parker and Angela await to take you on a second chance at love adventure.

CHAPTER ONE

"Snow! It's April." Angela Sewald pushed back from her desk. Great, the night just slowed down even more. Graveyard shift at the town's urgent care facility didn't slow down often. Spring break—the one week that the nearby universities and schools closed and most of Peyton Corners left town. The ski resort stopped advertising, knowing that freak spring snowstorms missed more than hit this time of year. Ski season was over in people's minds. Folks headed to Asheville or farther south for sun and surf during spring break.

Angela walked toward the automatic door, moving right to avoid the electronic eye sensor. White puffs billowed and scattered close to the door. She shielded her eyes, letting her night vision kick in. Out across the lit portions of the parking lot, she could make out the drifts and accumulating piles. Windblasts rattled the front doors. Crap, the arctic air reached further south than predicted. Her garden wouldn't see warmth and green shoots for weeks thanks to winter lingering a bit longer.

"Snow. One of those four-letter words your Mom didn't tell you about." A male voice spoke behind her. She knew that voice, sultry, deep and tinged with a hint of Southern huskiness. She pressed her lips together as well as her legs. She didn't need to turn around to verify the man standing behind her. Parker Jones's six-foot-three height didn't go unnoticed. Everything about him caught her attention. From his riotous blond curls to his brown eyes that glowed when he smiled. He oozed confidence and expertise. His Emergency Medical Technician uniform hugged his body, accenting his ass, long legs and ...Angela shook out her hands, flexing them. Running her hands over the places Parker's uniform hugged him best was the tip of where her fantasies ran.

She turned around, moving away from the window and door. "Hey, Parker. Didn't know you were still here."

"Yeah. Doc Stillwell headed out to Mrs. Carmichael's. Her granddaughter's baby decided to arrive now." Parker walked across the lobby and dropped on to the couch against the outside wall. The dark circles under his eyes stood out against his fading tan. Back four days from his Hawaiian vacation and with his shift partner Mitch laid up with the flu, two days

1

of sixteen-hour shifts' toll showed. "And Mitch's wife is sick. His mother is helping out."

Angela sat down on the chair across from the couch. "Wow. That keeps you on call?"

"Help is supposedly en route. With the storm, who knows?" Parker combed his fingers through his hair. "I sent Mandy home forty-five minutes ago."

"Good, her husband is on the road. I know she doesn't like leaving her mom and dad alone."

"She called before I came in to check on things. Glad she made it before the brunt of this damn thing hit." Parker looked up, a small grin on his face. "Doc said if the storm worsened to close up and head home."

"How the hell are we supposed to do that?" Angela clapped her hand over her mouth. She swallowed hard and ducked her head. She owned an all-wheel drive SUV. She also knew the winter precautions. Full gas tank, emergency supplies and clothes in the back seat, along with blankets and pillows. That didn't help the icy road conditions if the county hadn't plowed or treated the roads. At the rate the snow fell, her driveway apron would be blocked and impassable. Holing up with her best friend Tricia wouldn't work. Tricia took off for Las Vegas three days prior and forgot to drop off her spare apartment key.

Parker chuckled. "Believe me, I wish I knew a better answer than 'carefully.'" He sat upright, leaning forward to rest his elbows on his legs. He snuck a glance at Angela. He wasn't a good judge of height in numbers. He knew she came up to his chest the times they'd stood side-by-side. She looked up at him and he tilted his head down to get a good view of her. The uniform scrubs she wore didn't reveal much of her build or curves. The one time he'd seen her in other than work clothes was the company Christmas party. Some of the women wore dresses. Angela and others wore blouses and pants. Her red and green top and black pants showed off her curves. Hugged 'em in all the right places, if she asked him. She hadn't. Mitch's wife had elbowed him more than once when she caught him gawking at Angela. Yes, she caught his attention often that evening. Especially during the two slow dances they'd shared. Angela felt nice against him as they danced. A pleasure he'd like to indulge in again, this time without the dancing. He looked down as Angela lifted her head.

"Carefully. Right," Angela scoffed. She stood and started back toward the reception desk. "You don't live outside of town, do you?"

Parker sighed. He hated townhouse living. His schedule didn't leave much time for hunting for a single-family home. Most he looked at were outside his price range or too far out. Tonight he was grateful he lived in town and not out along some of the rural roads leading out of town. Some of those folks might not get out for a week like with the blizzard two months ago. "No, I don't. Tonight I'm thankful I don't."

Angela walked over to the couch, looked at him and dropped down beside him. "Route Forty-Two is going to be icy and dicey. I don't know how I'm going to get in my drive."

"That's the section between the city and county line, isn't it?" Parker sat upright, moving over a bit so Angela could sit without brushing up against him. He enjoyed her brief touch as she sat down. He wished she hadn't scooted away so soon.

"Yes, I'm tired of calling both to get a plow out my way. Private party rates are killing my bank account." Angela turned sideways on the couch and faced him.

"Well," Parker began as the reception desk phone started ringing.

Angela hurried over to the desk, picking the phone up on the fourth ring. "Peyton Corners Urgent Care."

Parker scooted to the front of the couch and stood. He walked to the entrance. Looking out, he grimaced. Ten or more inches of snow covered the parking lot and sidewalk. He glanced toward the employee parking section, checking on his pickup when he caught part of Angela's conversation.

"Yes, Doc, it's still coming down. No, the relief help didn't arrive."

Parker made his way over to the desk. He leaned on it, listening to the rest of Angela and Doc's conversation. "Notify the hospital and answering service we're closed and head home. Got you, Doc."

Angela's gaze met his. She pressed her lips together holding the phone away from her. Doc kept talking. His next line had Parker moving around the desk and reaching for the phone.

Give me the phone, he silently mouthed. Angela squinted at him and shook her head. Doc's voice got louder. "Angela, you can get home, right?"

Parker voiced his earlier statement. "Give me the phone."

He held his hand out, closing the space between him and Angela.

"Hey, Doc," Parker started speaking loudly, pointing to his hand at the same time. "I'll get Angela home or she'll stay with me."

"Not necessary," Angela countered.

Parker pried the receiver from Angela's hand and spoke again, holding the receiver to his ear. "Don't worry, Doc. I'll make sure we're ok. You take care of Mrs. Carmichael and the new grandbaby."

Parker waited for Doc's reply. A loud crackle and pop sounded, followed by silence. He handed the receiver to Angela. "Hang it up and see if our line works. I'm getting my jacket from my locker."

Angela hung up the receiver and started to turn. Parker moved behind her toward the doorway leading to the exam rooms and lab area. He paused at the door, turning back to her.

"Sorry for the caveman tactics. Bad roads mean we're gonna get one place and hole up. Make your decision. Either your place or mine." Parker pushed the door open until it clicked against the doorjamb leaving it open.

Angela licked her lips, blinked, and fisted her hands. Accepting his help didn't mean she gave up her independence. Parker was right. They'd get one place. Where was up to her.

She took her fanny pack out of the bottom desk drawer and laid it on the desk. She touched the speaker button on the phone base as she reached for the second set of keys attached to her pack. Crackles of static and loud hums rolled out of the speaker. She turned the speaker off and started locking her desk and file cabinets.

As she turned back to her desk, Parker came through the open door with his jacket over his arm. "Ready?"

"Almost. Give me ten more minutes." She took the other key fob off her pack. "Gotta get my coat and use the restroom."

"Ok. I'll meet you out front." Parker started putting his jacket on. "Make it five if you can. Got a text from Mitch saying it's whiteout conditions in places."

Angela nodded and trotted down the hall muttering. "Like I needed help making up my mind. Thanks a lot, Mother Nature!"

Parker smiled as he zipped his down jacket. Until they got on the road, nothing was final. He preferred his place since it was fifteen minutes away on a good day. Tonight might take forty-five to fifty. If Angela insisted on her place, he'd get them there weather permitting. For now, he needed to brush off his truck and check on Angela's SUV. He wanted to get her parked under the overhead awning closer to the building. It'd make digging her vehicle out after the storm.

He pulled on his black knit watch cap and quilted ski gloves. He glanced down the hall as he reached the entrance. The door started to slide open. A blast of arctic air blew in along with several snowflakes. He tugged the jacket sleeve cuffs down over his gloves. The air reminded him of his rescue training class on Mount St. Helen. Half up the slopes in early March with the winds blowing thirty to forty knots, the chill frosted their breath and a few pairs of glasses. Thank goodness, the instructor cancelled the campout or it would have taken until July for him to thaw out. He missed South Carolina's warm winters. Didn't miss them enough to move back and have his family hanging around his neck. Being the middle child cut down on the grief he got as a kid, but as an adult, he wished his mother would stop hinting about grandchildren or planning another wedding. Damn, she and her sisters were a competitive lot. He smiled as he stepped outside. He loved his family a lot. A bit of distance between them helped him have a life of his own, not one of their making.

The door slid closed behind him. He stood still, waiting for his eyes to adjust. The front of the building faced the street. To his left the uncovered parking area for patients took up most of the front and side portion of the building. On the right, the four handicapped spots along with seven employee parking spaces were under the covered awning. At the back of the building was an old garage that housed the ambulance and Doc's car when he was on duty. He squinted, looking toward the street. He couldn't make out a tire track. The few remaining ones in the parking lot were under the awning from when Mandy pulled out. At the rate the snow fell, getting to his place looked more doable than trying to make the drive to Angela's. He glanced back toward the door. He hoped Angela had boots with her. Getting her stuff into his truck was going to take both of them.

Angela double-knotted her hiking boots and stood. She took one last look around the reception area. Her coat, scarf, and hat lay on the couch. Her tote bag with her work shoes and uneaten lunch sat next to it. Her extra cell phone charger was in her coat pocket where she had stuffed it on her way out the door. The answering service said they would take care of notifying the hospital. Both had conference-called her cell to confirm everyone knew what was going on. She pulled on her quilted coat and wrapped her scarf around her neck. As she fastened her fanny pack around her waist, Parker came back in.

He stomped his feet, getting some of the snow clinging to him off. He looked up and spoke. "It's getting worse. Wind is picking up. I hope you aren't planning on getting home."

Angela pulled her crocheted hat on and finished zipping her coat close. She walked to the window and looked out. Snow swirled in batches, settled and blew again, creating another whiteout. She turned to Parker, waited until his gaze met hers. She wet her lips and spoke. "Not now. My downhill drive is iced and covered. I wouldn't chance it."

Parker nodded. "Hope you don't mind sharing my place for a few days. Let's get your stuff into my truck."

Angela walked back to the couch. She picked up her tote and started back toward the door. "In the back seat are my duffel bag, a small cooler, and a backpack."

"What can't go in the cap on the back of the truck?" Parker joined her at the door, holding out his hand. "I'll take your tote bag. I'll pull my truck up alongside your SUV."

"All of it can. Cooler has food and water in it. The duffel has clothes and the backpack has toiletries and a flannel blanket." Angela turned as Parker came up alongside her. "Survival stuff. The other stuff is in the back near the rear hatch."

"Other stuff?" Parker looked at her, his eyebrows raised.

Angela grinned. "Pillow and afghan. Additional warmth. An extra pair of boots."

"Essentials for sure. We'll take it with us." He took a hold of the tote handle and continued speaking. "I took my camping gear out of the truck last night. Thought about heading out to fish over the weekend. Glad I didn't go."

"I heard Mitch tell his wife your place has a wood burning stove. If electric and heat goes out, we may be camped out in front of it." Angela put on her gloves. "It isn't a gas one, is it?"

"Burns wood or pellets. I've got enough wood on hand to last several days. Pellets too. We'll get by." Parker started out the door and stopped. He turned back, faced her, smiling. "Question is can you rough it?"

"Don't underestimate this California girl. My parents believed in teaching us how to survive and respect the land. I'm a farmer's daughter." Angela walked past Parker, wondering what prompted her to let that part of her past out.

She wasn't ashamed of her family or their values. Living out in the country close to off the grid left her feeling alone, vulnerable, and estranged from many of her classmates and the few friends she had. A few years after her Grandpa Will passed away, she began to understand why he chose the life he did. Her affluent paternal grandparents wanted to shower her with money and privilege. None of which the rural farm community had. Everyone worked alongside each other like they did here at the clinic. People valued people, not things. Angela turned the brim of her hat down and her coat collar up. She hoped Parker's reception of her information didn't turn icy.

"Good to know. You won't mind helping out with cooking?" Parker asked as he moved up beside her. "I'm good at breakfast and a few dinner dishes."

Angela laughed. "I hate packaged food. Too much salt and chemicals."

"My sister's allergies required home cooking until she outgrew them. Short cuts saved me from takeout and fast food." Parker pointed at a truck across the parking lot. "I'll pull up beside you in a couple of minutes."

Parker started walking away from her. Angela watched him take one cautious step after another, all the while holding her Betty Boop tote in one hand. Other men would have left her holding the bag. Not bother asking about helping out, either. Nurses at the hospital said Parker was different. Two of his past dates confided he was a perfect gentleman the few times he went out with them. Angela pressed her lips together and started making her way to her SUV. Gossip didn't happen much around Peyton Corners. Too many people knew each other to let malingering rumors or tales run amok. The truthful tales got nipped in the bud by the churchwomen who read the tattle rag sheets they picked up at the supermarket two towns over like it was the national news.

Parker pulled his keys from his pants pocket. Glad for their warmth from his body heat, he worked the door key into the lock and slowly turned it. A click sounded and the inside lock popped up. He exhaled, noting how his breath fogged. Opening the door, he offered a quick prayer hoping his guardian angel wasn't on break. He tossed Angela's tote on to the passenger seat and climbed in. The door banged shut as he put the key into the ignition and pumped the gas pedal. Silence greeted him. He pumped the gas pedal again. He turned the key again and the engine sputtered. It coughed and wheezed, then revved into its familiar purring hum. Parker smiled. He fastened his seatbelt and put the truck into gear. He inched his way across the parking lot until he eased into the parking space next to Angela's SUV. The truck's headlights spotlighted Angela's ass as she leaned into the open door getting something out of the back seat. He swallowed, wishing his mind would focus elsewhere and not on being snowed in with the woman, he fantasized about more than once.

CHAPTER TWO

Angela straightened up once he parked. Her hat hung sideways on her head. She looked like she tussled with something and won the skirmish. Parker snorted. Humor would get him through for a while. Could he keep his thoughts on civilities once they reached his place? Keeping them there while he drove wasn't a problem. He didn't daydream and drive. Given how icy the parking lot was, his driving would take all his attention. Angela would understand without much explanation. Another positive in her favor.

Parker slid across the driver's seat until he could put both feet out on the snow-covered asphalt. Skating wasn't one of his more graceful sport attempts. He grinned as the image of his kid sister skating circles around him at the local ice rink came to mind. Tonight he wasn't trying to rival her in any way.

He swept one foot back and forth, testing for ice and snow packing. The sole of his boot dragged and scraped across the fallen flakes. Good, he didn't need to grip the truck for balance like he had before. He stood up and stepped forward taking half his normal stride. Moving fast would have him on his ass and cussing. While the thought of Angela rubbing liniment across his back and hips ignited a warm streak in his groin, other thoughts required his attention. Like watching where Angela was and loading the truck. Snow fell thicker than when he'd first gone out to check on his truck. If they didn't get on the road soon, making it to his place would take on snow-covered ice.

He reached the overhang of the carport as another blast of wind pushed snow off it. "Damn, that's cold," he cussed, reaching up to dust his head and hat off. "Gonna need a quick shower to warm up at this rate."

"If the electric holds out." Angela handed him the basket she held. "One reason I invested in solar panels."

"My townhouse co-op did the same last year." Parker moved to the back of the truck and opened the cap. He set the basket inside. "Came in handy when the last blizzard hit. Nice to have even lukewarm water available."

"Last freaky spring storm took three days to dig out." Angela went back to her vehicle and came back with two more bags. "Wonder how long it'll take this time."

Parker tipped his head back and squinted at the sky. "Well, I think. . ." Another blast of wind blew snow off the carport roof at him. "Ok! I get it, don't guestimate old man winter's stay."

Angela's laughter sounded behind him. He glanced over his shoulder. "Hiding?"

"No. Keeping the snow off me. You're doing a good job at it too." She grinned at him and stepped around him. "Would you get the body bag out of the rear please?"

"Body bag?" Parker shut the SUV's door and moved to the rear hatch.

"Yes, large bag that holds a lot of stuff. Not made for regular bodies." Angela stuck her tongue out as she faced him, holding out her hand. A beep sounded.

He walked over to her, glancing down at her hand. The outside lights glimmered off the set of keys she held. He reached for them——

"Damn, what the hell?" He wrapped his hand around Angela's. "Guess we don't have to worry about the exterior lights."

Angela's chortle told him she hadn't moved. Good. He waited until his vision adjusted, glad he'd left the truck running and the headlights on. "Can you see all right? Make it to the truck?"

"Yes," Angela replied, moving closer to him. "Stash the body bag in the cap. Hatch is unlatched. Can I get in on your side?"

"Sorry bucket seats." Parker carefully stepped back. He turned, blinking as his night vision kicked in more. The partially open hatch came into view. He moved forward. Step, shuffle, test for ice and step again. Ten steps later, he was at the SUV.

"Do I need your keys to lock it?" he called out, lifting the hatch completely open.

"No, keyless remote."

"Ok." He grabbed the body bag and pulled it to him. "Is this it? What's in it?"

"Yes. My other boots and extra gear." Angela called back.

Parker lifted the bag up on to his shoulder and closed the hatch. As he turned, a beep and the click of locks sounded. He followed his path back to the truck. As he passed Angela, he spoke. "Heard the locks click. I'll be back in a minute."

Angela watched Parker disappear around the back of the truck. Watching him lift the bag got to her. Knowing his muscular build and how his uniform hugged him when he moved certain ways set off warmth that she wished her face, hands, and feet felt. The temperature must have dropped more while they were loading her stuff.

She shielded her eyes as she made her way around the front of truck. The headlights gave off enough light for her to easily make out the end of the carport. More snow flew off the hood of the truck as she stepped out into the windblasts sending swirling snow around her. Step-swipe-step-swipe like she'd seen Parker do. Ice loved to find her and a bruised ass was always the prize. She wasn't going there tonight. Two more steps and she had the passenger door open. Heat rolled out greeting her as she opened the door more. Gripping the interior handle, she eased her way around the door and tossed her tote on the floor. She let go of the door handle, reaching for the overhead grab bar.

A loud clunk sounded, followed by metal latching closed. "Hold on," Parker called out. "I'll help you get in."

"Thanks. I can do it," Angela called back, lifting one foot up, ready to step into the cab.

"Yeah, I'm sure," Parker replied close to her.

Angela startled and jumped, falling backwards, her arms flailing as she tried to catch her balance. "What the hell?" she yelled, her feet sliding different directions. Frack, so much for getting one up on ice and avoiding a bruised ass.

"Got ya," Parker said, tight to her. She drooped against Parker, her head practically lying on his chest. Dignity and coordination drained out of her faster than a lit match could start a fire.

"Sorry," she murmured, raising her head.

Parker smiled down at her. He reached down, patted her cheek. "Don't sweat it. I caught you off-guard."

"Yeah," she replied, trying to stand up. "Let me get my footing. I found the ice we're trying to avoid."

Parker's chuckle warmed her cheek. "Bound to be some. Wind isn't warming things up."

Angela nodded and squinted as she looked down. "I think if you upright me and let me grab the door, I can get in."

"How about this instead?" Parker asked, scooping her up in his arms and sitting her on the passenger seat. "Quick and easy. Height and dexterity beats out wind and ice."

Angela grinned. "Thanks. Be careful getting in yourself."

Parker gave her a quick salute and closed the passenger door. She watched him carefully make his way around the truck, leaning on the hood with both hands, ducking as the wind buffeted him several times. A few minutes later, he pulled open the driver's door, jumping in. "Damn, that wind's got a nasty bite to it."

Parker turned, gripped the door handle with both hands, and yanked. Wind whipped around the door trying to send its icy fingers up his pant leg. He pulled harder until he slammed the door shut. He looked at Angela. She flashed him another grin and gave him a thumbs-up.

"All right. Seatbelt fastened?" he asked, fastening his.

"Yes. We're heading to my place or yours?"

"I know your place is closer. It's level roads to mine," Parker continued, "Best option is my place."

Angela didn't respond. He laid his hand on Angela's arm and asked, "Are you okay?"

Angela turned, nodding. "Yes, I'm fine. Trying to remember another way around the hairpin turn on to Main Street.'

"I know one through a couple back streets. Bet they aren't plowed." He put the truck in reverse and slowly backed up.

"Guess we'll figure something out when we get there," Angela said as he glanced in the rearview mirror. Large flakes of snow fell faster than when they first came out. They needed to make it to his place soon or they'd end up stuck out on the road somewhere. Ten minutes later, they were at the end of the parking lot entrance, ready to turn on to the highway. Parker glanced at Angela again. "My place, here we come."

"Yes," Angela replied. "Let's get there safe and sound."

Parker snorted as he eased on to the highway. "And no idiots out joyriding either."

Snow flew as he slowed for the first of five traffic lights at the outer edge of downtown. Stopping for whiteout conditions had cost them extra time, and driving blind wasn't an option. He'd rolled down his window twice to see if there was oncoming traffic at two of the crossroads he had planned on using. He glanced at the dashboard clock. Shit, forty minutes had passed. It took them forty minutes to drive what he covered in ten minutes in decent weather. If plows had gone through, there wasn't any evidence showing. Parker glanced at Angela. "I think we're going to have to negotiate the hairpin turn. If I take it slow and easy we should make it."

Angela nodded. "Halfway through the first part of the turn is the opening to Mama Lucia's parking lot. If we go through it, we come out on the second half of the turn which puts us closer to Main St."

"Yes," he said, easing the truck into the intersection as the light changed. "The lot is behind two office buildings. A level snow-covered lot is better than dealing with that tight turn across Fox Creek bridge."

"As my dad use to say, straight and narrow can be a good option." Angela glanced at him, grinning. "His grandpa was a minister."

Parker chuckled. "Hellfire and damnation type?"

"Only when needed. Great-grandpa could pulpit-bang with the best of them. He did the revival tent circuit in his twenties. Meeting grandma and falling in love settled him down."

"Sounds like your great grandpa was a character." He held up his hand as they came to the next traffic light. "I'm gonna need your help. I can't watch the street signs and keep my eye on the road."

"Great grandpa was." Angela rolled down her window, reached up and took a hold of the grab handle. "No cars coming. I hear faint beeps."

"Plow probably down the road. Is this Wilson East?"

Angela leaned against the door, squinting. "Yes. I can make out part of the road is plowed. One lane wide."

"All right. Here we go." Parker started turning into the lane. Angela kept watching where the headlights shined, noting how close they came to drifted and plowed snow.

"Ease it to the left. Drift on your right." Angela gripped the grab bar tighter.

"Thanks." Parker maneuvered the truck left and right until they were center of the lane. He let go a short shrill whistle. "Damn, I hope we're closer than I think."

Angela grinned even though Parker couldn't see her. "Yes. Two buildings down on the left is where the parking lot begins."

"Got ya. You watch too, okay?"

Angela rolled up her window, turned a bit in her seat. "Definitely. Mama leaves a bright red light on near the back door. It should stand out even in this."

Parker's chuckle reached out to her, embracing her in its warmth and comfort. Her grin deepened. She rubbed her lips together. If they got across the parking lot and out on to Main Street, the rest of their drive should be easier.

"Red light, here we come." Parker inched the truck forward. "Crack your window and listen for the plow truck. We don't want to run into each other."

"Right," she said, opening her window again. "I'm beginning to think I hate snow."

"Climate we anticipate. Weather is what we get."

"Never expected snow like this three weeks into spring." Angela tapped the windshield. "There's the red light." She glanced at Parker.

"See it. Where are the buildings?"

"First one coming up. You'll see a break between them. Keep going. When you see the light clearly. Entrance is nearby."

Parker cleared his throat. "See clearly. *Right.*"

"Well, better than we see it now." Angela let go of the grab bar, leaned toward Parker, and put her hand on his arm. "I'll guide you as best I can."

"*We'll* do our best." Parker slowed the truck, glanced at her and nodded. "First building counted."

They crept past the second building as a burst of wind blasted through their open windows. "Damn, that's cold," Parker cussed.

"Sure shit is," Angela said, chafing her arms. "Parts of the guardrails marking the entrance are sticking up."

"I see them. Here we go." Parker put on the left turn signal and started across the road, easing into the space between the guardrails.

Ten minutes passed before either of them spoke. Angela rubbed her gloved hand across the partially fogged windshield. "I think we're mid-parking lot."

"I agree." Parker put the truck in park. He rolled up his window and faced Angela. "Roll your window up. Let's get warm before we start moving again."

Angela rolled up her window, took her gloves off, and held them out close to the heat vent near her. "How much farther to your place?"

"About a mile down Main Street past Wooster Lane. Wind's died down some. Maybe we'll make better time." He turned in the seat. Angela's gaze met his. Neither of them looked away.

Silence mixed with the ping of ice pellets hitting the truck filled the cab. He pulled his gloves off, stuck them in his jacket pocket, and held his hand out palm up. "Put your hand on mine. I'll warm 'em between mine."

Angela looked away first. She slowly raised her arm, reaching toward him. Neither of them spoke as she laid her cold palm on his. He laid his other over hers, pressing up and down lightly. Each time he pressed against her, he felt her pulse. Slow, steady and strong. A faint flutter caught his attention and vanished until he pressed again. He looked up, catching her watching him. His pulse sped up. Need to take her in his arms, press his lips to hers, and reassure her flooded his mind and ego.

"Thanks." Angela pulled her hand out from between his.

"Welcome. Your other one too." He pointed at Angela's gloved hand.

She nodded. Pulled her glove off and placed her hand between his.

He repeated his actions and let go. "Give me both hands, palms together."

"Why?" she asked, holding up her hands, palms together.

"Chafing them will add warmth." He covered her hands again with his and rubbed. Warmth flowed off him on to her. It continued up over his wrists and along his forearms, working spirals as it inched its way toward his center right where his male urge awaited ignition.

Parker took his upper hand away, raised Angela's hands to his lips and kissed each knuckle. He tested for warmth and reaction. She jerked and began pulling back. "Wait," he said, gripping her wrist as best he could. "Need to test the other."

She lowered her top hand, turned the one over until her palm lay against his. He rubbed his lips over her knuckles and kissed each as he worked his way back across. He let go and faced the windshield. If her pulse was any indication, he affected Angela like she affected him. He got to her and she him.

Wind blasted against the truck, rattled the hood and shook it from side to side. Angela pulled her gloves back on. "Thank you. I think we best get going."

Parker put the truck into gear and started across the parking lot. He could make out the edges of the buildings where the exit onto Main was. The traffic light hanging over it swung back and forth with almost the same force as the last hurricane winds he'd dealt with. Not good. Wind shears would make drifting and blowing more prevalent. "Yes. The wind's picked up."

"No kidding. That light is swinging fast and furious. We need to get out of here before it comes crashing down." Angela took another swipe across the windshield with her gloved hand.

"I'll go as fast as safety allows." Parker pressed on the gas pedal a bit more, gripping the steering wheel tighter at the same time.

Forward they crept, the steering wheel trying to turn a different direction with each windblast battering them. He hunched forward, pressed on the gas pedal more and prayed. Timing their exit and turn onto Main needed precision he couldn't stop to calculate.

Fifteen minutes of fighting the wind, ice and blowing snow brought them to the edge of the parking lot. He pumped the brake, turned the high beam lights on and snuck a quick glance at Angela. She sat hunched forward much like him, looking straight ahead. Her hand wiped the foggy interior glass. She tapped the glass as she spoke. "A few more feet and we're there."

As if the heavens heard his prayer, took a liking to him, or old man winter decided to take a break, the wind died down. The traffic light halted part of its violent back-and-forth swinging. Parker wasn't bothering to ask what happened. He knew and words weren't needed. They'd gotten a break and he was taking it. "Hang on, we're going out."

CHAPTER THREE

Yanks and jerks of the steering wheel kept them from skidding across the road as the truck hit a patch of ice. Parker looked in the rearview mirror as he straightened the truck. Zigzag tire treads marked their path out of the parking lot and onto Main. Parker leaned back against the seat, heaving a sigh.

"I agree," Angela replied. "I hope we get to your place soon. I'd say we earned a stiff drink."

Parker snorted. "I'm for heat, washing up, and food. My stiff drink is hot chocolate with a shot of flavored coffee cream."

"Hope there's enough hot water."

"Well, we might have to share." Parker glanced at Angela, grinned as she shook her head. He added, "Five minute showers with each of us ready to wet soap and rinse."

"Been there. Done that. Remember, I've got practice living off the grid," Angela countered.

"Well, you may get to put it to use. We may be camping out indoors for the next few days." Parker pressed on the gas, causing the truck's tires to spin. "Hang on. I'm gunning it a bit."

He applied more gas. The truck jerked forward, flinging snow in the air behind them. Spinning of tires sounded as he tried applying more gas. "Open your window. Listen for when we get off the ice."

Angela rolled down her window and leaned out, looking toward the back of the truck. "We're almost clear. I'd take it easy on gunning it. Don't know if there's more ice in front of us."

"Right," Parker said, taking his foot off the gas pedal. He applied the brake, shifted the truck into second gear and pushed on the gas pedal. The tires spun. Ice and snow flew in the air and the truck jerked forward several feet.

"Looks clear from here," Angela pointed at the side mirror.

"Good," Parker said. "A mile and half to my place. I hope it's not an hour away."

Forty-five minutes later, Parker pulled up to the garage of his two-story townhouse. The outside lights flickered, dimmed and came back on, illuminating rows of parked cars. Several snow-covered cars sat in the additional parking areas close to the entrance to the complex. He pushed the garage door remote. Snow sprayed into the air as the door rose, spiraled around as wind caught it before settling on drifts and piles close to the edge of the short driveway. He pulled in, turned off the ignition and faced Angela. "Anything that you can leave in the truck?"

"Why do you ask?" Angela asked, unfastening her seatbelt.

"Two sets of stairs up and back down." Parker opened his door, hit the remote button and closing the garage door. "So what do you absolutely need tonight?"

"Food needs go up. Clothes and blankets." Angela opened her door and got out. "My backpack. I'll consolidate what I need in the body bag."

"All right," Parker said, exiting the truck. "I can carry some things too. I took my camping gear inside last night."

He started toward the door, stopped and turned back. "What is in your body bag?"

Angela laughed. "Towels and a couple of old afghans. Why?"

"It might be our best option to move a lot of stuff up all at once." He started toward the door again as the lights flickered, dimmed, and darkness engulfed them. "What a damn time for the lights to go out."

"Stay put," Angela called out. "I've got a flashlight we can use. Hang on."

Parker opened his mouth, ready to reply, when a cold hand touched his arm. Chills swept up and over him. He jerked and pulled, trying to get away.

"Hey. It's me," Angela said. A beam of light illuminated a spot on the floor near his feet.

"Sorry," Parker offered. "Kid sister pranked me by sneaking up on me in the dark a lot."

Angela snickered. "Older brother loved spooking me and my middle sister. Mom got him good though."

"Oh? How so?" Parker accepted the flashlight she pressed into his hand.

"He hated snakes. She tucked him in on a campout telling him to watch for snakes as she saw a few around the tent. Lights went out and my brother started screaming. Mom had put a dozen rubber snakes in the bottom of his sleeping bag."

Parker groaned. "Man, you traumatized him. Your mom was mean."

"Nah, she helped him dump them out and explained that it could have been a real snake. He needed to check and not just accept."

Parker heard Angela walk away. "Don't you need the flashlight?"

"Nope. Got one in my pocket." A thin beam of light arced through the air. "I learned from his experience too. I *always* carry a flashlight with me. Never know when you may need one."

"Yeah, snakes can be anywhere." Parker walked over to the door, shining the flashlight on the lock as he fumbled with his keys.

"Got ya. I've got my backpack on. Clothes, blankets and food in body bag. My other stuff can make it up in daylight."

"Good. I'll get mine after I unlock the door." Parker moved to his left, shining the flashlight ahead of him. He took a hold of the cold door handle, inserted his key and listened. The click of the key unlocking the lock had him almost grinning. Out of the storm and amongst his familiar things—home. The place where he felt secure and safe. Would Angela feel the same way if they were snowed in for a few days? Bright light momentarily blinded him. He blinked and yelled. "Hot damn. Light exists. Heat too ,I think."

"Great," Angela said coming up behind him. "Let's get upstairs while the lights work."

Parker took his backpack from her, put it on and he held the door open with his foot. "Cap hatch down and locked? You checked the cab for all your stuff?"

"Yes," Angela said, slinging the strap of the body bag over her head and on to her opposite shoulder. "You want to check the cap and truck before we go up?"

Parker hesitated, handed her the flashlight as he started to move away from the door. "Double checking never hurts."

She grabbed for the door. "I've got the door. And the flashlight." She shined the light in the direction of the truck.

She heard the jingle of keys, Parker muttering to himself, and the click of the cab door locks. He walked back to her, holding his hand out.

"What do you want?" She started to hand him the flashlight.

"Body bag. I can carry it easier than you can. No offense. I'm used to heavy lifting all day." Parker didn't lower his hand.

Angela shifted her feet, ready to say no as she moved into the small hall leading to the stairs. Several narrow steps greeted her. "Do the steps get any better?"

"Past the first, yes." Parker took a hold of the body bag strap. "I'm fine with carrying this."

Angela faced him. "I yield. I'd be too busy watching my feet instead of bounding up the steps."

Parker raised the strap off her shoulder. "Duck your head. You a stair watcher, eh?"

Angela nodded as she straightened her neck. "From way back. Slipped on a throw rug at my grandma Fiona's, slid on my ass across the waxed floor and tumbled down six steps."

"Ouch." Parker slipped the body bag strap over his head. "Go ahead of me. You can shine the flashlight if needed."

"Yup," Angela said clicking the flashlight off and hooking it on her fanny pack. "Bruised my ass, my legs and my ego."

Parker chuckled. "Please don't do that tonight. We need to get *us* up these steps safely."

"Top priority," Angela called out, reaching the top of the first set of stairs. "You weren't kidding about two flights of steps. I'm getting my cardio."

Parker waited until Angela started up the next flight before taking the first set of steps two at a time. As he reached the landing, he paused, watching Angela take the steps one at a time, placing her foot on the middle of each step. Her hips swayed as she stepped and moved. He'd caught her bending over, picking something up off the floor at work a couple weeks earlier. Her plump ass and hips set his hormones raging and his mind imagining how deep he could penetrate her in that position. Some women liked the feel of a man pumping in and out of her with a rhythm that had his balls slapping against them. Boney women were harder to hang on to with them bent over. With Angela, he'd give it a try. She had padding he wouldn't mind bumping up against. Then there was anal. Tried it. Wasn't wild about it. Some women were. Others were ok with it. Some looked at him like he'd lost his mind. He was going to lose himself in the traipse up the stairs watching the lush pert ass ahead of him.

Angela paused at the top of the second flight. She glanced back at him, rolled her eyes, and unzipped her coat. "Getting energized and invigorated too. Cool air feels good."

Parker stepped up on the landing next to Angela. "For sure. I'm up and down these stairs twice a day. Sometimes more."

Angela laughed. "We're both generating heat." She fanned herself. "Can't say we'll mind the crisp cool air if the heat is off."

Parker moved past Angela into the interior of his darkened living room. He hadn't planned to be back until daybreak when his night shift was over. Now he needed to find the light switch. He unzipped his coat, pushed up his sleeves and slid the body bag strap over his head and off his shoulder. "Stay put for a moment. I gotta find the light switch."

"You mean this?" Angela asked. Soft light flooded the living room. "Hope there's some warm water to wash up with."

"I can heat water on the wood stove. No problem." Parker dropped the body bag where he stood, shielding his eyes. "Thanks. Stairs to second level are along the back wall. Kitchen is to your left."

A loud rumble, sputter and hiss sounded. Angela looked around the living room. "What the hell?"

Parker pulled off his jacket. "Generator. Maintenance man lives in the end unit. The generator keeps baseboard heat running to keep pipes from freezing."

"Frozen pipes are hell to deal with. And Insurance companies love to deny your claim." Angela moved toward the couch, slipping her backpack off.

"They sure do. The complex owner put generators in for each triplex." Parker tossed his coat on the chair closest to him. "Maintenance may check on us if the storm lulls."

"Good to know." Angela took off her coat and laid it next to Parker's. "I'll put the food away. I've got sandwich makings. You hungry? I am."

"Could eat. You got any of your sweet pickle relish with you?" Parker started toward the kitchen. "Can you wait on washing up? I've got to get some camping gear out of my storage area off the balcony."

"Yes. Food comes first way my stomach is growling. How about hot water for tea? Ham and cheese sandwiches, okay?"

"Microwave is best option while electric is still on. Coffee carafe is in the drainer left side of sink. Ham and cheese is good." Parker slid open one of the patio doors. "Be back in a moment."

Angela filled the carafe, put it in the microwave and set the timer. She took her cooler out of the body bag and set it on the counter. The small kitchen reminded her of her first apartment after college. The small one bedroom rented for more than a third of her monthly pay. San Francisco was like that. High rents and exciting places to explore like the piers and restaurants in the tourist areas. Waiting tables had supplemented her income and paid for part of her grad school courses in medical assistance. Running a medical office took knowledge and expertise the local free clinic provided during her volunteer tenure. And look where it got her. . .snowbound with a hot hunk. Not a bad return given her possible other outcomes. Snowed in with a forlorn cat and a box of trashy romance novels from the sixties her mother recently sent her. No, even if nothing happened, live company was better than solitary for her.

She found plates in the cabinet closest to her and silverware in the drawer next to the dishwasher. Simple easy sandwiches with a few cookies and hot decaf tea would fill their stomachs. Parker wanted some of her relish. She smiled as she added a small dollop to his ham and cheese sandwich.

Her mother firmly believed the way to a man's heart was via his stomach. Angela tittered as she made her sandwich. Memories of her father chewing antacids after a few of her mother's meals flashed through her mind. Mom's cooking attempts at ethnic dishes sometimes missed the mark. She'd learned that easy on the spices was well worth it when it came to cooking. Parker had talked about his mom's homemade watermelon pickles at two company cookouts. She'd offered him a taste of her sweet pickle relish handed down from her grandma's great aunt. The rest as they say was like at first taste. And the kiss on the cheek she got when he found out she brought a jar for him to the last cook out. Since then, Parker had hung around more and sought her out. Maybe he was interested like Tricia said. Even her sister said if the man walked up and gave her a hickey, she'd still wonder if he was truly interested. Of course, her last hickey was back in high school outside the gym after a basketball game. Coach had caught them and her parents hadn't let her go out unchaperoned for three weeks.

Parker slid the patio door open letting in an icy blast of wind along with snowflakes dancing in the air until they settled on the floor, melting as they landed. He motioned her to him. "Need your help with the air mattress and pump. We're better off sleeping down here close to the wood stove."

Angela put her sandwich on the plate next to the one she made for Parker. She grabbed a paper towel and wiped her hands off. "Sure. How can I help?"

Parker held out a large tote bag. 'Take this and put it in the living room. I'll bring in the air mattress.'

Angela took a hold of the tote. Her hand brushed against Parker's. Warmth stronger than when they touched in the truck surged over her hand, up her wrist and curled around her arm inching its way upward until—she moved her hand away. Hots. . .she had to get them for the one person she never expected to be. . .she took a breath, looked away and acknowledged the feelings welling up inside her from the moment she knew where she'd end up for the next few hours or days. Parker was with her, taking care of her, and she him. They were talking about more than work or the latest schedule issues or anything other than themselves. He hadn't turned away when she'd mentioned her upbringing. There was something going on. Maybe this was the connection her siblings kept talking about—the one thing she didn't know how to make happen.

"Damn, it's cold out there. And I think it's going to get colder before the night's over." Parker tugged the large plastic bag through the patio door, stepped around it and closed the door. He locked it and pulled the blinds shut. Rubbing his arms, he looked toward the living room. The wood stove sat near the back outside wall. Heat radiated outward, warming the room and rising to other parts of the townhouse as circulation permitted. The flue and outside vent allowed for ventilation and control of the air flux within the stove. Tonight's wind meant he'd have to burn a low flame and check on it throughout the night. Another reason he wanted them sleeping downstairs.

"You're probably right," Angela said, reentering the kitchen. "Let's eat while we've got light."

Parker sat on the stool at the end of the eat-in bar. "Yeah. I need to get the stove lit too." He pointed to the sandwich close to him. "Yours or mine?"

"Yours. Microwave buzzed as you came in. I've got decaf tea bags and sweetener. Homemade chocolate chip cookies too." Angela took the carafe out of the microwave and filled the two mugs she'd put on the counter.

"I'm going to light the kindling in the stove. Then finish my sandwich. Tea sounds good too. Homemade cookies?" Parker took a bite of his sandwich and put it on the plate close to him.

"Another of my many talents. Home cooking from scratch instead of boxes. Though I do that from time to time too." Angela looked up at him, grinning as she handed him a tea bag.

Parker took the tea bag, put it in his mug and moved away from the counter. "Sleeping down here is our best option. I can keep an eye on the stove and we're warmer."

He opened the cabinet next to the fridge and took out a box of matches. "Air mattress and sleeping bags is an option." He glanced at Angela before he exited the kitchen. She hadn't asked about the bag he'd brought in. Was she curious or being polite about not asking? Lord, his mother had scolded him about that a few times as a kid. One vital thing he learned in EMT training was ask questions. Ask lots of them. He'd gotten used to being quizzed, questioned and grilled. It came with the job and it became part of him. Angela knew the drill too. It was second nature to her as well. What was going through her mind?

CHAPTER FOUR

Parker picked up several sheets of newspaper off the coffee table. Forgetting to put the last two days' newspapers in the recycle bin was paying off. He crumpled the sheets, balling them up tightly in one hand as he opened the door center of the potbelly shaped woodstove. Tossing the papers in, he leaned down and reached for several pieces of kindling and fire starter chips, tossing them into the stove. He straightened, struck a match, held it up, watching its flame grow and glow. Holding the match carefully, he leaned down again and reached into the stove laying the match on top of the paper and kindling. The paper caught the flame, igniting with a golden spark that lapped out over both paper balls and on to the kindling. He straightened and turned. Angela stood at the edge of the kitchen area watching him.

"Have I passed muster?" he asked.

Angela walked over to where Parker stood. He hadn't moved. It was if he waited for her to say something. His tone had changed from his confident one to a quieter, softer one that made her think he was shy or awaiting approval. She liked her men confident and strong. Strong in experience and unafraid of trying. Maybe she needed to speak up rather than stand back like she did at work. Unsure how Parker would take it, she could only act and see what happened.

She laid a hand on Parker's arm as she spoke. "Warmth and safety are important. Surviving is going to take both of us. I'm ready to help out."

Parker nodded. "Okay. I've got the fire started. Get two small logs out of the wood basket near the patio door."

Parker walked away, not looking back. She nodded anyway. She knew the size he wanted. Her father had taught them about open fire starting and keeping it contained. Parker's expertise about his stove she would learn firsthand. "There's a few smaller branches in here too. Want those for later?"

"Yes. Bring them, please."

Angela tucked four small branches into the crook of her elbow, cradling them against her. She gathered up a handful of smaller branches and twigs and moved into the living room. "Do you have a box or place you want these?"

"Wood crate against the wall. Bring me two of the small branches."

Angela dropped the branches into the crate along with her handful of twigs and other kindling pieces. She grabbed two of the branches and flexed them. Both cracked a bit. Good. She closed the distance between her and Parker. "These are dry and ready to break down to fit in."

Parker straightened and turned toward her, holding his hand out. She shook her head, dropped one of the branches, flexed the remaining one as a loud crack sounded. She handed Parker the two pieces. "I'll have the other broken up in a moment."

The wide-eyed look on his face said more than if he'd spoke. He didn't know this aspect about her. She almost smiled, but she didn't. There was a lot he didn't know about her or she him. Tonight was going to be different. Like a date and yet not a date. How much talking were they going to get done?

"Thanks." Parker took the broken pieces from her. He grinned as he bent down reaching for the other branch. "Been working out?"

She laughed. "Every day. You know what it takes to lift patients and move incoming deliveries."

"True. Let me take care of this branch. There's a bin behind me that holds fuel pellets. Fill the scoop and hand it to me."

Parker cracked the dry branch in two and placed it in the stove close to the other two pieces near the fire. The pellets would keep the fire burning at a low level emitting warmth without needing tending for a while. He straightened, turned and stopped. "Whoa. Sorry about that. I almost hit you."

"Don't sweat it. I'm watching what you're doing so I can help out." Angela held out the full scoop. "I'll take my turn checking on the fire too."

Parker nodded. He was learning about Angela from a side he might never have if Old Man Winter hadn't partied across the countryside one last time. "Let's finish eating and discuss how we're going to split things up." He walked into the kitchen, Angela following him.

"Sounds good to me. I know about roughing it and chores." Angela sweetened her mug of tea and drank some.

"Your parents sound like they took living off the grid seriously." Parker sat on stool he used earlier. He bit into his sandwich, chewed and swallowed.

He pulled out the stool next to him and patted it. "Sit down. There's no need for you to stand."

Angela slid her plate and mug across the counter. She moved behind him and sat down on the stool next to him. "Dad believed we needed to be self-sufficient. Mom's parents were old money. Fourth-generation San Franciscans. They kept trying to lure her and my sisters back with the promise of an easy life."

Parker dunked his tea bag, removed it and drank part of the lukewarm liquid. "Did they take them up on the offer? I know money can be attractive when you don't have much of it."

Angela snorted. "We had plenty of it. Dad drove a delivery truck for the local farm cooperative. He handled his dad's investments and money his great-grandfather left him. See Dad put his undergrad and grad school degrees to work as an independent investment counselor."

Parker chuckled. "I bet your grandparents were pissed when they found this out."

"Never told them. See Mom and Dad made sure we had the basics and earned the extras like our first car. They paid for junior college and beyond that we had to work our way through. My sister Bianca graduated with a four point GPA. She's CEO of her own investment firm."

"Damn," Parker said, setting down his mug. "And you?"

Angela winked and leaned toward him. "Bachelor's in nursing from Cal State Santa Cruz with honors. Cum Laude."

"Nice." He ate the last of his sandwich, dunked part of his cookie in his tea, and saluted Angela. "And your other siblings?"

"Biochemical Engineer, Nuclear Physicist, and owns own cab company." Angela saluted him with her tea mug.

"Frack. Maybe more of us should live off the grid. We might have done better in school." Parker popped the last of his cookie into his mouth and chewed. His two-year degree paled compared to her family and her education.

Angela put her mug in the sink along with her plate. She refilled the carafe and put it in the microwave to heat. "We had the love of learning instilled in us at a young age. My mom read to us. Dad helped us out with homework and quizzed us on current events as we read the paper to each other."

She reached for Parker's plate. "We snuck TV at our friends home when we stayed over or ate dinner. Sometimes we needed the internet for homework."

"Why Peyton Corners?" Parker looked away, fidgeting with the last half of his second cookie.

Angela took a deep breath. She'd run into this before—the you're better than me tactics some males played for their own ego inflation. She'd seen women do it too. One-upmanship wasn't her style. Everybody had worth. Parker showed it with every patient he brought in or comforted. He treated everyone as if they were his only concern. That touch and patient centric approach was one reason she'd noticed him. He practically practiced medicine like he was born to it.

"Why not is my first response." She held up her hand as she continued. "I like the hometown atmosphere and safe feeling. I'm not drawn to big cities. Tried that in college. Reminds me of a closet stuffed to the gills."

Parker looked up as she finished speaking. A smile curled his lips, his eyes glowed with his mirth. He nodded and pointed at her as he replied. "Now that I agree with one hundred percent!"

Angela laughed. The lights flickered at the same time and blacked out. Quiet followed. Several moments passed before Parker spoke again. "Got that flashlight handy? Looks like you're going to need it."

"I do." She clicked it on and laid it on the counter, pointing the beam across the sink and counter to where Parker stood. "I'll wash up these few dishes. Turn the sink on low stream so pipes don't freeze."

"Thanks," Parker said, walking away. "I'll get the pillows and towels from upstairs."

"Don't you need a flashlight?" Angela asked as a small beam arched over the back wall of the kitchen and across the window above the sink.

"Nope. Still got your penlight one from earlier. I'll call when I'm ready to toss stuff down the stairs. Be back in a few."

"Why, so you can see if you hit the broad side of the dark?"

Parker's laughter sounded and died as he walked into the living room. Silence followed. Nothing but the eerie quiet that leaves goose bumps and chills racing up and down arms enveloped her and filled the larger space where no light penetrated. Angela inhaled, counted and exhaled, letting go a long deep sigh. She picked up the sponge off the back of the sink, turned on the cold water so that it trickled out and did the same with the warm. She wet the sponge, reached for the bottle of dish detergent sitting on the windowsill when a loud bang, rattle and shaking of the patio doors sounded.

A screech filled the room. She glanced around as best she could. "Damn Mom Nature is fussing tonight," she said out loud.

"I agree," came a voice from the dark.

She let out another high-pitched eek, dropping the detergent bottle and sponge in the sink. She grabbed the flashlight, turned with her other hand fisted ready to punch whoever was there.

Parker's face came into view as she lowered the flashlight. He squinted, shielding his eyes as he moved into the kitchen. "Hey. How am I supposed to see?"

"By not spooking me and sneaking up." Angela lowered her fist. "I don't punch like a girl."

"Thanks for letting me know. Not that I planned on finding out." Parker closed the distance between them. "I want to know did you bring anything to sleep in?"

Angela took several short breaths, ready to spout a sarcastic reply. Pressing her lips together, she inhaled and exhaled a few more times until she could calmly answer. "Thermals is the best I got. I don't carry baby doll pjs with me in this weather."

Parker knew his answer better be clear and concise. Angela's tone left no doubt she would have punched him, ready to do harm and do more if needed. "Good thing to have too. I'm offering a sweatshirt and a pair of sweatpants."

Angela snorted. "Right. They'll fall off me. Thanks for the offer but—"

"Hang on," Parker interrupted. "They're ones my nephew left behind on his last visit. He's your height."

"Oh," Angela said, her tone softer. "I appreciate the offer. The sweatshirt for sure. I don't like tight things when I sleep."

"He cut the elastic cuff out of the pants. They're loose too."

"Probably why he left them behind."

Parker laughed. "That and he paid forty bucks for them. Swore he was going to Tennessee State. Bugged my sister until she bought them."

"Sounds like my niece and her UCLA stint."

"Didn't go?" He started back across the living room, shining the flashlight in front of him.

"Dropped out freshman year. Transferred schools and didn't tell her mom until time to pay the rest of the semester's tuition."

"What? How'd she pull that off?" He stopped at the bottom of the stairs.

"Transferred to UC Irvine. Within the UC system, it's allowed. Believe me, my sister was ready to go to LA and quiz my niece royally."

"We didn't get away with stuff like that." Parker started up the stairs. "I'll be back down in a few."

"Yell when you need me to help with things. I'll be in the kitchen." Angela's flashlight beam disappeared as she entered the kitchen.

Parker grinned at his thoughts as he continued up the stairs. They were talking like two good friends. Banter and easy responses for the most part flowed. How would the rest of the night and into tomorrow go? They'd worked together for over two years; the same shift for the last six months. Spent time on cases and nights working side-by-side with little or no time to get into serious discussions. The kind that allowed two people to get to know each other beyond the superficial stuff. Had they moved past friendly banter in the last few hours? Did surviving the harrowing drive to his place count? Or her reaction to his catching her off-guard? He wouldn't know unless he asked the question. Put forth his interest in her and see what happened.

He yawned as he entered the guest room at the top of the stairs. His nephew called it his room though he hadn't visited in two years. Parker located the sweats he sought and added the slippers his nephew left behind too. Angela could use them instead of wearing her hikers. He was ready to get out of his boots and into his own moccasins. He carried the sweats and slippers into his bedroom at the back of the house. The large master suite included a full walk-in shower he'd loved to use if the blasted electric had stayed on. Generator didn't put forth enough energy to chance running the tankless hot water unit. Damn, he'd forgotten to tell Angela about the cast iron kettle he used on the wood stove. Glancing at his watch, Parker blinked. It was midnight already. No wonder he was beat. He'd worked ten hours straight before they left the clinic. Bedtime was upon them. He wondered how Angela was holding up. Gathering the towels and flat sheets he wanted along with the extra toiletries he kept back, he stuffed the items in the laundry bag he used to take his laundry down to the washer. He grabbed two last items, draping them around his shoulders. He usually slept naked. Comfortable pajama bottoms and the quilt his grandmother made him for his thirtieth birthday would remind him he had company.

Chuckling at his inane thoughts about clothes and sleep, Parker walked back toward the landing. With heat, both of them might not mind being naked. Cold, snow, and minimal heat pushed naked and exploring each other's bodies right out of his mind. Well, almost.

Angela stopped once she entered the kitchen. She glanced behind her. Not that it did any good. Pitch-black darkness greeted her. She'd seen Parker start up the stairs. Heard a few creaks and steps as he walked around. Rolling her shoulders, she let go a deep sigh. Tension wasn't her norm around Parker. What brought it on? Yes, he had scared her. Caught her off-guard. Was her autopilot stuck on self-protect mode? What had her angst raging into overdrive? They'd come through the rough drive to his place. Parker hadn't . . .hadn't what? Hadn't made a move on her other than to make sure they were safe and sound. Sleeping next to him, alone with him and in his home ignited feelings. Ones she'd thought about in passing when she'd daydream about him or in her fantasy dreams. Was part of her waiting to see if the rest came true? Or was reality better than anything she'd imagined? Either way, she needed to get her angst under control and shift into relax mode. The last she'd looked at her watch it was closing in on midnight. The hour she usually shucked her clothes, took a quick shower and dropped into bed, nude beneath her flannel sheets and wool blanket. How soon were they going to stop fighting their exhaustion and inflate the mattress he'd talked about?

She walked to the sink, laid her penlight on the counter and began washing the few dishes they'd used. Taking her mug out of the microwave, she remembered asking about warm water to wash up. What else did Parker have that she could heat water in on the wood stove? Any size cooking pot would work. Keeping an eye on the pan was important. Newer pans burned if their bottoms got too hot. Cast iron or a Dutch oven would work best. As she rinsed the dishes and laid them on the towel she found hanging from the oven handle, she tried recalling the cabinets she'd seen before the lights went out. Two on either side of the window. Another set close to the stove and. . .bingo! The large one below the drawer Parker had gotten their utensils out of. Picking up the penlight, she shined it along the counter until she saw the drawer and cabinet she wanted.

Angela opened the cabinet. Shining the flashlight into it, the beam hit the item she wanted. A cast iron Dutch oven. She laid the flashlight on the counter, leaned down and took the pan out. Parker called out as she set the pan in the sink under the water trickle flowing.

"I'm tossing things down the steps. I'll be down in a moment. Need to turn water on up here too." Two thuds sounded, followed by a couple of whoosh like sounds and lighter plops as she made her way into the living room.

Holding the flashlight out in front of her, she saw the pile. Pillows, maybe a blanket or two. Clothes and slippers. She reached the bottom of steps and shined the light up the steps. Towels and a small bag sat on the top step. "You need help?" she called out.

"No. I'll be down shortly. Gather that stuff, please. Hate to slip and fall."

Angela nodded, even though she knew Parker couldn't see her. Neither of them needed to take unnecessary risks. Safety mattered until the storm let up or stopped. She pulled the blanket and pillows out first, laying them on the couch she found midway into the room. Then the clothes and slippers.

"Okay, ready to come down." Parker said, illuminating the stairs with his flashlight. "I found a couple of battery-operated lanterns and a few candles I forgot I had."

"I got the steps cleared. Also found a Dutch oven that I'm filling with water." Angela tossed the clothes and slippers on the couch on top of the pillows and blankets.

"I have a cast iron kettle I use to heat water on the stove to help humidify the air. It's on top of the stove." Parker handed her the bundle of towels he carried. "No problem using the Dutch oven. Have you noticed the time?"

"Finally, yeah. Going on midnight or after by now. I wanna wash up a bit and get to sleep. You?"

CHAPTER FIVE

"Right with you. I'll inflate the air mattress. It's queen size." Parker dropped the bag he carried on the couch on top of the other things already on it. "I'll sleep on the couch."

"Shared warmth is best in these temps." Angela started back toward the kitchen. "Rather have us snug and cozy in our sleeping bags and blankets over us."

"Better than sleeping on the hard cold floor, for sure." Parker undid the ties on the plastic bag he brought in earlier.

"True." Angela called out from the kitchen. "Question is, do you snore?"

Parker laughed. "How the hell am I supposed to know?"

"Oh, come on. Your girlfriend or an ex hasn't complained?"

"No live-ins to render that verdict. As to exs, well, most of them weren't the stay long type. I'm single and looking. You?"

Silence followed. He could hear Angela moving around in the kitchen. Water sloshed and the clatter of metal against metal sounded then quiet took over. What had he said? He answered honestly. Maybe too honestly? Too soon? What was going on?

He laid the air mattress on the floor and unfolded it. Upending the bag, the foot air pump tumbled out. Nudging it out of the way, he picked up his flashlight and moved into the kitchen. Shining the light along the floor, he looked around. Where was Angela? He kept turning until he saw her feet. Raising the beam slowly, he stopped when he got close to her waist. She looked at him, flashed a weak grin, and tried to turn away. Water sloshed out of the oven and onto the floor.

"Sorry." Angela tried to move without spilling more water. "I can be such a klutz."

"Stay put. I've got plenty of towels. Don't sweat this." Parker put his flashlight on the counter, opened a cabinet and grabbed some of the towels in it.

"I'm so sorry." There was no mistaking the tears in her voice.

He dropped the towels on the floor, kicking them toward her with his foot. He reached for the pan. "There's nothing to this. I upended a whole bucket of water trying to mop the floor after a pipe burst last summer. I damn near slid on my ass across the floor twice. Learned about not wearing wet socks on a damp tile floor."

One giggle sounded. Then another as he got closer to Angela. He took the pan from her and moved toward the sink, still talking. "There's a bit of warm water still in the line. Let me run some of that into the pan. You can wash your face and brush your teeth with that. Sound good?"

"Uh-uh," Angela replied in between yawns. "I'm dead on my feet. I think my adrenaline has dried up."

Parker set the pan the in sink, turned on the hot water tap and let it run for a few minutes. Barely warm water flowed out, then a burst of very hot water followed as cold began to take over. "Okay. You've got water to wash with. In the morning, I'll heat more and you can clean up in the half bath. Stay put. I'll get a washcloth for you."

Angela sighed as Parker exited the kitchen. His honesty and concern touched her more than she realized. Part of it had to be her tired state, right? A man who wasn't sweating water on the floor. Cleaned up the mess without cussing or fussing and was making sure she could wash her face and brush her teeth. Had she missed something? Her sisters and mother told her men like this didn't exist. Her father's mild temperament boiled over when trouble happened or she and her siblings had fought. Her parents had some loud vocal disputes from time to time. Parker appeared to be at ease with life's ups and downs. "Thank you," she called out.

"You're welcome."

Standing in the dark, fanning herself as the temperature outdoors and inside slipped lower felt surreal. Unreal in ways she hadn't thought about like Parker's cool-headiness wasn't just a part of his job, it was who he was. He led without being overly dominant and partnered at the same time. She fanned herself more as memories of his interaction with a patient's four-year-old came to mind. Squatted down, so he and the child were eye-to-eye, Parker talked with the toddler until she stopped crying and accepted the juice box he held out. Hungry and tired, the girl curled up on his lap, falling asleep while her mother received discharge and care instructions. Watching him pick up the child and cradle her to him as he walked out the door with the mother told her more about him than if he'd said he liked kids. Where did she go from here? Could she keep her hormones and psyche in check as he lay next to her? Should she offer to sleep on the couch?

"Here ya go," Parker said as he reentered the kitchen, shining the flashlight along the floor. "Don't sweat things. Take a breath. Prep yourself for sleep."

Angela moved toward him. He knew emotions and lack of sleep could rock things in directions neither of them was ready for. Keeping them safe and warm took priority. He'd sleep on the couch wrapped up in the quilt and a sleeping bag if necessary. On the air mattress with the sleeping bags between the quilt and the flannel sheets he'd wrap around the air mattress, they'd stay relatively warm. If Angela wore the sweats, she'd probably overheat. If the temperature dropped inside more, she'd want them handy. He knew he wasn't risking hypothermia and he sure the hell wasn't letting her chance it either.

"I put a trash bag in the commode for us to use since we don't want to risk water freezing or issues with pipes if the generator goes off." He laid his hand on Angela's arm. "Let's get the mattress inflated. Do you know Ninety-Nine Bottles of Beer on the Wall?"

Angela's snort and snicker reached inside him and loosened the valve of his growing angst. She wasn't closing down on him. Good. In the morning, they could talk more. Reach agreements on how they'd go about things. For tonight, they were safe and warm. The powers-that-be were watching out for them. They had to be. They'd gotten here, they were inside, fed and ready to tackle sleep. He bet come a new day and with sleep, they'd be ready to take on the day and work together for their common good.

"*Oh, do I.* My mother told my dad he had to come up with a cleaner version of it for us kids. She didn't want the neighbors thinking they'd turned their kids into a bunch of rowdy bar-goers."

Parker laughed as he bent over to attach the pump's hose to the air mattress. "I bet he changed it and handed you root beer to sip in between verses."

"Yes, in the dark brown bottles similar to the ones his beer came in. My mother had an old-fashioned conniption fit over that one until she took a good swig and almost spit it out."

Parker lost it. He dropped the hose, wrapped his arms around his middle and started howling. Peals of laughter filled the room. The beam of Angela's penlight arced across his face. He laughed harder. Angela's laughter mingled with his. Five minutes passed before he could speak. He wiped the tears from his eyes as he straightened. "Your dad is a corker. He must have pranked your mom a lot."

"They believed laughter and love were a priority. We weathered hard times by learning how to make do with what we had. Taught me about creativity and pulling together."

"Sounds wonderful and tough at the same time." Parker picked the hose back up, inserted it into the air mattress and started pressing his foot up and down on the pump pedal. A whoosh of air sounded, followed by a small squeak as the pump filled with air again. "I think the Dutch oven is almost full. You want to go ahead and get ready for bed?"

"Thanks Parker," Angela said, picking up his nephew's sweatshirt and pants off the couch and walking away from him.

"For what?" he asked, picking up his pumping pace as he mentally sang another round of root beer bottles on the wall.

"For caring. Listening. Relating. Talking. Being you." Angela's light disappeared as she entered the kitchen. "And understanding."

Parker opened his mouth, ready to dismiss the compliments and thanks. Something his mother had called him on more than once. Growing up the middle child between two sisters and a military father wasn't easy. Praise and compliments were few and far between. His father was gone more than he was around. Mom worked two jobs leaving them in each other's care. He shut his mouth, pressed his lips together and swallowed his response. He continued pumping until he formatted another answer. "You're welcome. I'm glad you're here."

Silence filled the room. Sounds of water splashing, and clothes rustling sounded. The pump groaned as it filled and exhaled its breath into the air mattress. Parker stopped thinking about root beer bottles on a wall and started softly humming a love ballad from his youth. In the other room, the woman he'd noticed, thought about and admired was preparing to sleep with him. Willingly preparing, too. His last few dates had ended with a kiss on the cheek and a verbal "Yes, let's get together again" that hadn't happened. A night together like in the old days his great-grandmother used to talk about bundled into a bed with lots of pillows and blankets between them. The way she and great-granddad courted.

Angela laid the sweatshirt and sweat pants on the counter. They looked big enough to cover her hands and feet with room to spare. She dipped the washcloth in the water in the Dutch oven. Not quite cold and certainly not hot water covered her fingers and soaked the cloth. She plunged the cloth into the water more, sucking in air at the water's chillier temp as she reached deeper into the oven. "Damn, that's cold," she whispered, pulling her hand out of the water. Wringing out the cloth, she glanced over her shoulder toward the living room. It was practically pitch black in the room. There was no way Parker could see what she was doing except for the small area illuminated by her penlight. Cold water and soap didn't do well together. She rubbed the bar across the cloth a few more time and laid it down. She worked the cloth across her face and neck, rinsed it and readied for the chilling rinse.

"How you doing in there?" Parker called out from the living room.

"Almost done." Her teeth started to chatter as she rinsed the last of the soap off her face and neck. Thank goodness she didn't wear makeup. Tinted face lotion and lip balm was all she needed. The night shift didn't bring in patients looking for glamorous nurses and doctors like the soap operas and television shows portrayed. Day shift didn't either, except the receptionist and medical assistant covering the front wore scrubs that reminded her of the nurses at the hospital. The doctors on duty wore either their usual green scrubs or a lab coat over their shirt, tie and dress pants.

Pulling her long- sleeved scrub top off, she grabbed the sweatshirt and slipped it over her head. As it settled around her neck, she took off her bra and shoved her arms into the sleeves. Coolness raked across her skin, causing goose bumps to rise. The material began to warm with her body heat as she reached for the sweatpants. Bending down to undo the double knots of her hikers laces in the dark wasn't going to be easy. She was going to have to step out of them, work her scrub pants and thermal underwear off without chilling. Right. In the dark, unsure where she placed her foot and dancing around trying to get her thermals out of her socks. Just wasn't going to work. Angela licked her lips and spoke. "Umm, I've got a problem."

"What?" Parker started into the kitchen shining his flashlight on her. "I'm here to help."

Angela looked up to where she could see part of Parker's face and back down at the darkness engulfing her feet and legs. She sighed. "Well, it's called double knots and ..." Her voice trailed off.

The beam of Parker's flashlight panned over her shoes. He approached her holding out his flashlight. "I'll untie them for you. Hold my flashlight."

"I can untie them. It's getting them, my pants and thermals off, and into the sweats without chilling. That's the issue."

Parker stepped back. There was no mistaking the unsaid "no thank you" to his offer. He caught his bottom lip between his teeth, halting his response. He nodded, noting this wasn't his baby sister yelling help. He needed to ask before he started doing. Just because someone said they had a problem didn't mean he had to solve it. Sometimes talking it out was the best solution. "I'm gonna change in the half bath. Would sitting on the couch solve your problem?"

Angela didn't answer for several moments. He inhaled and exhaled several times, ready to offer another option as she replied.

"That's a great idea. I do need help with the double knots. Thanks." Angela moved toward him.

"Sure." Parker backed up, shining his flashlight in front of him. "I'll change and meet you at the couch in, say, ten minutes?"

"You got it." Angela flashed him a smile he caught a glimpse of as she turned away. "I'll brush my teeth and meet you there."

Words failed him. Confidence oozed out of her in ways he'd only noticed when he brought patients in and she took over. Yet, she shied away from him earlier as if he'd gotten too close. Too next to her as he cleaned up the spilled water. Parker walked out of the kitchen, picked up his pajama pants and thermal top off the couch, going on to the half-bath. He halted at the door, listening, waiting and ready to go if Angela called out again. Nothing but the sound of water running greeted him. All right, she stymied him and intrigued him at the same time. Apparently, there was a lot more to Angela than her easygoing friendliness with him. The friendship they'd developed over the last six months brought them to this point. Parker stepped into the half-bath as a shrill howl sounded as another blast of artic air swept down and over the triplex rattling the patios doors. Yes, he got it. Mother Nature and Old Man Winter were helping out by snowing them in together. "Look," Parker muttered as he closed the bathroom door. "It's not like we couldn't get here on our own."

Another blast of wind shook the building reminding him if they could, why hadn't they?

Angela rinsed her toothbrush, scooped a handful of water out of the Dutch oven, pressed her lips together hoping her teeth didn't start chattering, and quickly raised her hand to her mouth. She slurped the cold water in, rapidly worked it around her mouth, and spit it out. "Damn, that's cold."

She put her toiletries back in her duffel bag. As she picked up the sweat pants, her top and bra along with her penlight off the counter, she glanced out the kitchen window. A few snowflakes danced across her view. Patches of moonlight cutting through the overhead cloud cover illuminated the branches of a close-by tree. Icicles mixed with snow decorated the tree limbs reminding her of Christmas and the unknown surprises inside the wrapped presents beneath the tree. What would morning bring? Would what they'd shared wrapped in the cocoon of darkness continue in the light of day? Or was there more to reveal like the nesting dolls her friend from Finland had gifted her with one Christmas? Angela exited the kitchen sure of one thing. Whatever tomorrow brought, she and Parker would be unwrapping it together. They had to wrap up the air mattress first. Then themselves before any unwrapping could start in the light of day.

As she made her way into the living room, Angela shined her penlight around the area familiarizing herself again with the layout. Once they turned off the flashlights, darkness was their top blanket. Silence would enclose them in its cocoon until dawn or they turned on the flashlights again. Was she ready to sink into the intimacy this all represented? Closeness that stepped beyond sharing space, verbal discourse and knowing another person was there with her. A unique combination would enwrap them into a oneness that could bring them closer or drive them apart feeding on the fear of the unknown. Either way, she was part of it as was Parker.

She laid her penlight on the coffee table, shoved the pile of towels and blankets together, and sat down with her scrub top and bra in her lap. She started to lay them aside as the bathroom door clicked open. Stuffing her bra into the sleeve of the top, she quickly folded the top in half and laid it next to her. The thought of Parker finding her bra unnerved her more than the thought of sleeping next to him, very close to him did. Sleeping next to Parker wasn't the same as having sex with him. Yet the depth this added to their. . .words failed her. They'd moved beyond coworkers with tonight's interaction so far. Did the word friends work? Was there a description? She didn't know.

One thought filled her mind: *Now mattered. Nothing else.* Analyzing took more energy than what she had. No flashes of uncertainty whipped through her. For now, she was sure of one thing—she needed sleep. She reached down, undid the double knots of each hiker and loosened the laces. Sleep got top billing as soon as she got her hikers and scrub pants off.

CHAPTER SIX

Parker stuffed his flashlight in his hikers and picked them up off the floor. He draped his uniform and thermals over his shoulder. He shook his head as he exited the bathroom. It felt weird to be wearing clothes knowing he was going to bed. His usual routine of strip, drop his clothes where they fell and drop into bed wasn't happening. Part of him wanted to say, 'Hey, do you mind if I strip and flash you as we get into bed?' He grinned at the inanity of his thoughts. Things that were habit and like a litany your body and mind went through expecting the same result. He bet Angela had had her moments too. Well, tonight wasn't usual. Neither was it completely unusual. The place and timing might be key factors.

He looked up as he moved forward, noting the thin beam of Angela's penlight outlining part of her leg as she sat on the couch. Did she still need help? He'd fumbled with the cold wet laces of his hikers twice before he got them untied and off.

"Ok," he began, walking toward the couch. "Ready to help. What do you need me to do?"

Angela looked up as part of the light from his flashlight illuminated her face. "Sorry. I musta dozed off. I got the knots undone. Just waiting on you."

Parker laid his clothes on the chair opposite the couch. He set his boots on the seat of the chair and took the flashlight out of them. "Ok. Let's get the sleeping bags and blankets set up. I'm ready to sleep."

"Me too." Angela stood up. His nephew's sweatshirt hung down to her knees. She still wore her thermals and socks. Good. The extra layers under the sleeping bag and blankets should keep her warm if the inside temp dropped.

Angela picked up one of the flat sheets and faced Parker. "Both of them wrapped around the mattress?"

"Yes." Parker reached for the sheet, adding, "One on top of the other. Then sleeping bags. Blankets on top of them."

Angela let go of the sheet, watching Parker. He shook out the sheet, billowing it over the mattress, smoothing it as he tucked excess under the sides, bottom and top. He looked up. "Ready for the second one."

"I've got it. Are there cases for the pillows?" Angela unfolded the sheet she held, shook it out until it billowed out over the mattress. She knelt and began working the extra under the corners and edges like Parker had until the double sheets lay smooth and taut on the mattress.

"Yes. Had them in with the towels. Where did they go?"

Angela looked up. The outline of Parker's firm ass covered with paisley print pajama pants greeted her. She licked her lips, pressed them together and looked away, not before she caught the outline of his balls and cock as he bent over further. Her mouth went dry. She didn't mind the view. Caught her off-guard. Worth the unexpected view, nonetheless.

"I might have covered them up when I moved the towels and sheets to sit down." She stood up, moving closer to the couch. "Hand me the towels. I'll lay them on the back of the couch."

"Here." Parker thrust his hand out, clenching a towel at her.

"Got it." Angela took the towel, folded it in half and laid on the back of the couch.

"Here's two more." Parker tossed another towel to her, followed by another.

She caught both, laid one down, folded the other in half and placed it on top of the first one. As she began folding the third towel, Parker straightened up.

"Found 'em." He grasped two pillowcases in his hand. "Pillows are by you. Trade you a case for a pillow."

Angela snickered. "Sure. Here you go." She tossed a pillow at Parker, catching him in the chest as he turned toward her.

"I'd start a pillow fight if I wasn't so damn tired." He quickly pulled the pillowcase on the pillow she'd tossed at him.

She picked up hers, pulled on the case and replied. "I would too. Sleep is demanding my attention real bad."

"I'm with you." Parker unrolled two sleeping bags on top of the mattress. "Which side you want?"

"Either. Makes no difference to me." Angela tossed her pillow on the mattress. "I may get up once to use the bathroom."

"Me too. Since I know the living room better, why don't you take the side closest to the half-bath?" Parker tossed the other pillow on the mattress. "It also puts me close to the stove. I can check it easier."

"Sounds good to me." Angela stretched, yawning at the same time. "Hand me my penlight and the sweatpants please."

"Sure," Parker said, holding both out to her. "Take these slippers too. Might be a bit big since they were my nephew's."

Angela laid the penlight on the end table close to her. She put the sweatpants on the arm of the chair that held Parker's uniform and thermals. "Thank you. Can we move the table closer so it's easy to find the penlight?"

"Yes." Parker set the lamp from the end table on the floor. He pushed the table forward until it was flush with the edge of the chair. "Any closer and you might hit it. Don't want you getting hurt."

Angela smiled. "Agree. Thanks again. I'm ready to crawl in and pass out. You?"

"Right beside you after I get these blankets on top of the sleeping bags." Parker handed her one end of the quilt. "Help me get it on both sides, please. I'll put the afghan across the foot where we can get it if needed."

They worked together smoothing out the quilt and the afghan, then turned them down to where each of them could unzip their sleeping bag and get in. Angela sat on the air mattress, reached for her penlight as she glanced at the other side of the mattress. Parker stood near the stove.

"Problem with the stove?" she asked, ready to get up.

"No. Checking the fire. It's burned down to glowing embers. I'm adding a half scoop of pellets to keep a low flame going once it burns down more." Parker opened the stove door, tossed the pellets in and closed the door.

Angela heard the thump of the scoop hitting the side of the bin as she turned off her penlight and lay down. "What about checking on it?"

"I sleep in spurts. Couple of hours at best. Then awake for a bit. I'll check on it then. Smoke detector is battery-operated so we'll hear it if needed. I adjusted the flue." Parker got in beside her. "Thanks for caring. I appreciate it."

Before she could reply, he turned off the flashlight and lay down next to her.

She blinked, trying to voice her reply. Instead, her eyes closed and her breathing slowed. Sleep claimed her lulling her into a deep slumber filled with images of a warm green spring.

Parker turned on his side, moved carefully closer to Angela. Proximity helped with sharing body heat and warmth. Cuddling closer might frighten her. Consent mattered. Until Angela gave it, he wasn't assuming. He stretched his arm out until his fingers touched her hair. Knowing she felt secure with him mattered. Right now, sleep mattered too. Tomorrow they could talk more. He inhaled, counted to five and exhaled as he envisioned sleep enveloping. Twice more he repeated the relaxation process. On the start of the third time, sleep pulled him deep into its embrace.

Parker rolled over, cracked open one eye and glanced at his watch. The illuminated dial showed four-thirty A.M. They'd gone to sleep somewhere between midnight and one. He chafed his arms as he sat up, reached for his flashlight and turned it on. He blinked several times, letting his eyes adjust to the beam of light. As he rose facing the stove, he glanced behind him. Angela wasn't in bed. Where was she?

He picked up the flashlight, ready to go looking for her, when the bathroom door clicked open and the beam of her penlight shone across the floor. "You ok?" he asked, moving toward the open door.

"Yes. Nature called and I sat contemplating life for a few minutes. You all right?"

Angela closed the space between them, stopping when they were toe-to-toe.

Parker exhaled, nodded and spoke, realizing she couldn't easily see him nodding. "Yes. My bladder nudged me awake along with a couple of weird dreams. Also time to check on the fire."

"How can I help?" Angela asked stepping past Parker closer to the stove.

"If the embers are red hot, add a scoop of pellets. If they're glowing, time to add a couple pieces of wood and a few pellets." Parker headed toward the bathroom. "Just check on the coals or embers. I'll be out in a moment."

Angela opened the door of the stove. Heat rolled out, warming her face and chest as she leaned down to get a good look at the embers. Red-hot areas like her dad taught her to look for lay center of the ring of ashes from the earlier fire and flames. Several gold glowing areas lay toward the back.

She straightened as Parker exited the bathroom. "There's patches of reds and golds in the center and along the back."

"Good," Parker replied coming up behind her. "A low flame will keep the heat going. The baseboards are warm to the touch. Means generator is still working."

"Who'd thought knowing all this stuff would come in handy in the twenty-first century?" Angela moved around Parker and perched on the arm of the chair. "I keep reminding myself that my parents weren't as bad as I thought they were."

Parker chuckled. "Oh, I can relate."

"How so?" Angela asked.

"I spent my junior and senior high school years thinking my dad was a real jackass." Parker closed the stove door and faced her. "I've got the munchies. Wanna split a honey and peanut butter sandwich? Maybe hot chocolate?"

Angela grinned. She knew that feeling. Dinner breaks came when she could catch them on busy nights. Snacking later on got her through a very busy night or if she ate dinner in between triaging patients.

"Sounds good. How you gonna make the hot chocolate?" She stood up, turning her penlight back on.

"Instant. Best kind when you got the 'I want chocolate now' munchies. Canister is in the cabinet close to the coffee maker." Parker turned toward her, the beam of his flashlight illuminating something he held. "Mind filling the kettle? Hot water makes the stuff taste better."

Angela took the kettle and started toward the kitchen. "More experience speaking?"

"Sorta. Made a sandwich one night. Started eating it and remembered mug in microwave. Except. . ." Parker stopped speaking. Had he done that deliberately?

"Except what?" Angela turned back.

"Didn't turn the microwave on. Too tired to care it was cold. Tried to gulp it down. Never again." Parker's snort followed. "I managed to warm the remaining half cup. And downed twenty ounces of water in the next couple of hours."

Angela smirked. "Never too old to learn, I guess."

"Yup. And additional lesson learned. Don't multitask when tired."

Angela pressed her lips together and walked into the kitchen. Mirth bubbled up. She wasn't going to multitask walking into the kitchen in almost pitch-black darkness laughing and trying to watch where she was going.

She set the kettle on the counter. Two open cabinets later, she found the hot chocolate canister. "Is the scoop inside or measured by spoonfuls?" she asked, calling out.

"Plastic scoop should be inside. Clean mugs are in dishwasher."

"We can use the ones from earlier. I washed them." Angela noted where the mugs and spoons were on the counter as she set the canister next to the kettle.

"Sounds good. I'll make the sandwich in a moment. Bread is next to the toaster. Peanut butter and honey are in the cabinet over it."

Angela stuck her finger into the narrow stream flowing out of the tap. "Brrr! That's cold." She pulled her hand back, thrusting her finger into her mouth, quickly closing her lips around it. Warmth started to seep back in as Parker entered the kitchen.

Parker shined his flashlight around the kitchen. Angela stood close to the counter. He moved the light up her torso until he reached her shoulders and neck. She stood with her finger in her mouth. Her lips puckered around her finger. His hips jerked. His cock nudged the fly of his pajama pants more. Were his dreams prophetic? Blessed with precognitive insight except it wasn't his cock in her mouth. Lips pressed together, he inhaled and exhaled twice, willing his obnoxious id to stop pumping him full of on-fire hormones. Focus. He had to, needed to focus. On something other than sex...not that it hadn't crossed his mind and dreams a few nights prior. Grabbing Angela and making out in a cold kitchen would warm much up. Well, maybe a few libido pulses and boy did it. Consent was a key item. Right now, he needed to quell his munchies and get back to relaxed. Four hours of sleep wasn't enough to make too many rational decisions on. He blinked and asked, "You ok?"

Angela pulled her finger out of her mouth. A small pop sounded. She grabbed the kettle, taking its top off and plunging it into the sink. Parker lowered the flashlight and sidestepped around Angela. "Sorry I caught you off guard again."

"You didn't catch me off guard. I'm fine. Just don't like cold water." Angela turned toward him. "How much cocoa in each mug?"

"A couple of spoonsfuls. Half cup at this time of night helps me get back to sleep."

Angela set the kettle on the counter. "Doesn't some hot chocolate have caffeine?"

"Some does. I make my own. All organic ingredients. Cocoa, powdered milk, and mini marshmallows." Parker laid his flashlight on the counter and reached for a mug. "Go ahead and put the kettle on the stove. I'll make the sandwich and bring it in with the mugs."

"Kinda like a late night-early morning picnic." Angela picked up the kettle and her penlight and exited the kitchen.

Parker laid both hands on the counter, took a deep breath, closed his eyes, and let go a deep sigh. Letting barriers down wasn't easy. He and Angela had a great work relationship. They teamed up, got the job done and read each other's body language well. They knew what needed done because they'd done it over and over. Taking things to the next level was different. Very different for either of them. A workplace romance wasn't supposed to happen. At least that's what a lot of folks believed. He wasn't sure. For now, he needed to start easing those barriers away. His and hers both. Jumping over them without preamble only reinforced them.

He opened the loaf of bread, took two pieces out and laid them on a paper towel. Just like the peanut butter he spread on each slice of bread, each of them probably had sticky spots. He sure did. He'd dated attractive women before. Usually locals that his buddies introduced him to. Someone like Angela from a large city, West Coast sophistication—like her moneyed grandparents and with a degree, what could she see in him? Then she hadn't acted like some of the. . .he wasn't using the word. Calling names didn't change what people felt they were entitled to. Lacey had made it more than clear he didn't fit her bill of what a man was. Money that didn't come from blood, sweat, and hard work. She wanted old money, long time passed from generation to generation. She was working until she met and married her millionaire. Last he heard, she was divorcing for the third time. Parker wiped the knife off, closed the peanut butter and put it away. He picked up the honey dispenser, turned it over and shook it until honey flowed down toward the top. Flipping the lid open, he squeezed the bear-shaped bottle until a large dollop covered part of the peanut-buttered slice of bread. As he closed the lid, he sighed knowing that getting Angela to squeeze him might take a bit more finesse than what he had at four-thirty in the morning sporting a hard-on that wanted attention. He laughed as he cut the sandwich in quarters.

"What's so funny?"

"Oh shit!" Parker yelped, fumbling the wrapped sandwich. "Damn, woman. You snuck up on me."

"I'd say turn about but you ain't either of my brothers. Or my kid sister." Angela caught the sandwich between her hands. "I think we need a few more paper towels. This is sticky."

Parker pressed his lips tighter together, shaking his head, trying to keep his response to himself. Licking Angela's fingers off might be a comeback that she'd banter back. Right now, he wanted more. To lick other places and bury himself deep within her as they rocked from one orgasm to another. Catching his bottom lip between his teeth, he pressed hard against it. Taking one deep breath after another, he swallowed his first response.

"Did I say something wrong?" Angela asked, worry evident in her tone.

"Nah," Parker began. "My mind wanders and takes walks where I have to censure it from time to time."

Angela moved very close to him. "I get it. Retorts are sometimes better left unsaid. Don't sweat it." She leaned closer and kissed his cheek.

Parker swallowed hard, fisting his hands tightly, or he'd reach out tangle his fingers in her hair, press his lips tight to hers and take the kiss to another level. This wasn't the time to go there. Light of day and more discussion might yield where they went next. For now, it was time to eat and get back under the blankets where it was a hell of lot warmer. "Let's get back in bed. It's warmer there."

CHAPTER SEVEN

Angela started toward the living room, penlight in one hand, sandwich in the other. Had she done something wrong? Parker went silent after she'd kissed his cheek. Damn had she caught him off guard again? Another faux pas? Shit, when had she misread him?

It's dark. How can you read him? Her conscience scolded. *Stop worrying about being right and be yourself. He's got a mouth. He'll tell you if you fuck up.*

Great—the one word her parents used when she or her siblings really messed up. Messed up royally, as her grandparents used to say. Fucking up was akin to being damned her parents often said. That was like asking for the earth to open up and swallow you. She sure shit didn't want to fuck up. She took two quick breaths reminding herself that errors happened and apologies worked. Permission whether understood or spoken also came into play. Assuming wasn't always a good thing.

She laid the penlight on the end table along with the sandwich. She started toward the bathroom ready to wash her hands when Parker called out. "Be there in a moment."

"Ok. I'm going to wash my hands and use the bathroom." Angela quickly made her way to the bathroom. Daylight was growing. Dawn soon would take over and a new day would begin. Was she ready to face Parker in the light of day? Most of the time they worked during the dark of night.

Parker set the mugs with spoons and cocoa mix in them on the table along with some damp paper towels. He took the roll of dry paper towels out from under his arm and set them next to the wet ones. He glanced toward the partially drawn blinds covering one of the living room windows. Dawn was upon them. He hoped they could get back to sleep comfortably. He needed more than four hours to function beyond inept. He wasn't going there again if he could help it. They needed to talk and come to some understandings. He liked what he'd learned about Angela so far. Could he convince her to become friends, maybe friends with benefits or more? He wasn't a betting man nor was he making leaps to more without communication and an agreement from her.

He opened the stove door, assessed the embers and remaining coals. He tossed a full scoop of pellets in, added some wadded paper and a lit match. Soon yellow flames licked at the pile of pellets and paper. Raking through the coals with a fireplace rake, he mixed the glowing coals and embers with the growing fire. No need for wood for now. As he closed the door, Angela exited the bathroom. Her gaze met his. She yawned and looked away. She looked pretty good to him—tousled bed hair, thermals, socks and sweatshirt didn't detract him.

"Fire's going. It'll warm up in here more soon. Let's eat and drink. Talk a bit and sleep more. I doubt we're going anywhere soon. I'll check outside later." Parker lifted the kettle off the stove and touched the side of it. "Still cool."

"Sleep sounds good. A bit of food and talk too." Angela sat down crossed-legged on her sleeping bag.

"Strange surroundings. Unique situations. Both can rob you of deep sleep. For me it's letting go of work. So many people you want to help. Some you can. Some you can't." Parker set the kettle back on the stove. "It's going to be a bit before the kettle is hot."

"That's okay." Angela lay down on her side. "I can wait for the hot chocolate to go with the sandwich."

Parker sat down on his side of the mattress. He glanced at the stove, noting the glow through the glass window in the door. "We'll hear the kettle boil."

He chuckled. "I haven't said that since I was in London."

"You were in London? When?" Angela asked, tossing the part of the afghan over her.

Parker lay down on his back and pulled part of the quilt over him. Tucking his hands behind his head, he continued talking. "My freshman and sophomore years of high school. My family lived there for two years."

"Your mom or dad's job transfer there?"

Parker rolled on his side, leaned on his elbow and propped his head up with his hand. "Dad's. Military moves you around a lot."

"Oh yeah. My grade school bestie moved every year until she started middle school. I got good at letter writing. No internet at home and the time differences were difficult to mesh time to chatter when I did get internet access at school."

"Mom wanted my sisters and me to have real time with our dad as much as we could. She moved around the world for a few years so we got that." Parker let go a deep sigh.

"Why the sigh?" Angela asked, snuggling down into the covers.

"Once dad made command rank, things changed. He pulled foreign duty stations close to the action. Too close to hostilities or fighting. Family safety mattered."

Angela took a hold of his hand. "I'm sorry you lost him."

Parker squeezed Angela's hand. "Thanks. We lost him before that. He took more interest in his troops and job than us. Mom worked two jobs to help make ends meet. Even my sisters and I worked."

"Not easy knowing someone else matters more than you. Especially with your parents." Angela moved closer to him.

"At first no. The two years in London opened my eyes to a few things." Parker let go of Angela's hand.

"Like what?"

"Prestige and demands come with promotions. I went to a public school instead of the base one. You are judged by who and what your parents are if it's known you're a military brat."

"Sorry that happened. It isn't different elsewhere. You're new. You get judged. Even if you aren't." Angela rolled on to her back, bunching her pillow up under her head and neck.

"Sounds like you got your share of it too."

"Yeah. Cliques happen. It's like they're part of life. I don't get a lot of them." Angela looked at Parker. "Did you enjoy your time in London?"

"What I remember of it, yeah. History came alive. Field trips were central. Visiting places as we learned about them came to life in different ways. Understanding why something happened is essential to identifying why you don't forget the lessons learned."

"Like your dad ignoring you?"

Parker snorted. "More like divorcing us. He tried to make up for it when he got home on leave. His absentee parenting taught my sisters and me the importance of self-sufficiency."

"Parker?" Angela asked.

"Yeah."

"Mind if I change the subject?"

"Did I say something wrong?" Parker asked, sitting up.

"No. I'm just wondering. . ." Angela stopped speaking.

"Wondering what?" Parker turned more toward her.

"Why we're talking like this now? Sharing stuff we might not have if we were at work." Angela sat up, hugging her knees to her.

"Good question. I like you. We've worked together on and off for the past two years. Most nights we're so busy, we pass each barely saying hello."

"True. It's like we've been waiting to have this conversation. There's a comfort level to it."

"Well four months ago at the Christmas party, we did break the ice more. I enjoyed talking about holiday traditions. And I wanted to ask you to lunch. But my shift trade came through." Parker laid his hand on her arm. "You kissed my cheek earlier. Why?"

"Felt like the right thing to do. Darkness shields us. We don't see much with the flashlights. Even with dawn breaking, how much are we really seeing?"

"Good point. Feeling and hearing are the senses we've depended on. Others are kicking in with the light. What about what your heart is saying?" Parker stood up. The hissing of water caught both their attentions. He grabbed one of the folded towels off the back of the couch and wrapped part of it around his hand. He lifted the kettle off the stove, filled their mugs and set the kettle on top of the wood pellet bin.

Handing Angela one of the mugs and a spoon, he spoke again. "I had to learn to trust me. My dad made decisions and issued orders for so long he tried the same approach with my sisters and me. Didn't work well."

"What happened?" Angela took the mug from him.

"Mom saw us mature. We'd managed to take on more responsibilities and learn from our mistakes. Dad didn't get we'd come through stuff without his help." Parker stirred his hot chocolate, picked up his mug and sipped. "Hmm. . .good."

"Agree," Angela said as he sat down on the couch, resting his mug on the arm of the couch.

Angela set her mug on the coffee table and started to get up. She glanced at Parker as she straightened. He watched her in between sips. If he'd done this at work, it would have unnerved her. Set her on edge. Workplace romances were a big no-no in her book of relationship rules. She'd observed the uglier side of working close up with your love interest or spouse. Poor Doc Stillwell's wife had quit on him and filed for divorce shortly after the urgent care center opened. The demand of twenty-four-seven- on-duty life got the best of her. Romance and family were very difficult to mix with a medical job. Even some of the doctors and nurses who managed to get past rough spots said it wasn't easy. Tight together almost every day could be nerve-wracking. She'd seen it with her parents. Denying her attraction to Parker wasn't going to solve anything.

She picked up her mug and sat down in the chair across from the couch. As she set her mug on the side table, she asked, "Ready for half of the sandwich? My stomach is growling."

Parker set his mug on the coffee table. He leaned forward with his hand out. As if on cue, his stomach loudly growled. He looked down and back up, smiling. "I think my vote is voiced."

Angela laughed. She picked up the paper towel, tore it in two and laid part of it on Parker's hand. Next, she tore the sandwich in half. She laid Parker's half on the paper towel. "Here's your half."

"Thanks." Parker wrapped the paper towel around part of his half and took a bite.

Angela bit into her half, savoring the sweet honey and peanut butter mix. She quickly ate the rest of hers. She reached for her mug as Parker picked up the thread of their earlier conversation.

"My life wasn't easy. Not that any kid's life is. I think military kids go through rougher times because we never know if our parent is coming back."

"Knowing your mom or dad is in harm's way or might even die hits hard. I interned with a community hospital in Los Angeles. Seeing the at-risk families and kids makes you wake up and be thankful for what you got." Angela sipped her hot chocolate, settling back into the chair.

"It sure does. Thanks for making the sandwich." Parker folded the paper towel in half and wiped his hands with it. He stood up, walked over to Angela, holding out his hand. "I'll take your half."

Angela handed him her half. He opened the stove door and tossed them in. "Adds to fire fuel. Easy clean up."

He sat back down on the couch. "I'm gonna say one more thing and then change the subject. I'll explain why in a moment."

"Okay."

"My dad took it hard when they evacuated him from Afghanistan in 2005. Getting shot didn't deter him from taking care of his troops. He never left the war. Two tours in active fighting took away the dad we knew as youngsters. He committed suicide ten months after that." Parker grabbed his mug, swirled the rest of his drink around, raised the mug and looked at Angela. "Here's to personal wars and the healing that still leaves scars visible and invisible."

"To life. To living. To understanding." Angela leaned forward, holding her mug out to him.

Parker touched his mug to Angela's. He pulled away, blinking back the tears that formed. Talking about his dad still hit him hard from time to time. Blaming himself or trying to get into his dad's head stopped when a shrink in Charleston took him aside after a long shift dealing with a thirty-car pileup. War affected everyone. Even those that stayed safe at home. Healing came with acceptance. Sometimes that didn't happen. His dad hadn't left the war. It came home with dad. Haunted his dad until he sought silence the only way he knew through death. Dad had seen so much of it that he knew no other way.

Parker downed the last of his hot chocolate and set the mug on the coffee table. He stood. "Thanks for listening. I get caught up in the pain if I look back too much. Every day I move more into permanent healing. I'll take our mugs into the kitchen."

Angela handed him her mug. "Thanks. I can't finish my chocolate. Can I help with anything?"

"Not until it's lighter in here. We need more sleep. I've got a crank radio in the kitchen we can use later." Parker said moving into the partially illuminated kitchen due to daylight streaming in through the window over the sink.

Angela quickly used the bathroom and returned as Parker exited the kitchen. She walked over to him. Her arms spread wide. "I think we both need a hug."

Parker nodded and slipped his arms around her waist. "Yeah. Living alone can be hell when the past sneaks up on you. Hugs are good. Cuddles too." He let go and kneeled on the air mattress. "Mind if we do some cuddling? It'll help me get back to sleep."

"Well. . ." She didn't voice her uncertainty. Tired and her mind at half-throttle, she wasn't sure what to think or say. She covered her mouth as she yawned.

Parker lay down on his back. He patted her side of the air mattress. "My grandparents bundled as they courted. I'm good with that."

"Bundled?" Angela perched on the chair arm, twisting part of the sweatshirt around her hands.

Parker rolled on his side facing her. "Yes. An old-fashioned way of keeping the couple chaste during cold spells. They grew up in northern Quebec. Temperatures dropped to below zero often during the winter."

Angela shoved the sleeves off her hands, chafing them several times. "It's chillier than when we went to sleep in here."

"Temps change between dusk and daybreak. It's warm over here. Get in your sleeping bag and warm up. With the quilt and afghan between us, we can still cuddle without a lot of tight touching. Sound good?"

Angela swallowed hard, pressed her lips together, and inhaled. Tapping her fingers against her leg, she counted by fives to fifty and stopped. Exhaling, she nodded. Not sure if Parker could see her response, she said, "Yes. It does."

Parker sat up, straightened out his sleeping bag and got in. He tossed part of the afghan over him, stuffing the rest of it between him and her sleeping bag. Angela kneeled on the air mattress and arranged the quilt and her sleeping bag so part of the quilt bunched up against the afghan. She crawled into the sleeping bag and covered up. She glanced at Parker.

He reached out and cupped her cheek. "It's okay. We've revealed a lot. We're short on sleep and cold."

"Will it warm up in here later?" she asked rubbing her hands on her legs.

"Depends on if the sun comes. The solar panels might help the baseboards put out a bit more heat. If we need a bigger fire, I'll get one going. We know how to get through this."

Angela sighed, snuggling deeper into the pile of covers over her. "Yes, we do. Sorry I'm skittish. Trust takes time for me."

Parker scooted closer. He leaned tight to her, rested his forehead against hers. "Got ya. Don't over-analyze. Go with what feels right. No means no. I respect boundaries and limits."

He brushed his lips over hers and pulled back. "Turn on your side away from me. I'll spoon to you so you can curl into me. Shared warmth should lull us back to sleep."

Scoots and moves back and forth set the air mattress to rocking like a boat bombarded by waves. Angela grabbed the side of the mattress, looked back over her shoulder and said. "This is worse than sleeping in a waterbed."

Parker burst out laughing. "I tried that once. Damn near got seasick. Said never again and donated the damn thing to a community yard sale."

Angela caught her bottom lip between her teeth. Images of her six-foot-two brother shinnying in and out of his waterbed flashed across her mind. She bet Parker had done the same. Her brother kept trying for six months to get used to his water mattress. After the second repair leak thanks to his cat sticking her claws into it trying to ride out a wave attack from Dillon turning over, their mother had drained the mattress and tossed it. She burst out giggling, as Parker started moving again.

"Okay, I'm settled. You?" Parker asked.

"As good as I'm going to get." Angela reached between them, pulling more of the quilt over her.

"Good. I'm going to put my hand on top of the quilt so I know where you are if I turn over." Parker patted her close to her waist through the sleeping bag and quilt.

"All is good." She tucked one hand under her pillow. Bunched part of the quilt around her other hand and took several deep breaths. Lack of sleep had her on high caution. Parker hadn't done anything suspicious. Her tried and overactive imagination had turned on past memories that weren't necessary. After they slept more, she'd explain. Until then, knowing Parker was next to her felt good. Warmth penetrated her cold hands and body. She closed her eyes, focusing on the dream she'd had before waking. A day at the beach with her family.

Parker felt Angela's breathing deepen and slow. He smiled. She was easing back to sleep. Good. He understood caution and vigilance. When they awoke next, day would be upon them. What came next depended on the weather and what they needed to do to survive and thrive until they could dig out. He took a deep breath, exhaled and repeated his earlier relaxation exercise. Soon his mind focused on memories of his Hawaii vacation and warm surfs. Sleep deepened his breathing.

CHAPTER EIGHT

Six hours later

Angela clasped her knees tighter to her. Parker lay on his side facing away from her, snoring softly. Her ex-husband had snored a bit louder when he was overly tired and fell into a very deep sleep. Doug had chosen a life that embraced travel and risk. A lot of risk. Stock car racing took precision handling that a thrill seeker like Doug loved. She'd mourned when he left. Smiled when she learned of his wins. And wept a few tears when he was forced to retired due to one too many crashes. He'd made money and then some. Last she'd heard he'd followed some young wealthy socialite to Greece. That was four years ago. Why had he entered her thoughts now?

Parker rolled over, mumbling in his sleep. She couldn't make out what he said. He settled down and kept on sleeping.

Glancing at her watch, Angela exhaled. Ten A.M. Her stomach growled twice, protesting its emptiness. By now, she'd usually showered, dressed and puttered around the house doing morning chores. Today wasn't a usual day. Three days ago, birds chirped outside her bedroom window as they sat in the tall oak at the edge of her property. Today. . .only the wind and the crackle from the two pieces of wood she'd added to the fire in the stove sounded along with Parker's intermittent snores.

Her stomach grumbled and growled again. Angela let go of her legs, straightened them, stretched and slowly moved to the edge of the air mattress. Parker kept on sleeping as she stood.

She smiled as she worked her way around the chair and end table. They had created a nest pushing the chair and end table closer to the mattress after shoving the coffee table down and tight to the couch. Near the wood stove, safe and warm they'd bundled together ready to wait out the storm raging outside. Now she had a storm raging inside. One that had her wondering if she'd said too much or not enough. Like Parker said early this morning, neither of them had messed up. In the light of day when coherent thoughts returned, she agreed with him. The things they'd shared were close to personal and yet some of what she said other co-workers knew about. Only Tricia and her family knew about Doug. Doug happened back in San

58

Francisco. A continent away. Six years earlier. No, she wasn't going to talk about Doug yet. Maybe if Parker was serious about his statement about looking, she would. Still, how could a stud muffin like him not have a steady lady? Here she was with him. She'd hugged him. Kissed his cheek and—oh my yes, he'd kissed her even if it was a quick brush of his lips over hers.

Angela slipped her feet into the moccasin slippers Parker had handed her last night. A bit large, they flopped a bit as she walked in them toward the kitchen. She didn't care. Her body heat would warm them and they were much better than sliding around the cold tile floor in socks.

She paused near the patio doors wondering if she dared look out. Look out and see what Mother Nature and Old Man Winter had delivered. They'd survived the first brunt of the storm. At times during the night, the shrill whistle of the wind cut through the dark silence. Its eerie pitch reminded her of the thriller movies her father and brother Dillon loved to watch. The ones that set her overactive imagination wandering down paths that gave her nightmares. She knew better now. Thanks to her brother's ingenuity and love of building, he now built sets and electronics for many of Hollywood's studios. A burst of wind rattled the patio doors. The outdoors could wait. No matter how much snow had fallen, roads were probably still impassable. For now, she'd let that wait. Nesting with Parker felt safer than venturing outdoors. Her stomach grumbled. Yes, food mattered.

Angela pulled open the kitchen window blind. Patches of snow clung to the outer sill and edges of the window frame. Bright sun streamed in illuminating the sink and spilling out across the floor. Shielding her eyes, she looked out the window. Snow and ice icicles decorated the close-by tree limbs. The branches of the nearby juniper tree waved up and down as the wind swept through it. Old Man Winter hadn't loosened his grip yet. Shrugging, she turned away.

The jars of peanut butter and honey sat on the counter alongside the loaf of bread. At least she'd gotten the knife in the sink. Behind the peanut butter and honey sat the hot chocolate container. Angela opened the cabinet above the items and looked inside. She smiled as she picked up one of the items. Parker believed in quick and easy without it being overly processed. Powdered milk sat next to a container labeled pancake mix. Inside, written on cardboard, was a list of the ingredients and how much of each. Nodding, she set the mix on the counter along with the box of powdered milk. Basic pancakes didn't need eggs though the extra protein would help. If he had any in the fridge next to the stove, she'd have to open it quickly and close it to keep the interior cold air intact. Maybe they could put some items out on the patio, depending on the outside temperature.

She opened the fridge, peered inside and shut the door. Without a flashlight to be sure what she saw, Angela opened the cabinet she'd found the Dutch oven in last night. She bet Parker had a cast iron skillet or griddle. Most campers did. Cooking over an open fire or gas stove took pots and pans that withstood the heat and use. Her mother kept a set specifically for camping. Bingo! She set a skillet, griddle and a couple of unlined saucepans on the stove. Clean up would be easy with a bit of soaking, soap and water combined with good old fashioned scrubbing. The way she'd learned to do dishes until her first apartment—then the dishwasher got varying use.

As she walked back into the living room, Parker sat up, combing his hands through his hair. "Good morning," he said, stretching.

"Good morning." Angela held her hand out to the stove. Heat radiated against her palm. Not oven temperatures. Hot enough to warm the immediate area nearby. If she built the fire up, the top temp would heat a pan enough to cook the breakfast she had in mind.

Parker stood up, stretching again. "You okay?"

Angela nodded. "Yes. Caught another five hours until my bladder nudged me. Dozed until the wind started up again along with my stomach protesting."

Parker chuckled. "Nature does demand our attention now and then. Like now for me." He stepped around Angela and trotted toward the half-bath. 'Give me ten and we'll decide on breakfast."

"Sure. I've been investigating your kitchen and fridge contents." Angela picked up her penlight off the end table.

"Good," Parker called out entering the bathroom. He quickly pushed the door part way to. A pisser hard-on was one thing. A boner from dreaming about sex with Angela—that was something else. He lifted the toilet seat lid, shoved the waistband of his briefs and pajama pants down and sat down. Easiest way to be sure he didn't make a mess. He'd have to change the bag out later. It was a bit stinky in there. He closed the lid, washed and dried his hands. As he rummaged in the cabinet over the toilet hopping to find an air freshener cone, his stomach loudly growled. He grabbed the first cone he came to, pulled the plastic top up and sat it on top of the tank. Floral scents filled the air. Not his first pick for air freshener scents. Something more manly like pine or vanilla like in his bathroom upstairs came to mind. Hey it was better than stink of piss and shit emanating through the room. He shook his head. Discretion wasn't where his thoughts went. Simple earthy and easy to understand was all his mind could handle. He needed coffee before he could claim he was even a bit civilized. Well at least his thoughts. His outward exterior was all manners and couth. That was slowly ebbing away if he didn't get food and coffee soon. He checked the baseboards before walking out of the bathroom. Still slightly warm to the touch. He'd heard the generator sputter and spit a couple of times during the night as he rolled over. Depending on how long the sunshine held, the solar panels would help raise the interior floor heat. Things were looking up. He was ready to ask Angela about fixing food.

Parker stopped dead in his tracks. The sight in front of him was one that made him swallow twice, clench and unclench his hands, and remind himself to breathe. Yes, breathe, and think about not walking over and patting Angela on the ass. She was bent over in front of the stove with the door open, tending the fire. Walking up and fondling her without permission would either get him slapped sillier than his stupid id already was or cause her to drop what she was doing. Putting out a fire or treating burns would dash all hope of laying more foundation on what appeared to be a growing comfort and bond between them. No way was he going to risk that. He pressed his lips together and took one last breath before he spoke. "Thanks for taking care of the fire."

Angela straightened, facing him. "You're welcome. I hope you don't mind I decided on breakfast for us."

"Fine by me. I'm not overly finicky. What did you decide?" He sat down on the couch, rummaging through the pillows and towels until he found his moccasins.

"Pancakes with honey and a couple of eggs stirred in. Bacon and cheese toast."

"Sounds heavenly. You find all this in my fridge and cabinets? I ain't shopped this week yet."

Angela laughed as she passed him. "You have a dozen eggs that need using. Found an open bacon package in the meat drawer and a few cheese slices too."

"Good. Stuff needs used up. Hope we have enough things on hand to carry us through the next two or three days." Parker yawned as he slipped his slippers on. "Man, I need coffee."

"Taking care of that too. Found the filters for the coffee maker and a can of coffee. If you've got a couple of rubber bands, I'll show you how to make coffee in a saucepan."

"In a saucepan? Rubber bands might have them in the drawer where I keep the bag ties." Parker moved forward, preparing to stand.

"Yes, saucepan. Not quite filter drip coffee but just as good. Stronger if you let it brew too long. Like a tea bag, only more of it."

"Good thing to know. I don't have to unearth my camping coffee pot. How's the temp holding in the fridge?" Parker stood up, leaned down and picked up the afghan, folding it.

"Decent. There's still ice in the freezer. I snuck a peek to see what was in there."

"Glad you did. I cook basics. Nothing fancy. Bachelor food at best." Parker headed into the kitchen.

Angela followed him. "Do you have an ice chest? Outside thermometer shows five degrees. We can put stuff in it on the patio. Keep things chilled better."

"I like how you think. Practical and observant." Parker turned and faced Angela. "Things I find attractive. By the way, I was serious earlier about looking."

Angela arched an eyebrow, folded her arms across her chest, and gave him a once over up and down look. "Well, you snore. Not as bad as my ex. And paisley print pj pants aren't a fashion statement. Not that I'm attracted to men who wear suits all the time."

He couldn't smile. No just couldn't. Mirth and smiling might. . .might what? Cut the silence? Change the mood? Or had Angela just said she found him acceptable? Maybe she was attracted to him? As much as his ego egged him to ask more questions and find out, the more his psyche said shut up and get food and coffee in him first.

"Agree. Neither one of us is making any fashion statements. Oversize sweatshirt and thermals aren't the latest out-and-about trend either." He opened the drawer closest to him and began searching through it.

"I doubt either of us is going out and about any time soon." Angela pulled back the blind from the patio door, peering out. "Snow drifts are lining most of the patio. About halfway up the railing posts."

"Damn," Parker said, moving closer to her. He took ahold of the blind, pulling it back more. "There's about twelve or more inches out there. No telling what the front and roads look like."

Angela let go of the blind and moved behind him. "If you'll put a couple more logs on the fire. I'll get the bacon ready to start cooking. Pancake mix just needs water. They'll cook up in the bacon grease."

"Just like when you're camping." Parker let go of the blind and started toward the living room. "I've got a hand crank radio we can listen to later. It has a plug for your cell phone charger."

Angela nodded. "I brought my spare battery. It's fully charged. Also a power pack. The crank will save on using those."

He stopped before exiting the kitchen. "Sure will. We might be snowed in more than a couple of days. You okay with that?"

Angela looked up from putting bacon in the cast iron frying pan next to her. "Isn't going to do much good if I'm not. Seriously though, I'm fine. May need to do some laundry by hand if it goes beyond two or three days."

Parker shot her a thumbs up. "I can string a clothesline in the upstairs bath. I promise not to peek at your unmentionables."

Angela tittered. "Thanks. I promise not to assume your boxers are all pink paisley print."

"Touché," Parker called out, continuing into the living room. "Fire should be going good in a few minutes."

'Great. I'll put this on and then get the coffee going." Angela said, walking into the living room carrying the skillet and a meat fork.

Parker straightened as Angela approached him. "Watch where you stick that fork," he teased, picking up several small pieces of wood.

Angela made two short jabs with the meat fork away from him. Shaking her head, she replied, "Not the kind of meat I'm hungry for at the moment."

She set the frying pan on the stove and stepped back from him. Parker tossed the first two pieces of wood into the stove, picked up the ashes rake and stirred the embers close to the main flame burning close to the center of the ring of partially burned wood and ashes. Raking the red embers toward the main flame, he gauged the fire would pick up shortly. That left time to heat the skillet and not burn the bacon. A lesson he learned cooking over an open flame with the grill just inches from the live fire. He laid the other pieces of wood close to the flame and embers.

Closing the stove door, he stepped back. Angela was nowhere in the living room. He heard her moving around while he tended the fire. Noting where she was or what she did wasn't his main focus then. Now she was. Each of them was feeling shy and standoffish. Revealing more of themselves in the dark of night was different than in daylight. Add to it, they each were still unsure and afraid. Afraid to drop the socialized boundaries workplaces often required. They weren't at work nor were they going to be for at least twenty-four to forty-eight hours more. He knew better than to push, poke or prod when it came to relaxing with a co-worker beyond the subtleties exchanged during work hours. He wiped his hands on one of the towels on the back of the couch. Moving around the couch, he called out. "Angela, are you okay?"

"Kinda," Angela answered. "Hunger and lack of caffeine setting in. I need to find my hairbrush. Part of me is feeling grungy."

"I sorta get it," Parker said moving into the kitchen.

Angela looked up, setting her backpack aside. She pointed at the coffee filled filter sitting next to the medium-sized saucepan half-full of water. "Coffee's ready to brew once the bacon starts."

She started to turn away from Parker. He didn't need to see the tears threatening to flow or her angst over bed tousled hair and sniffing each time she reached for something swearing she smelled stale and sweaty. Last time she felt this way she was trying to impress a guy she'd met for a breakfast date after an overnight shift at work. Shit, when had that feeling started? Were her hormones in overdrive? Had thinking about Doug ignited this? Or was she feeling vulnerable because her morning routine wasn't happening? Some days routine kept her going. She'd admit she was a creature of habit. Some days more than others. Like this morning. She was out of her element and comfort zone.

Parker laid a hand on her arm. "I don't know what's going on. I'm getting strange vibes and yet I know the feeling of, man, I want a shower and food. Am I on to something?"

She nodded, pressing her lips tighter together. She took one breath after another, focusing on the handle of the drawer in front of her. Her heart skipped a beat and then fluttered as anxiety ebbed and flowed through her. Insecurities and past taunts waited their turn to flare and spark into being. Exhaling, she glanced at Parker.

He slid his hand up her arm, moving closer to her. "How about a hug?"

CHAPTER NINE

Angela started to pull away. Parker stepped back. "Did I say something wrong?"

She shook her head. "No. Ever have one of those deja vu feelings? One where you hear your parents telling you about manners/"

"Oh man, have I. It's like you're on edge trying to be excellent and feeling like you're not."

"That's where part of me is at. Nothing to do with you. The most I lounge around is while I wait for coffee to brew. Even then I usually shower and dress before I make breakfast."

Parker held up his hand. "Now I get what's going on. We live alone and function at our own levels. When others are present, it's like our company manners spring into action."

Angela let go a deep sigh. "Yes. That and other things. Ones I'm not sure I can describe."

Parker closed the space between them. He laid one hand on Angela's shoulder, his other on her forearm. He waited until her gaze met his. "I'm offering a hug. A way to break the company ice surrounding either of us. We're friends, right?"

"Yes, we are."

"Good. I think a good morning hug is a great way to move into the day." He slid his hand up Angela's arm, stopping close to her shoulder. "You open to a hug?"

Warmth sparked deep inside of her. From some place she hadn't imagined, her heart. The place she hadn't thought about. Not because she'd closed it off. Or shut off her deeper passionate feelings. It was Parker and what he was doing. He checked in, asked and didn't take. Maybe she could let her guard down more. Relax and feel safe.

"Yes, I am." She placed a hand on Parker's waist. "Ready for it too."

Parker grinned, looped his arms around her neck and moved tighter to her until their feet touched. "You decide how tight and how long."

Angela slid both arms around Parker's waist and leaned toward him. They touched from their chests down to their waists. She closed her eyes, tipped her head back, and wet her lips.

Parker stood still, taking in Angela's moves and reactions. She held him loosely and yet. . .was she asking for more tipping her head back and licking her lips? Could he kiss her and not distract them from the fact they needed to get back to the bacon he could smell cooking? Perhaps he could. Reading silent signs had never been a talent he developed well. Vitals, physical appearance concerning health, or life and death issues he got. Those he knew because textbooks and instructors explained them. He'd seen and experienced them first hand. Non-verbal signals aka body language—that left him guessing. Guessing and taking a chance. Well, he was going to take a leap of faith and go where his gut said to go.

Dipping his head, he brushed his lips along Angela's cheek, pressing one kiss after another along her jawline until he reached her ear.

Angela murmured as he pressed his lips to her ear, softly saying, "I think the bacon is cooking. Smells good."

Parker pulled back and rested his forehead against Angela's. "I'd kiss you more. But that bacon smells damn good. I hate to waste a chance at a good breakfast cooked by someone else. Coffee and cereal get boring after while."

Angela snickered. "All right. I'll cook breakfast. You can decide about lunch and dinner later. Right now I need to check the bacon."

She squeezed Parker tightly one more time and dropped her hands. As she stepped back, Parker did the same. He moved to her left, leaving her room to get past the counter. She picked up the pan full of water. "When it boils we add the filter. Take it off the stove and let it steep until the water is the color of how strong you want your coffee."

Parker grabbed the coffee-filled filter and followed her into the living room. She picked up the meat fork from on top of the pellet storage bin where she'd left it. As she set the pan on the stove, the partly full teakettle began to steam.

"Got an idea how we can do two things at once with hot water." Parker reached for the kettle. "We can make coffee in here. And you can use the water in the pan to wash up with after we're done eating."

"True. There's the Dutch oven too. Can you add a half cup of water to the pancake batter and mix it up? This bacon is cooking faster than expected." Angela turned several pieces of bacon. She glanced over her shoulder, adding, "I need something to put this bacon on."

"Got both under control." Parker stuffed the coffee-filled filter into the kettle, put the lid back on it, picked up the pan of water and took it into the kitchen with him. He grabbed the roll of paper towels off the counter, put them under one arm and took a large serving platter out of the cabinet closets to the stove. As he entered the living room, he looked for the best place to put the platter. Closest to Angela was the wood pellet bin. He set the platter down, took the roll of paper towels out from under his arm and unrolled several sheets, layering them on the platter. He caught Angela's nod as he turned back toward the kitchen. "Platter is for the bacon. I'll be back with the batter in a moment."

He added the half-cup of water, cracked the two eggs sitting next to the bowl into the batter and tossed the shells into the large trash bin marked compost items near the patio door. It took him two drawers to find the medium-sized whisk he wanted. Air helped make the pancakes fluffier he remembered his mother saying during one of her Sunday morning cooking lessons with him. Stirring the batter thoroughly twice, he added three more ingredients to the mix: cinnamon, honey and nutmeg. Two more stirs got all the makings mixed. He put the batter-covered whisk in the sink, took a large serving spoon out of the utensil drawer and picked up the bowl. He continued stirring as he entered the living room. "Batter is ready. Where do you want the bowl?"

Angela pointed to where the platter had been. "On there for now. Can you set this on the coffee table, please?" She held the bacon-filled platter out to him as he sat the bowl down.

"I got it. How goes the coffee?" Parker took a hold of the platter with both hands, making his way around the couch and set the platter on the coffee table.

"About done I think. If it boils much more, it might come out bitter or ultra-strong." Angela added two spoons of batter to the skillet. "I take mine with milk and sugar. You?"

"Mostly black with a bit of sugar. Often I add milk to cool it down. I'll take the kettle into the kitchen and let it steep a bit more before taking the filter out." Parker wrapped his hand in the towel he used earlier to wipe his hands on and grasped the handle of the kettle.

Twenty more minutes passed as they worked in tandem moving things between the living room and kitchen. Parker took a turn cooking the last batch of honey cinnamon hotcakes while Angela prepped the bread for toast. She showed him how to toast bread in a skillet until it was almost as brown as if he used the toaster. Adding half a slice of cheese to each finished the cooking. Angela walked into the kitchen with the skillet in hand. "Okay this can cool off in here. We need forks, spoons, plates and napkins. Please pour the coffee."

"Right on it." Parker set two mugs on the counter, adding two spoons of honey and powdered milk into each mug. He poured the kettle-brewed coffee into each mug, inhaling as he did. "Man that smells divine. Who'd thought coffee could steep like tea?"

Angela paused near him. Her hands full of utensils, napkins and plates. "Ready to eat?"

"Oh, yeah." Parker picked up both mugs and headed into the living room. He paused as he reached the coffee table laden with a platter of bacon, honey cinnamon hotcakes, and four slices of cheese toast. Simple fare. Yet it looked like a feast. A feast he was ready to partake of. He set the mugs on the coffee table, glanced at Angela and grinned. "Looks awesome. Smells great. And I bet it tastes good too."

"Thank you." Angela handed him a plate with four hotcakes and two pieces of cheese toast on it. "Help yourself to the bacon. I like mine with the cheese toast like a sandwich."

"I'll try it after I'm done with the hotcakes. Do you want honey on yours?" He set his plate on the end of the coffee table close to the kitchen.

"No, thank you." Angela set her plate and mug of coffee on the end table. She sat down in the chair, kicked off her slippers and propped her feet on the air mattress close to her pillow.

Parker sat down midway down the couch, reached for his plate and glanced at Angela. Her hair was still tousled. She had put her glasses on midway through cooking, admitting her contacts were bothering her. She'd avoided him for several moments. Damn, he hadn't gawked, had he? It took a few looks to get used to the change. Not that she looked bad in glasses. The silver wire frames complemented her. No detraction as far as he was concerned. He used reading glasses when he was on the computer for quite a while. Hazard of his continuing ed classes. "Mind if I ask you a personal question?"

Angela set her mug down, not wanting to grip it any harder. She'd barely gotten two sips of coffee down her along with a couple of bites of hotcake. Had he deliberately waited until she had her mouth full to ask a loaded question? She held up a finger, nodded, and wiped her mouth with her napkin. "At the moment, I do. I don't handle discussions well until I'm about halfway through my first mug. No offense. I'm sure we've got things to talk about."

Parker wiped his hands on his napkin, set his plate on the coffee table, and picked up his mug. "I salute your honesty. I'll put this out there. When you're ready I'd like to know how much water you need to wash up."

Angela sipped her coffee. "Depends on what we can heat and how much water is needed for dishes, too."

"We'll tackle it when we're done eating." Parker set his mug down and reached for another hotcake. "These are good. Very good."

"Thank you. Your mix and my cooking. What is in the mix?" Angela set her mug down and started eating another hotcake.

"Nothing unusual. Flour mix of rye, rice and oat. A bit of sourdough starter. Helps with rising if you don't have eggs handy. Thanks to my younger sister's wheat allergy I learned to cook gluten-free before it became the norm."

"I know that feeling. We had a lot of fresh and organic ingredients too. Co-op trading, local farmer's market and what we grew." Angela set her plate aside, slumping down in the chair more.

Parker pointed to the platter holding the last eight bacon pieces. "I ate maybe four or five pieces. How many you want for your sandwich?"

"Two is fine. You want any more?" Angela yawned, arched her shoulders and leaned forward, stretching her hands and arms out in front of her.

"No. Too much fat and salt all at once. Don't need to send my cholesterol levels skyrocketing." Parker put his pieces of toast together, cheese on cheese, and took a bite.

"I can use the bacon in another dish. Right now I want to sip my coffee and enjoy the moment." Angela picked up her mug and sat back in the chair.

Parker nodded, leaning back against the couch. Several quiet moments passed. No wind. No ice crystals pelting the windows. Even the fire seemed to enjoy the interlude. No crackling of wood. Just warmth and peace. Parker inhaled and exhaled slowly. He ate the last of his cheese toast sandwich, downed the last of his coffee, and set his mug down. Settling back against the couch again, he closed his eyes and let his thoughts run where they wanted to go.

He knew he wanted to kiss, hold, and touch Angela more. To the point of pleasuring them both. How did he tell her he found her sexy even now? It wasn't just how she looked. Her confidence. Her sense of humor. It wasn't as warped as his. It came damn close. They worked well together. Teamed up to get the job done. She understood practicality, easy and simple ways of doing things. Though some people didn't find organic and off-the-grid cooking easy. He sure did. Convenience had its role too. But processed, packaged and loaded with chemicals. Not much of that in his kitchen. He liked his junk food—chips and pretzels when the guys came over for poker. That was few and far between now due to the shift he worked.

The thunk of Angela's mug on the end table roused him from his dozing, causing him to focus again on her. Coming right out and telling her he wanted her, found her attractive and was interested in learning more might not be the best way to move forward. He'd taken some liberties in the kitchen. Backing off some might be in their best interest. Offer an apology and check-in? Yeah, that probably would help out a lot.

Parker opened one eye, glanced at Angela, and sat up. She sat with her legs crossed, tapping her steepled fingers against her chin. She appeared to be staring at something and yet not anything in particular. The picture that hung on the wall across the room was an Australian seascape print a friend from his time in London gave him. The teal frame and aquamarine background drew his attention when he gazed at it. The photo definitely had its appeal. He started to move forward. Angela glanced at him, lowered her hands, and rocked forward.

Angela grabbed one of her pieces of cheese toast and bit into it. Finding the words to describe her uneasiness and turmoil hadn't been easy. She still wasn't sure how to voice her thoughts. Parker had shown and said he wanted more. He was interested. Yet, lingering images, past feelings. . . and she took two more bites of her cheese toast. She needed to stop feeling so damn vulnerable. He hadn't done anything she hadn't agreed to. Tuning into what they'd talked about mattered. Maybe that was the starting point of their next discussion. One that had to wait until she felt more presentable and in control. She finished her piece of cheese toast, placed her hands on the arm of the chair and stood up. "Heating water is a priority. I need to wash and dress. Then we talk more. Okay?"

Parker nodded as he rose. "Sure. I understand. Let me check the upstairs temperature. Can you put the kettle and Dutch oven on to heat?"

"Kettle and pan I used earlier. The Dutch oven maybe a bit more than I can lift." Angela started toward the kitchen. Parker followed her.

He entered the kitchen first. "I'll fill the Dutch oven and put it on the stove. While I'm upstairs, could you please get a couple of trash bags out from under the sink? I'll clean up the half-bath while you're washing up."

"I'm on it." She filled the kettle and pan, set them on the counter and opened the cabinet under the sink. Cool air rushed out, chilling her face and hands as she reached for the box of trash bags. No frost or ice appeared on the pipes or back wall as she looked deeper into the cabinet. Insulation from the snow and the interior insulation held. She drew a deep breath and let it go. Images of burst pipes and dealing with evacuating vanished. She hoped her pipes and place fared as well. As she straightened up, Parker exited the kitchen, carrying the Dutch oven. She laid the two trash bags on the counter, picked up the kettle and pan, following Parker into the living room. He stood by the stove.

"I'm going to check on things upstairs. I'll be a few moments." Parker moved to the stairs, pausing as he took a hold of the railing. "I want to know if I've done something wrong."

Angela placed the kettle and pan on the stove next to the Dutch oven. She faced him, her lips pressed together. She glanced at him, looked away and glanced at him again. She shook her head and moved toward him. "Wrong? No. We're in an unusual situation. I'm not sure if we're overreacting or trying to read more into what's said or unsaid."

He nodded. "I feel like one of those bobbleheads that goes around bobbing without really saying much."

Angela grinned. "Don't worry. I think we've reached a place where each of us needs to regroup into a mutual comfort zone."

"Thanks for seeing that. I'll check upstairs. Get your stuff together that you need and I'll be back down in a bit." Parker bounded up the stairs, taking them two at a time. Comfort for him was cooling down his gonads and focusing on turning their time together into a date. How in the hell did he do that?

CHAPTER TEN

Angela inhaled slowly, counting by twos to a hundred. She'd already exhaled by the time she hit fifty. Focusing on something other than Parker's pajama pants pulled tight around his ass as he trotted up the steps might get her calmed down. They'd touched briefly as they hugged. Then he kissed her. Nibbled her jaw and—Angela gulped. Parker's hot breath against her ear damn near had her creaming her panties. And neither of them had seen the other naked yet. She gripped the arm of the couch, counting again as she took another deep breath. By the time she reached ten, she exhaled, rolled her eyes and wiped her sweaty palms on her thermals. She didn't know if sex would happen or it wouldn't. She did know each of them had to want it. Mutual desire was so much sweeter and wonderful when two people connected. Maybe that was where all of this was leading. After that, then what? Forecasting what she'd pack for lunch the next day was as far as she got. Hunches sometimes played out. Other times. . .well, going with the flow for now felt solid and right.

"You ready?" Parker called out.

"No. Not yet. Take your time." Angela stood up, pulled her scrunchie out of her hair and walked into the kitchen. Her duffel bag sat near the mail-covered table close to the patio door. She smiled as she picked the bag up and sat it on a chair. Parker sorted his mail almost the same way she did. Catalogs, bills, and junk mail took up the upper third of the table. The lower portion held opened envelopes with dates written on them along with the words important or file. One pile had a chartreuse sticky note on it marked W file. Gee, Parker hadn't learned the fine art of taking the trashcan and recycle container over to the table and feed them as he went through the mail? She glanced over her shoulder. Of course, he could teach her a thing or two about sorting mail too. His trashcan and recycle container weren't still sitting by the table waiting to get fed. Working overnight shifts changed a person's priorities. Sleep and food often topped the list.

Angela unzipped the middle section of the duffel. She took out a quart-size storage bag laid it on the table. Inside it were a change of underwear, socks and a sports bra. Holding the section open wider, she could see two more bags inside. Two more changes. Not that she had to worry about a bra much since she wasn't at work. The outer zipper pocket contained a sports one and a sleep one. Either offered enough leisure support. Also kept her nipples from being too obvious when her thoughts and hormones sent mixed responses that she'd rather not be apparent until they talked more. She zipped the middle section closed as she heard Parker coming down the stairs.

In the large back section, she found a pair of denim leggings and a long sleeved t-shirt, her post-workout clothes. She could put her thermals back on if needed. Otherwise, she planned to wrap up in the afghan. She draped the clothes over the back of the chair as Parker entered the kitchen.

"Found the radio. Also found these." He set a stack of paperbacks on the table next to the radio. "Even got a deck of cards, a word tile game and a couple of other board games. A few letter tiles are missing."

"No problem. We can cut up paper or cardboard and write on the missing letters on it." Angela picked up one of the paperbacks. An old noir detective story. As she read the back, she nodded. "My bobblehead turn."

Parker snorted. "My mother left a few boxes of my stuff she found in her attic last time she visited. I hadn't finished going through the first box yet. These were in it."

"Saturday nights were family nights growing up. We took turns reading to each other. G-rated books most of the time. My dad loved detective stories. His granddad had a stash of them that dad read over and over."

"Maybe we can create our own time together like a campout date?" Parker said and turned away fussing with the radio.

"Most of my campout dates were very chaperoned." Angela zipped the duffel closed and set it on the floor. She glanced at Parker as she leaned down to pick up her backpack. His gaze briefly met hers and he looked away.

She straightened, moved closer to Parker and laid her hand on his shoulder. "I'm not saying no. I'm saying maybe we're making our own date or dates depending on how long we're snowed in."

Parker faced her. He shrugged. "I'm not upset. Just unsure how to . . ."

His shrugged again and turned back to the radio.

Angela slid her hand down Parker's arm. "Unsure how to what?"

Parker pressed his lips together. He needed a second cup of coffee. And a whole lot more sleep. He hadn't slept more than four hours at a time. Keeping an eye on the stove and Angela had kept him from much REM sleep. Sleep he needed without remembering all the weird dreams and dozing in between thoughts that didn't cohere even with most of him awake. He pressed his lips tighter together. Blurting out his first thoughts wouldn't make sense. How did he explain uncertainty, a bit of fear, and a whole lot of wanting to get past tiptoeing around their attraction? Then was it mutual to the same level for both of them. He glanced at Angela. She hadn't moved. She watched him like a cat ready to pounce. This mouse needed to speak, not squeak. Not roar like a lion. He needed to say what he felt without over explaining.

He turned and faced Angela. "I've asked women out. Gone to ritzy places, dropped money, and had second and third dates as a result. Even done buddy ones with women friends. But. . ."

Angela hadn't looked away or frowned. She hadn't grimaced when he said buddy. She appeared to be listening. Actually, hearing what he said. That garnered her several points. She patted his arm as she spoke. "This one doesn't fit your experience? It's different. Maybe very different?"

Parker swallowed hard. Was he that easy to read? Was he wearing his emotions on his face as his grandmother used to tease him about? He wet his lips, exhaled and replied. "Yeah. And I'm not sure how to make a first date after I've slept with a woman before we agreed to date."

Angela clapped her hand over her mouth. She snorted twice and dropped her hand. "I'm not laughing at you. It's the irony of the situation. You want time to talk with someone. Get to know them. And have leisure moments where you get beyond superficial things like weather, job, and maybe politics."

"So true. You know, we might be there and not realize it. We've talked about weather. It affects our job almost daily. Our job enters into everything we do during the eight hours we work together. Well, politics?"

Angela held up her hand. "Can we agree to disagree on that for now? I'd hate to ruin a good campout date with an argument."

Parker laughed. "I agree to disagree on politics. It makes for a much more interesting debate when we do discuss it. So we're having a good campout date?"

"Yes. You're a good host. You're thoughtful, caring, and kind. I knew that from work. I've learned more about you in the time we've spent together than if we'd actually gone out on a real date."

"Really?" Parker took a hold of the radio's crank and started turning it. "I don't know whether to be impressed or worried."

Angela picked up her clothes off the back of the chair. "Stop worrying. We're talking. We're interested in what the other is saying. Right now, I need to wash up. Do something with my hair and shift gears into daytime mode."

"Understood. Do you need toiletries? Soap, washcloth and a towel are in the bathroom upstairs. It's at the rear of the hall."

"Thanks. I hadn't gotten mine out yet. I'll brush my teeth when I come back down." Angela started walking away. He kept her within his vision until she entered the living room.

He turned back toward the table, focusing on the crank, trying to not focus on the way his cock kept nudging against his briefs. A quick jack off hadn't cooled his gonads every time he thought about Angela upstairs nude.

Angela stopped at the top of the stairs. She was about to enter Parker's private domain. The man cave area as her father used to call his office and den. The place where he sought refuge from five noisy children and his wife. Once in a while he'd invite one of them in to share one-on-one time with him. Or help with homework. Often she and a couple of her siblings would follow him up the short staircase to the landing, the outer area of the cave. The place where her father would affectionately hug them and shoo them away. They'd run down the stairs, noisily giggling and chattering.

She gripped the banister firmer, took a deep breath, exhaled and stepped into Parker's domain. Looking left and right, she noted three open doors. As she moved across the floor, she noticed the soft light illuminating the bathroom interior creating an intimate feeling to it. Close to the bathroom was a closed door. Possibly a closet or another room. At home, a similar door led to the staircase to her attic and storage area.

Putting one foot in front of the other took concentration if she wanted to avoid her curiosity. Peeking into the other doors without permission wasn't polite. Not that either of them had waltzed along that edge in the last few hours. They'd skated close to falling off and stumbling in a fast roll down the hill into how good and perfect either of their etiquettes could be. She smirked and shook her head. That was a hot topic waiting to ignite once she went back downstairs. For now, she wanted to wash away yesterday's work grime and the sleep from her eyes. Warm water from the kettle she carried mixed with the cold coming through the pipes would give her a quick thrill as her grandma Fiona used to say. The chill of the cold mixed with enough heat to perk the body up. And washing quick was the answer.

Angela laid her clothes on the counter, set the kettle close by and pushed the door partway closed. The counter's coolness felt good against her hand. Not overly chilled, yet with the heat emanating off the kettle it wasn't cold. She pulled the plunger for the sink, filled the basin halfway from the kettle and put the washcloth into the water. She quickly stripped off the sweatshirt, wincing at the cold air rushing over her breasts and arms. Lathering the washcloth took a bit of work. Soap and cold water didn't have a great love relationship. Working the cloth over her arms, face and underarms took more time since rinsing the cloth required watching where she put her hand instead of trying to do it by feel like she did at home. Squinting, she rinsed the cloth and ran it over her face, arms, and under arms. Cold water dripped from the cloth down and across her nipples. Shivers like the icicles she'd seen hanging off the tree limbs and patio railing jolted through her. She tossed the cloth on the counter and grabbed the towel flinging it over her shoulders like a cape. Pressing her lips firmly together, she fought against the urge to chatter her teeth, sending her interior and exterior into a huge shivering contest.

She opened the bag holding her clean underwear. She tossed the towel on the counter, put on her bra and pulled on her long sleeve t-shirt. Thrusting her arms through the sleeves of the sweatshirt, she paused. The interior of the shirt was still warm from her body heat. Part of her wanted to curl up inside and not come out until spring thaw was officially in full force. Not that was going to happen anytime soon given the amount and depth of last night's snowfall.

Trying to wash between her legs and mons was going to take a tactical approach if she left the sweatshirt on. It wasn't coming off until she had shucked her thermals and panties. Taking a hold of the waistband of both, she shoved them down and off along with her socks. She quickly put the slippers back on. The bathroom floor was *cold*. Damn cold. Too cold for bare feet or even sock-covered ones. How the baseboard heating system kept the pipes from freezing, she didn't get. All the pipes she'd checked last night were wrapped with insulation. Leaving the doors open on the kitchen sink cabinet had helped offset part of the cold penetrating through the outside wall. Even the half-bath had sink pipes were wrapped. She bet the bathroom ones were too. Swirling the cloth around in the cooling water, she dismissed checking the pipes here. Chilling wasn't on her to-do list. Lathering the washcloth took more time than she liked. Shivers threatened to claim her again. Goose bumps formed on her legs, growing and multiplying as she washed and rinsed.

Grabbing the towel again, she dried and flung it over the shower curtain rod. Pulling her panties and leggings on took longer than anticipated. Chills and shivers were gaining ground, numbing her a bit. She blew on her hands and chafed them together. Tipping her head back, eyes closed, she voiced a prayer. Not that she was overly religious. But, calling on deity to come forth with some sunshine wouldn't hurt. Faith, prayer, and being thankful along with asking for help got people through rough spots. Not that she was in one. She wrung out the washcloth and tossed it over the shower curtain rod next to the towel. Her teeth started chattering as she put the toilet seat lid down. Pulling on the sweatshirt took more effort this time. She knew she needed to get back to where it was warmer before she began to chill much more. She tossed her thermals over her shoulder, stuffed her panties and both pairs of socks in the plastic bag and exited the bathroom. Moving at a trot, she crossed the floor wondering what if Parker knew how chilled the upstairs had become. As she started down the stairs, she heard Parker call out.

"Ah, fuck! More snow? How damn much more?" Parker turned the volume up as the weather forecaster continued.

"Sorry folks. Looks like Old Man Winter is sitting on his ass and braying loudly with the wind chill factor in the single digits. We're expecting another one to two inches on top of the three to four we've already got throughout the area. Temperatures start to rise close to the weekend. Mid-thirties by Saturday."

"Doesn't sound good." Angela said behind him. "Hate to wear out my welcome."

Parker spun around. "Honey, you can't. Digging out's the issue. Temp is going to keep things icy and packed. Not going to be easy. Gonna take time and be done in chunks."

"I can help." Angela moved toward him, clutching her thermals and a plastic bag.

"I'm sure you can. I'm not angry. Just frustrated. I charged my cell phone as I cranked. Got three texts from Doc. And a quick call from the maintenance man."

"Okay. And?"

"Doc, Mrs. Carmichael, her daughter and the new grandbaby are doing fine. He called the hospital and they know the clinic is closed until further notice. Maintenance man said generator is holding up ok. He may stop by later to check on us if he can get out again."

Angela reached for her duffel bag. "What did the third text say?"

"To behave with three smiley faces and a winking one."

Angela snickered as she picked up the bag. "Did you respond? It's not like we're misbehaving."

"Nah. Figured let Doc and his imagination run wild. Keep him entertained between cribbage games with Mrs. Carmichael and her son-in-law."

Angela looked away, unzipped her duffel and stuffed her thermals in it. She rummaged in the plastic bag before she put it the duffel. She held up a pair of pink and blue stripped socks as she faced him. "Not too wild, I hope. Well, at least keep it at PG-13 rating."

Parker burst out laughing. "Ain't mine to censor. Nor mine to ask about. We're not kissing and telling. Even if they figure things out." He walked over to Angela, brushed his lips over hers and pulled back. "Meanwhile, I need to wash and get dressed too. Be back down in a few."

As he started to exit the kitchen, Angela called out. "Kettle is still up there. Not very warm. It's rather cold up there."

"Yeah, I know. Good for stimulating blood flow so I hurry up and get it done as my father used to say. Winters in England can be brutally cold." Parker took the stairs two at a time. "I'll be back down in a few."

Angela moved to the edge of the kitchen, catching Parker bounding up the stairs. Did he have a hard on? Or was she imagining things? The front of his pajamas tented out like his thoughts had been on something else before the weather forecast cooled things down a might. She wasn't taking bets on how fast the chill upstairs would change the direction of his thoughts.

CHAPTER ELEVEN

Parker slowed as he reached the top of the staircase. Cool air raced over his face and hands as he turned toward his bedroom. Upping the temp throughout the house demanded attention. Attention he wasn't prepared for at the moment. His mind ran rabid with the idea of snuggling naked with Angela in a double sleeping bag. Shared warmth fell second to having her uptight and real, like where his dreams and a few masturbation fantasies had gone.

But what if she said no? Yeah, his conscience and ethics prohibited him from taking. Mutual desire, mutual want and satisfaction made all the difference in the pleasure and orgasms. Pleasuring his partner brought him as much joy as his own orgasms did. He'd been blessed to have a few partners that enjoyed giving him pleasure in return. Surrendering and letting the female lead added an edginess to their coupling. Two of his encounters with this led to intense orgasms for both he and his partner. He'd helped another regain her confidence and security in her attractiveness. It'd been a few months since he last heard from Linda and her husband Brad. Parker wondered how his four godchildren and their parents were faring in North Dakota.

As he entered his bedroom, he glanced at the hall thermostat on the wall close to the bedroom door. It read forty-four degrees. Not good. If the outside temp dropped much more, the inside pipes could freeze. Opening cabinets and keeping the water dripping would help. Opening the hot water spigot would help allow water and air to flow as well. Damn, why couldn't winter just give up and let spring come on as it should? He laughed at the mendacity of his thoughts. Like one season had muscles to edge the other out or duke it out fist-to-fist. Shaking his head, he continued into his bedroom, grabbed his jeans off the chair closest to his closet, another sweatshirt from in the closet along with socks and underwear. He stopped at the dresser close to the closet and opened the top drawer. He pulled out the first t-shirt he came to. He blinked, sighed and continued out of the bedroom. His sister's orange South Carolina college t-shirt gift wouldn't show under his sweatshirt. He swore the shirt should have come with sunglasses or a bloody dimmer switch.

Talk about neon orange. The thick material of the shirt would add an extra layer under the sweatshirt.

He entered the bathroom and partially closed the door. He noted the towel hung over the shower curtain. He'd use the same towel Angela had. Picking up a new washcloth off the stack in the linen shelves behind the door, he tossed it on the counter next to his clothes. He cupped his hand around the kettle. More cold than warmth caressed his palm. So much for a warm wash-up. Cold water it was. He pulled the stopper and dumped the rest of the water from the kettle into the sink along with the cold water trickling out of the faucet. Turning the hot water spigot on slightly, more cold water flowed out. Shucking his clothes, he gritted his teeth and wet the washcloth. He worked the soap across the cloth, lathering it as fast as he could. Cold wetness under his underarms and across his chest were nothing compared to the shock his cock and balls were going to get next. Parker inhaled, took ahold of his cock and slipped the cold wet soapy cloth down and over him. There was no way in God's green earth he was putting that any nearer his balls. They'd shrivel up tighter than a green plum to quote his granddad.

Parker rinsed the washcloth, ran it over his cock and rinsed the cloth again. This time he wiped his chest, arms and underarms, then one last plunge of his hand and the cloth into the very chilled water. He wiped over and around his neck and face. He reached for the bar of soap. It shot out of his hand and on to the floor. "Come back here, you," he yelled. "Damn it. I'm not washing the floor."

As he bent over to grab the bar of soap, footsteps sounded behind him.

Angela hastily pulled on her socks, shoved her feet into her slippers and trotted toward the stairs as fast as she could. Another thud sounded, followed by Parker cussing and yelling more. All she could make out was "soap and water on floor." As she reached the top of the steps, nothing but silence greeted her. Lord, had Parker slipped and hit his head. Was he out cold? As she trotted toward the bathroom door, she prayed that nothing bad had happened. She started to push the door open and enter the bathroom, her mouth open, ready to say something. She stopped dead in her tracks. Her mouth hung open. She tried to speak. Nothing came out. Swallowing wasn't happening either.

In front of her, bent over with his ass in the air, his balls dangling down and part of his cock in view, was Parker, intently looking for something between the toilet and tub.

She closed her mouth, blinked, nodded and pressed her lips together. This view wasn't one she could have summoned up even on her best story nights. Not that she would have said out loud what this luscious vision was. Here in plain view and very real...oh, definitely very real. If she reached out she could...

Angela drew back her hand. Goosing Parker was verboten. Embarrassing either of them topped that list too. She backed up, enjoying the view a bit longer. She stopped backing up halfway across the floor. Wetting her lips, she called out. "Parker, are you okay?"

Parker clasped the washcloth wrapped around the soap and straightened. He froze as Angela came into view. She moved a step closer. He gripped the soap and washcloth tighter. If she got closer and he turned around . . .how did he explain his hard-on? Being buck-ass naked? He licked his lips, ready to answer when the absurdity of it all slammed down on his ironical obtuse sense of humor. He inhaled rapidly, trying to push his mirth back down. Laughing hysterically wasn't going to help. Taking a slow deep breath, he nodded. Nodded again and moved behind the bathroom door. He let go a deep sigh and spoke. "Yes, I'm fine. Give me about ten minutes and I'll be out. It's damn cold up here."

He shoved the bathroom door almost shut and continued washing up. He speedily dried and pulled his briefs and t-shirt on. As he finished fastening his jeans, he opened the door more. "Do you mind waiting at the top of the steps so we can go down together?"

"Sure," Angela answered. Her tone was flat. He didn't blame her. Given what just happened, he'd be skeptical too.

Angela didn't look back. She kept walking until she reached the top step. Part of her wanted to go down the steps and let Parker guess where she was. Not that she could go much of anywhere. Snowed in limited her movement to down by the stove, wrapped up in the afghan. So much for sulking like a teenager. Pretty much like a pre-teen. She was well past that. What was it Doug used to say? Her ego reverted to its childhood every time she felt slighted. Angela took a deep breath and stepped down one step, sitting on the landing. Chafing her hands over and across her upper legs, she glanced back at the bathroom door. She could see Parker in the mirror as he dressed.

She pressed her lips together tightly, rubbed her hands faster on her legs. Time had come to admit something to herself and maybe out loud to Parker. She was interested in him. Attracted to him. And after seeing him naked. . .the man had a body that she could ogle for hours. He had a nice cock and his balls. . .oh, running her tongue up and down those. Fanning herself, she inhaled slowly. She'd seen his hard-on before he jumped behind the door. Oh, yes, he was fine and studly. Very fine. Was he serious about his earlier question? He was truly interested in her? That was one item she needed to ask about. Talk about moving outside her comfort zone. A hunk desired *her*—that defied her imagination. Then again, this wasn't fantasy anymore. It was reality. Angela stood up, ready to move back toward the bathroom, when Parker exited. His neon orange t-shirt caught her attention. Possibly in a way he hadn't planned on. That thing needed a dimmer switch and a pair of sunglasses to look at it.

"Where did you get that?" She pointed at Parker.

Parker glanced down, shaking his head. "Kid sister's gift. Her sorority had 'em made up for Halloween. The thing must glow in the dark. I haven't gone outside with it on for fear of getting arrested for wearing such an object."

Angela snickered. Lowered her arm and snickered again. "You poor thing. The things we do for our siblings."

Parker chuckled. "It's an extra layer under this." He held out his sweatshirt and put it on. "I wear it to bed now and then with my pajama pants."

Angela held up both hands. "Whoa! Pink and green paisley print pajama pants and that together?"

Parker vigorously nodded. "Yes. My grandmother said my pajamas covered me quite well thank you."

Angela clapped her hand over her mouth and turned away. She wrapped her other arm around her waist. Pressing her lips together behind her hand didn't help. Eeks and eeps of laughter rang out. She tried turning around. All she could do was lean on the wall and laugh.

Parker walked by her, stuck his tongue out and continued down the stairs. "When you're done peeing your pants, let me know. I can do some hand laundry for you."

Angela straightened and followed Parker down the stairs. "I can do my own laundry. Thank you. Covering up for grandma is important, I'm sure."

Parker dropped down on the couch, pulling the afghan partly over him. He'd broken the ice more. Not in the way he'd hoped to. Still, taking the edge off things had gotten them downstairs and talking. "Yes. I've flashed my mother and grandmother a few times. Not something I care to repeat. I don't know who was more embarrassed."

He held up part of the afghan and patted the couch. "Come on and sit down. I'd like to talk about something."

Angela hesitated. He glanced at her hands. She wasn't flexing them. Not sure if that was a good thing. His body language skills weren't the greatest. She appeared to be considering his offer. Parker wet his lips, ready to say more when Angela moved around the coffee table and sat down next to him. She reached for the afghan, saying, "It's chilly in here."

He nodded, handing Angela part of the afghan as he spoke. "I'll get the fire going more in a moment. I want to talk about what happened upstairs."

"Umm, okay." Angela scooted away from him. "Do I owe you an apology?"

Parker turned so he faced Angela, clearly able to see her before he answered. "No. I owe you one. You might think I dropped the soap on purpose."

Angela took her hand out from under the afghan and took a hold of his. "How could I know that? If you did, so what? It's over unless you plan on making more of it."

Parker looked away, wiped his sweaty palms down his jeans. He looked back, waiting until Angela's gaze met his. "Make more of it, no. Want to talk about it more, yes."

"What more is there to talk about?" Angela started to pull her hand away.

Parker gripped Angela's hand. "Please don't pull away. We've hugged, kissed and slept together. Now you've seen me naked. Well, partially seen me. I think we've crossed a threshold."

"Threshold?"

Parker nodded, loosening his hold on Angela's hand. "Most people go on dates. They get to know each other. Take time to find out things and try each other out."

"True." Angela pulled her legs up and tucked them under the afghan. "Go on."

"Well. . ." Parker paused, squeezed Angela's hand and said. "Remember when I said I was looking for a girlfriend last night?"

"You mean when you said you were single and looking?"

"Yes."

"I thought you were letting me know I didn't have to worry about explaining being snowed in with you."

Parker grinned. "A good surmise. It's true, you don't. I'm going to let you in on a secret."

"Oh?" Angela hugged her legs to her. Parker felt her gaze rove over him like she expected him to throw off the afghan and yell surprise.

"Yeah. One I probably should have told you a while ago." He paused again, letting the weight of what he was about to say sink in for both of them.

Parker leaned forward, stretching his other hand out toward Angela. "I'm very interested in you. I like what I see. Now that I'm getting to know more about you, I want to see if we can take this further."

"Further how?" Angela wrapped more of the afghan around her.

"That's a good question. I'm not exactly sure. Talk more. Drop the rigid rules that we've tried to show and do. Really talk about what's going on between us. Like are you interested in me? Are you attracted to me?"

Angela cupped her hands one around the other and blew on them. How did she answer Parker's questions? Was he looking for a fling? A let's do it and when the snow melts nice knowing you? Doing you? She could do the same thing too. Each of them was taking a chance. A chance that could fail or pan out into more. Where it went neither of them was sure. She looked up, blew air out her puckered lips and said, "How about you get the fire going while I answer? It's damn cold in here!"

Parker nodded. "Okay. Seriously, please answer. I'm cold too." He rose and moved behind the couch, still talking. "I don't want to lose a friend either. We also can't keep on dancing on the edge of things."

"I agree. Our friendship is different due to a lot of things. Most co-workers spend time talking about superficial things like you pointed out earlier." Angela drew the afghan up around her, snuggling into it.

Parker opened the stove door. "Fire has died way down. The bits of sunlight peeking through the clouds will heat the solar panels enough so the radiant heat may turn on. That will keep the chill down for a while." He picked up the branch he'd laid on the arm of the couch and snapped the branch in two. He tossed it in the stove along with two scoops of pellets. He faced her.

Angela held out part of the afghan. "Come on in. It's warmer in here than out there."

Parker chuckled. "Yes, shared body heat does help ward off hypothermia."

"It sure does. My parents bundled us kids in together when cold snaps would hit. Sometimes snow fell down to the two thousand foot level and the wind swooped down with it. Even the cats and dogs would burrow in under the covers." She looped part of the afghan around her shoulders and scooted closer to Parker as he sat down. He turned toward her. She smiled and said, "I do have an answer for you."

Parker tucked the afghan around him. He looked at her, winked and just kept looking at her.

Angela inhaled, rubbed her lips together, and exhaled slowly. Voicing what she'd been thinking about, dreaming about and even pumping up her courage to say over the last few months was about to be real. *Very real.* Once she said it, there was no going back. She opened her mouth to speak when a hard rat-a-tat-tat sounded against the front door.

Parker sighed. Who had the damnedest messed-up timing? He tossed off the afghan, rose and silently prayed it wasn't someone needing help. Though he and Angela wouldn't turn them away. He looked through the door's peephole. Outside, wrapped up in a Santa hat and thick wide neck scarf, was Matt, the complex's handyman. Parker undid the chain lock and deadbolt. Wind and blasts of cold air rushed in as he opened the door. "Come on in, Matt. It's colder than a working deep freeze out there."

Matt stepped in, stomped his feet knocking some snow and ice off his boots. "Thanks. Can't stay. Stopped by to check on you and let you know the snow removal service maybe out in the morning. Don't worry about your driveway. They'll clear it late in the day or day after."

"Appreciate the info. We're holding up okay. Could stand a bit warmer temp but nothing a few blankets and layers can't cure. You?"

Matt laughed. "Sharing a bed with two huskies keeps you warm and sweating. Honestly, I'm working up a good sweat clearing walkways some. Be careful if you go out. Some spots are slick. Good to know you are all right."

Parker let Matt back out and shut the door. As he turned, Angela came up behind him. She stopped when she got where he could see her. "Sounds like we're here for a day or two more."

"Yeah. Time for that conversation we were trying to have. Now as you were saying. You have an answer for me?"

CHAPTER TWELVE

"Yes, I have an answer for you," Angela replied. She started back toward the couch when another two raps sounded on the door. Sighing, she did an about-face, ready to answer the door when Parker moved in front of her.

"Let me get it. You can't tell who might be out there. No offense. I know my neighbors." Parker turned and stepped up to the door. Peering out the peephole again, he started laughing. "What does Matt want now?"

Parker opened the door. "You forget something?"

Matt held out two large plastic shopping bags. "Yes and no. Mrs. Pescalli cooked up a large batch of soup and several dozen cookies before she left on vacation Tuesday. More than I'll ever eat. She wanted me to share with the other tenants. Here's yours. Now back to shoveling walks."

"Thanks. Let me know if you need help." Parker took the bags.

"Sure will." Matt stepped off the porch and moved on down the walk to where his snow shovel stood up right in a snowdrift.

Parker shook his head and closed the door. "Appreciate the food. I'd appreciate less interruptions too."

He sat the bags on the coffee table. "You were saying you had an answer for me."

Angela glanced at the front door, the coffee table, and back at Parker. "Before we start talking again, does that need to go into the fridge?"

"Shouldn't. It's been outside. Probably cold enough we don't need to worry."

"Okay, then. I'm sitting down. We're having this conversation. *Without* any more interruptions, I hope." Angela plopped down on the couch, grabbed part of the afghan and covered her legs. She glanced at him. "Are you sitting down? Or poised to answer the door again?"

Parker suppressed his comeback. Angela was right. They needed to have this conversation without any more interruptions. He stepped between the coffee table and couch, moving very close to where Angela sat. He kicked off his moccasins, picked up part of the afghan and sat down, scooting closer to Angela. "I'm done answering the door. Matt is busy shoveling snow and checking on the other tenants."

"Good. I do have an answer for you." Angela looked at him again, not looking away.

Parker propped his feet on the coffee table and covered his feet and legs with the afghan. He laid an arm along the back of the couch, laying his hand on Angela's shoulder. "I'm ready for your answer."

Angela turned slightly so she faced Parker. His gaze met hers, roved over her face and he smiled. Talk about tension, apprehension, and nerves. Both of them were ready to accept a *no*. When neither of them had said no. Where they went next depended on how he took her answer. She wasn't going to find out unless she voiced it. "I," she began, leaning back on the couch and more into his touch. A touch that felt so right and yet could be gone. This moment took risk. A risk they both went into knowing the outcome was uncertain. She licked her lips and continued. "I find you very attractive. I like you a lot. We share common values and get along well."

Parker rubbed his hand over her shoulder. "Thank you. Do you think we can take this further?"

"Like what?"

"Like dating. Seeing each other outside work. Spend more time together. Explore what we've got going." Parker started to pull his hand away.

"Please don't pull away. I like when you touch me. It's. . ." Angela looked away. If she admitted her fear and insecurity, would he back off? How much more could she reveal and be comfortable with the outcome? Doug's voice yelling 'inadequate', the one word he used every time they fought, echoed through her mind. Not good enough.

"I won't pull away." Parker put his hand back on her shoulder and moved tighter to her. "Go on with what you're saying. I'm listening."

"It's—it's reassuring." She inhaled quickly, pressed her lips together before she could say more. Parker didn't need to have all her insecurities and quirks laid out. They were agreeing to get to know each other better. At least that's what she thought they were discussing.

"That's good to know. Consent and informed are very important to me. I don't like being taken advantage of, nor do I do that." Parker slid closer to her. "Is it okay to put my arm around you?"

Angela nodded. "Guess I'm being a bobblehead again."

Parker leaned over and kissed her cheek. "It's okay. Yeah I say that a lot. Reassuring someone, even myself, is a priority with me. Are you all right?"

"Yes and no. There's a part of me that says you don't know the real me. The me that comes with a past that even scares me at times." Angela moved closer to Parker to the point her legs and upper torso almost touched him.

Parker looped his arm around her shoulders and hugged her. He laid his forehead against hers. "I'll let you in on a secret. I've got one of those too. Maybe everyone does. We deal with them as best we can. Some may do it better. I doubt they don't have their moments too."

Angela looked away, blinking several times. She inhaled and slowly exhaled, wondering what came next. How much had her doubt, her internal fear and misbelief swamped her courage, conviction and determination into the dank darkness of believing she wasn't good enough?

"Hey, you got me wondering, do I owe you an apology?" Parker cupped her chin, tipping her head slightly back. "What's with the tears?""

He let go of her chin. He reached up, using his thumb, and wiped away two tears that fell partway down her cheeks.

Angela rubbed her lips together. Parker deserved an answer. One they could both move forward from. She sniffled, took a couple of deep breaths and answered. "Uncertainty. Fear. And worry. Part of it is my past reaching up to knock me upside the head. Another portion is not recent luck in dating or even a short-term relationship." She let go a deep sigh, turned and slouched against the couch, resting her head on Parker's arm.

Parker traced Angela's cheek with his fingers, running them up and down before he cupped her cheek. He wanted to pull her closer and cradle her against him. Talk about a hard knock. Why did people think they had to cut others down? Make them feel less just to pump themselves up. He didn't understand it. Never would. He bent, kissed Angela's cheek again, and slouched next to her as best he could with his arm still around her. "Here's something I rarely share. I ain't had the greatest success either. My older sister is married and has a couple of kids. My mother keeps egging on about more grandkids. She's got step-grands by her second marriage. Me. . .I'm trying to find someone who I want to have dinner with a couple times a week and watch TV with. You?"

Angela giggled. "My parents have plenty of grandkids between my brothers and sisters. They still make sure they have their yearly discussion about how they want me happy and with someone. I think it's a litany repeated since life began. Procreate and get with someone to do it who sticks around to help raise said offspring."

Parker snorted. He looked at Angela, grinning. "My turn to nod. Seems like we get the same message from our families. Find someone. Settle down and raise a brood. Shall we see if we can do this?"

"Ah—not sure that's the object of this conversation. It might be a bit too early to propose. We don't even know if we. . . ." Angela shut up, sat up and said, "Never mind. That topic isn't part of what we're talking about."

Parker sat up. He turned toward Angela, laid his hand on her forearm as he spoke. "Oh, but it is. I'm gonna say the word and then change the topic in a few. Sex. We're attracted to each other. You possibly saw part of that when I flashed you upstairs. I've seen the way you look at me from time to time at work. I'm guessing you got the hots for me. Now let's talk about food."

Angela caught her bottom lip between her teeth and worried it. Talk about hitting the nail on the head, to borrow one of her cousin's parents' favorite sayings. Parker hadn't minced words. He'd laid it out full and bare. No misunderstanding where he was coming from. He knew she wanted him. He wanted her and wasn't afraid to admit it. Yet, he knew it was time to clear the air and let each of them process what they'd said.

"Are you hungry already?" Angela reached for one of the bags Matt had given them. "I wasn't paying attention to the time."

Parker stood up and opened the bag closest to him. "Not exactly hungry. More like the nibbles. Coffee and a few snacks usually get me through. Too much coffee and I won't sleep well again. I've got decaf tea stashed somewhere, too."

Angela chortled. "You're like my sixteen-year-old nephew. He is always munching on something, fruit or veggie snacks. Drinks soda like it's water. Until coach told him he was ruining his endurance and game stamina."

"Another reason why I tend to drink decaf and lots of lemon water. Flush out my system along with the caffeine. One cup of caffeinated coffee is all I do. Right now I think we both got the munchies." He pulled a plastic storage bag out of the bag he held. "Ooh, these look like Mrs. Pescalli's rum raisin oatmeal chocolate chip cookies. Talk about sweet and gooey. Sometimes she mixes in toffee chips along with butterscotch ones too. Oh man she made me two dozen of them for my birthday last year. I doled those out cuz I could have eaten all two dozen the first day she gave them to me. "

"How about you get the kettle from upstairs so we can brew some tea? I'll see what the soup already has in it. Maybe I can crumble up the leftover bacon and add it. I think you may have the makings for drop biscuits too. I believe I remember how to wrap them up in aluminum foil and bake them around the edge of the fire." She reached for the bag Parker held.

He pulled the bag back. "I'll share. Yes, I'll get the kettle. But first, I want a kiss and a hug."

Angela watched Parker move around the couch, carrying the plastic bag of cookies. Was she willing to give him what he asked for? Actually, stated a want instead of asking. Sometimes you had to put out what you needed to find out if it would get fulfilled.

"Stop," Angela said, backing up. "First, if I do give you a hug and a kiss, it's because I want to now. Don't read anything more into it. Like thinking you can swoop in for more without asking. Second, if I say no now, doesn't mean you can't ask again later. Got it?"

Parker stayed where he was near the end of the couch, close to the chair and coffee table. "I'm glad you're stating your boundaries. They're important. I got 'em. Also I accept no as an answer. I'd share the cookies even if you say no."

"Thanks. It's about trust. An area that takes time to build." Angela walked into the kitchen. "I do trust you some. Or I wouldn't be here."

"I figured that out too. Trust works both ways. Without it, no relationship can survive and thrive. Even friendship is a working relationship." Parker said following her. "How about you decide on the hug and kiss after I bring the kettle down?"

"Sounds good." She turned to catch Parker's reaction. She missed it because he was gone. She could hear him almost running up the stairs.

Parker paused at the top of the stairs. He gripped the banister firmer. Shit, did Angela think he rushed upstairs to push her to answer him? He needed to rephrase his way of thinking and speaking to include Angela. Damn, he had to refocus. Be more aware. Had he lived alone too long?

Or was this the partnering aspect his mom talked about with respect to relationships? Even friendships. He owed Angela an explanation. Meanwhile, the upstairs was cooler than earlier. Checking on the radiant heat took priority. He grabbed the kettle and started back down the stairs.

"Hey, Angela," he called out as he reached the last step. Silence greeted him. He hesitated, cocked his head listening and leaned toward the kitchen. More quiet. Almost an eerie silence that sent shivers racing across the back of his neck. Was she giving him the cold silent treatment or had something happened?

Parker made his way past the couch and into the kitchen. No sign of Angela. He set the kettle on the table. He glanced around the kitchen. Patio doors were closed. The bag with the soup container in it sat on the counter. Where was Angela?

"Thermostat reads forty-five degrees. Energy level is at half way mark. Why haven't you kicked on?" Angela's voice sounded from the far end of the living room.

Parker maneuvered around the couch and into the corner alcove close to the half-bath. A thin beam of light spilled out on to the wall. Angela had found the utility closet and was trying to turn something on. "Can I help?" he asked, opening the closet door more.

Angela jumped. Turned with her fist pulled back, ready to punch. "Sure can stop scaring the shit out of me."

"Good idea. What are you trying to turn on?" Parker asked, backing up a couple of steps.

"The radiant heat. It kicks on at home when the solar panels reach a certain temp and energy level. Yours don't?" She clicked the flashlight off and stepped out of the closet.

Parker held his hand out. "Flashlight, please. There's a switch in between them that you have to turn on. It's partway up the wall. I miss it too. Keep thinking it's between them and it's not."

She laid the flashlight in Parker's hand. "Not in an obvious place. That's why I couldn't find it. I hope there's enough juice to get the coils heated. Warmer floors would be nice."

"Also have coils in the walls too. I bought the place as an investment. Never figured I'd be living here." Parker shined the light up the wall a bit above the temperature gage and the energy meter. "There you are." He reached for the beige-colored knob.

"I can get it," Angela offered. "Keep the light on it and let me past you."

Parker moved back and to the side. "Turn it to the right until it clicks to start the electricity flowing to the coils. It usually takes about thirty to forty minutes to heat up."

Angela brushed against Parker as she stepped into the closet. Partnering with him felt good and right. It was like mutual respect flowed between them. She took hold of the knob, turned it to the right and stopped as a click sounded. "That's done."

She backed out of the closet and shut the door. Facing Parker, she slipped an arm around his waist hugged him and kissed his cheek. "There's your answer to your hug and kiss request. Maybe next kiss will be on the lips." Angela moved back and walked away, not before she watched Parker's mouth open and close. She raised her hand, fingers and thumb splayed and dragged her hand downward as she continued into the kitchen. She'd caught Parker off guard.

Parker smirked, clicked the flashlight off, and didn't bother suppressing his Cheshire cat grin. Only four other women had caught him off guard like that. His sisters and mom and an ex-girlfriend he knew from high school and college. Angela joined that elite group. A very definite strong point in her favor. Yes, he was seeing where maybe the unusual circumstances they were in might not be so bad after all.

He walked into the kitchen, over to where Angela stood with her back to him. He leaned close and whispered. "Oh, you scored big on that one. Bonus points. Welcome to the elite group to catch Parker off guard."

He stepped back, reached for the kettle and added. "I'll get this going and check on the fire. Maybe we can play Gin Rummy while the biscuits and soup cook."

Angela glanced at him and winked. "Part of an elite group. Gee, does that make me special?"

"Sure does." Parker filled the kettle and faced Angela. "I hope you get to meet the other members at some point."

"I do too. We've got to be pretty special to be elite." She started to lean toward him with her lips puckered.

CHAPTER THIRTEEN

Parker pressed his lips to hers and moved back. Angela watched him walk away, into the living room, whistling as he did. The jaunty tune he whistled set her to smile and humming along. She couldn't quite place the words. The ones she remember talked about home, hearth and sharing it with the one you loved. *Love?* Damn, was that what her psyche kept nudging her about? The warm feeling she got sitting next to Parker? The same more intense part of it when he held her close as she admitted part of her fears? She stopped humming, pressing her lips firmly against each other. One deep breath followed by another helped keep her heart from beating faster. All right, so maybe she cared more than she could admit out loud.

She took the soup container out of the bag, holding it up where she could see what was inside. Chunks of potatoes, white and sweet, along with peas and corn and diced carrots stood out against the dark brown broth. Mrs. Pescalli possibly used a beef-based broth. Adding the left over bacon would add extra seasoning. She set the container on the counter and opened it. Leaning down, she inhaled. Pepper, sage, and onions greeted her. Definitely a homemade base. Spices didn't stand out from processed broth. Picking up a spoon off the towel she laid the dishes she washed earlier to dry, she stirred the soup, noting small chunks of meat. Fishing one out, she tasted it. "Oh, yes. Beef simmered slowly off the bone. I've got to get Mrs. Pescalli's recipe. This is good."

"She is a good cook. She ran the local diner before Mama Lucia bought her out. Is that her beef stew soup?" Parker said from behind her.

"Will you stop sneaking up on me?" Angela turned, holding a spoon full of broth out to Parker. "One day you're going to get hit and I'm not going to be at fault."

"Good point. I'm sorry I did it again. I've got to change how I operate. Think about two instead of me on my own." Parker reached for the spoon.

"Don't beat yourself up. Being aware is the important part. I've got to remember you're here too. It's different. So we live and learn." She handed the spoon to Parker. "I think it's beef vegetable soup."

Parker took the spoon, tasted and nodded. "You're right. That's good. I bet she mixed her beef stew and vegetable soup recipe together. I taste a hint of oxtail in there."

"Your taste buds are that sensitive?" Angela took the spoon and laid it in the sink. She picked two strips of bacon and started crumbling them into the soup. "I tasted the beef and could tell it was homemade stock. Can't tell difference between oxtail and beef bones with meat on them broth."

"Fat is slicker with oxtail bones than beef ones. There a bit of fat slicking the top of the container is all. That with drop biscuits slathered with honey. Hot tea and the cookies. A delicious dinner." Parker sat down at the table.

"It's going to take a while for the soup to heat through. Biscuits are going to need watching once they start baking." Angela crumbled the last bacon strip into the soup and thoroughly stirred. "Is it okay to use the Dutch oven on top of the stove?"

"Sure is. I use it over an open campfire. Before you start cooking, I'd like to talk more. I put the kettle on to heat. Sit in here or back in the living room?" Parker pushed back from the table. "Your choice."

"What more do we need to talk about?" Angela put the lid on the soup container and leaned against the counter, unsure if she wanted to discuss sex or let out more of her past. Maybe Parker needed to confide more. Or was she feeling uncomfortable with her new realization?

"You mentioned your past scared you. I admitted some of mine did too. I suspect there's things we're worried about sharing. I know I've not said a lot about my past." Parker started to stand up.

Angela walked over to the fridge and opened it. "How about we talk while we decide what needs to go in an ice chest outside? I get antsy about these subjects. Doing something helps me focus. It keeps me from being overwhelmed."

"Emotionally swamped. I know that all too well. I'm good with working and talking at same time." Parker looked at his watch. "Damn, it's four-thirty. The day flew by."

Angela stepped back from the fridge, holding up two plastic bags. "Don't know what this is. It smells bad and is very green inside."

Parker pulled the trash bag out of the garbage can and rushed toward Angela. "Last week's salad fixings. Bachelor life doesn't always keep up with clearing out the fridge." He held open the bag, trying to get it under the two bags without slipping on what they dripped on the floor.

"Looks like you need a roommate or keeper." Angela turned back to the fridge. "What else am I going to find in here?"

"How about you take out things that look salvageable and leave the rest for later?" Parker ducked his head adding, "I'll clean the fridge out after it's warmed up and the electric is back on. Or are you applying for roommate and keeper job? Position is open and I'm low on qualified applicants."

Angela glared at him, shook her head and went back to the fridge. "Get the ice chest, please. Let's get this dealt with, then we'll talk about when to start dinner cooking and what you feel the need to confess."

Parker tried to quiet his groan as he started toward the living room. Angela looked around the open fridge door and added. "Penitence is good for some things. Great-granddad used to say, fessin' up helped people sleep at night. Grandma used to mutter, only if fessin' up corrected the situation."

"I agree with your grandma. I'm not confessing anything I haven't already shared to some extent. It's what we think that makes us unacceptable or unattractive that I'm talking about," Parker called out from as he opened the second door close to the utility closet and peered in.

"I guess I'm okay with that. I'm not finding much to put in the chest. Still need to get it out where the cold can keep it fresh a while longer," Angela said, closing the fridge door.

Grabbing the large Styrofoam chest and lid, Parker started back toward the kitchen, continuing the conversation. "Whatever there is, I can pack snow around it if there's no open containers. As to fessin' up, can I say I'm enjoying being snowed in with you?"

Angela laughed. "Permission to fess up about that is permitted."

"Gee thanks, ma'am. *I feel so much better now.*" He set the chest on the counter and began putting items into it. "In the drawer close to the stove are some plastic sandwich and storage bags. Would you get some, please? The cheese and lunchmeat can go into two of those." He picked up the egg carton. "I had another dozen eggs in there?"

"Actually two half dozen and two left in a third carton. I think you need to organize your shopping better." Angela held up a bowl half full of eggs. "Do you like egg salad?"

"Yeah. Love it with fresh baked bread. Of course, not asking you to go that far."

Angela handed him two quart sized storage bags and a gallon one. "Let's set something straight. I don't mind cooking. I don't mind helping out. I appreciate when you kick in and help out. What I do *mind* is you apologizing for voicing your boundaries, making your needs known without checking if I'm on the same page, and sneaking up on me. You've hit two out of three."

He put the meat and cheese in bags. Then put them along with an unopened box of butter into the gallon bag. He laid them on the bottom of the chest and put the eggs on top. He reached for two containers that sat close to the chest. "These too?"

"Yes. There's cut-up vegetables in one and shredded cheese in the other. I can use them to make another meal. You've got a couple of packages of chicken that are froze solid. I think those will be ok overnight in the ice chest. I'll cook them up tomorrow."

"Man, I must be in deep shit as my dad used to say." Parker started toward the patio door carrying the full ice chest, the lid under his arm.

"No. I'm guilty of faux pas too. I prefer to discuss this after you're done with the snow and cold. I'm not looking to get beaned with an iced snow ball." Angela stuck out her tongue, blew a raspberry at him and exited the kitchen.

Parker shook his head, grinning too. Angela hadn't held back. She told him what bugged her and stayed toe-to-toe with him. Man, she was garnering brownie points left and right. Did he tell her? Admit he loved what he was seeing? Wait, he used the L word? When the hell had *that* happened?

Around the time you mentioned proposing, his conscience chided him.

"Oh hell, I wasn't serious about proposing," he muttered, opening the patio door. A gust of wind blew snow at him as he stepped out onto the patio. "No one asked either of you, Mother Nature and Old Man Winter."

A hefty blast of wind battered him and blew snow off the roof almost down the back of his sweatshirt. He straightened, looked left and right and toward the sky. "In the chest with the snow please. I get you think the two of us are avoiding the heat of the issue. Neither of us is looking to jump in bed, get off and walk away. We're talking and moving forward."

Parker shook his head, quickly scooped snow with his bare hands into the ice chest, stopping to blow on his hands a couple of times in between scoops. With the chest half-full, he put the lid on, added a brick on top of it and went back inside. As he closed the patio door, he heard Angela enter the kitchen.

"Kettle is boiling. I overheard your discussion with Mother Nature and Old Man Winter. I agree with your sentiment. Now let's make some tea and move on with our discussion. I've got the mugs and tea bags already. Please bring the honey and spoons in with you."

Parker was sure his mouth hung open. Talk about straight to the point. Well, all right, continue their discussion they would. It didn't look like he needed a shovel to dig his way out of a pile of manure. Angela had grit and wasn't afraid to show it. Nice! He grabbed two of the spoons off the counter along with the jar of honey. Where this part of the discussion went he didn't know. Topic was up to Angela for the moment.

Angela filled each mug she'd set on the coffee table with hot water. She added a tea bag to each with a couple more close by. She liked her tea strong. Sometimes off-brand teas needed a second bag to brew decently. Off-brand teas she'd encountered usually used tagless tea bags. Those she used took two bags to brew a decent cup of tea. As she set the kettle back on the stove, Parker entered the living room carrying two spoons and the jar of honey. He laid the spoons on the coffee table next to the jar of honey.

"I'm gonna check on the fire. Then we'll talk. If you have an item you want to discuss first, let me know." Parker raked ashes into the ash urn close to the bin. Tendrils of smoke rose up and died down as he raked more into the urn. He added two scoops of pellets and three more limbs. "I'll need to bring in more wood before it gets too dark."

"Sunset isn't for an hour or two more. Daylight savings time." Angela picked up her mug and drank. "Bitter. Needs more honey. Do you want an extra bag in yours?"

"No thanks. I prefer my tea lighter than my coffee. Got sick off super-strong tea while in London." Parker sat down close to her. As he added honey to his mug and stirred, he asked, "Got a particular item you want to discuss first?"

Angela took a couple of sips of her tea, set the mug down and faced Parker. "Yes, I do. I need to talk about Doug."

Parker held up his spoon. "One moment. Let me get some of this in me. It's still damn cold out there. Need to warm up a bit."

He drank twice and set his mug down. He faced her and leaned back against the couch. "Who the hell is Doug?"

Angela wrapped part of the afghan around her, tossed part of it at Parker. "Cover up, please. I don't want you chilling. Doug is my ex-husband."

Parker pulled the afghan over him and glanced at her. "Your what?"

"My ex-husband. Let me explain, then you can ask more questions."

"Okay." Parker faced her. "Go on."

"I met Doug my senior year of college. Happy hour at a local bar close to campus and the hospital where I worked and interned. We caught each other's attention from the moment we were introduced by mutual friends."

"I understand."

"We dated for a couple of months. He traveled for work without saying what it was. I was busy finishing up classes and dealing with issues surrounding my great-grandparents' estate."

"Not an easy place to be."

"No. Doug appeared to support my taking care of things and finishing classes. He kept traveling more and more. Between trips, he proposed. I accepted, figuring he'd tell me why he needed to travel as much as he did. I knew he worked for a race driver. I didn't know who the driver was until he ended up in the ER one night and damn near died due to a racing crash."

"The son of a bitch never said anything? That is fucking selfish," Parker blurted out. "Sorry."

"That's okay. I felt the same way. Pity does strange things to you. I believed his admonishments that he wouldn't drive more and he wanted to settle down. Kids and the white picket fence."

"You believed he'd change. Been there. Done that too. Man, I'm sorry."

Angela sighed and flashed a weak grin. "The marriage lasted about six months. He kept driving and wanting me to finance his cars. Bigger, faster and more challenging races. When he totaled a twenty-five thousand dollar specially built car drag racing in Mexico and never told me until I got the settlement statement from the insurance company. I walked out and filed for divorce a week later."

"Questions permitted?"

"Not yet. Doug's favorite thing to throw at me was, I was never good enough. Inadequate in bed and keeping his attention. He wanted it all to center on him." Angela picked up her mug and gulped down her tea. Her hands shook as she set the mug back on the table. She glanced at Parker ready to hear his barrage of taunts and insults.

Instead, he motioned at her. "Come here. I want to hold you. Just quietly hold you."

Angela took a deep breath, held it. Glanced away and exhaled. She'd voiced one of her strongest fears. Inadequacy haunted her every time she considered something. Vulnerability didn't set well with her. The fortress she tightly cocooned herself within worked to a point. Did she lower her drawbridge and let Parker in? Take the risk that he wouldn't find her lacking. Could she get past her own doubts and fears?

"Are you sure?" she asked, her gaze meeting Parker's.

"Very sure." Parker leaned back against the couch, spreading his arms wide open. "We all need a safe place. Somewhere we feel secure and respected. I'm offering you such a place."

He nodded, smiling too as he continued. "I'd beat the shit out of Doug for you. But that wouldn't solve anything either. People like him are scarred and scared too. They just won't admit it."

Angela let go of the end of the afghan she tightly held, looking at it amazed she hadn't worn the yarn apart with all her running her hands back and forth over it. She tossed the rest of it off her, smoothed her wet palms down her leggings and stood. Parker pushed the afghan off him and patted the empty space very close to him. He nodded again and patted. "Come on and sit down. I'll let you in on one of my secrets when you're ready."

CHAPTER FOURTEEN

Angela shook her hands, took a step forward and leaned down. She pushed the afghan further away from Parker. Turning, she said, "Quiet holding sounds good. I'll let you know when I'm ready to hear your secret."

Parker nodded. "Yeah, I'm bobbleheading again. I'm big on visual and words backing each other up when necessary. Like now. I'll hold you until you tell me let go. Okay?"

Angela flashed him a weak grin and briefly nodded. "One thing more we've got in common. . .being bobbleheads."

Parker chuckled as Angela sat down next him, leaving some space between them. "Things in common are good. Do you agree?"

"Yes. I think that if I'd taken the time to look at what Doug and I had in common, I might not have jumped at his proposal or gone out with him." Angela pulled part of the afghan over them.

"Hindsight is always a hundred per cent. Its past views and actions. Thanks for sharing. You ready for me to hold you?" Parker laid his arm on the back of the couch. "Ready when you are."

He watched Angela, waiting to see if her silent language gave him any clue. She'd leaned back against the couch when she sat down. No stiffness or rigid posture. Subtle signals she felt some comfort around him. Trust was a gut-level reaction. One that he learned about after his dad's death. Suicide took a person's life and slammed into those remaining just as hard. Sadness and guilt ate at him for a long time. Letting go and accepting other peoples decisions weren't his responsibility sank in about two years ago. He looked away as he loosely looped his arm around Angela's shoulders.

"I'm ready," she said, scooting closer to him. "Thanks, Parker."

"For what?" he asked as Angela nestled against him.

"For being you. For being a friend." Angela kissed his cheek. "For caring. It means a lot."

Parker shifted slightly, settling him tighter against Angela. He reached under the afghan until he found her hand. He entwined his fingers with hers and squeezed. Angela tilted her head back, looked up at him, winked and slumped down into his embrace. Quiet filled the room. The occasional crackle and pop from the logs burning in the stove sounded and faded. He felt Angela's breathing deepen and slow. She squeezed his hand again and turned toward him. She leaned close and pressed her lips against his cheek and turned away again, staying pressed against him.

Parker's right hand lay sprawled on her shoulder. His other loosely held her hand. Silence and just being occupied the space and room. No one fussed at them or anything else called them to leave this moment. This time. This space. Peace, tranquility and . . .contentment—yes, contentment with here and now filled her. Maybe Tricia was right. Finding someone who she could be herself with mattered. Took priority for her after all the bad and burned relationships she'd had. Maybe finding peace within herself and accepting she'd survived was okay. At home, the ticking of the kitchen wall clock would pull her back into her harried gotta-do frame of mind. Right here, right now, she didn't care that there were other things they could be doing. Holding each other mattered more. She turned again, faced Parker and said, "Thank you. When you're ready to share your secret I'm ready to listen."

She felt Parker take a deep breath and let it out slowly. He repeated this twice more. Angela started to move away. Had she upset him? Said something wrong?

Parker tightened his hug. "Wait, please. Blurting things out ain't my style. I've got scars from doing that. I need to know you're ready to go to that level with me. It's not like we're going to be able to back away from what's going on here."

"We're getting close and deep?" Angela asked.

"Thought we crossed that bridge when we talked last night and spent the night curled up against each other. Then I may be wrong." Parker kissed the top of Angela's head as she scooted closer and settled back against him.

"It began something. What I'm not totally sure. I'll admit I'm interested." Angela looked up at him. He could feel her short breaths along with her rapid pulse.

"Interested is good. I'm interested, too." Parker worried his bottom lip between his teeth for a moment and added. "I've been interested for quite a while."

Angela sat up and turned so she faced him. She blinked, shook her head, and glared at him with one eyebrow arched like she was trying to see him better. "What did you say? I don't think I heard you correctly."

"What do you think I said?" Parker slipped his arm off the back of the couch. There was no going back to the peaceful moment where Angela lay against him. Easy comfort was gone. He counted to five and repeated the question. "Seriously, what do you think I said?"

"You've been interested in me for a while." Angela began to move further away.

"Stop!" Parker yelled. "Moving away isn't necessary. I'm not pushing you away. I'm sharing something that I kept secret for a reason. Hear me out okay?"

Angela nodded. She pulled her legs up under the afghan and leaned back against the couch. "Sorry. Defensive posture. Another one of the scars from Doug and a couple of other bad relationships."

"Hey, I get it. Believe me when I say both of us haven't had an easy go of finding someone. That's part of why I kept my interest quiet." Parker held out his hand. "It's easier talking when I know you're not going to jump up and run off."

Angela looked down at Parker's hand. He'd offered it palm up. The sign of peace. He wasn't pulling away. He'd called her out from her rush to pull away and build another fence between her and someone who cared. Why? That was the big question egging her to not put her hand in Parker's. Yet, she couldn't lay her fears on him. He hadn't done anything other than share a secret. He wanted to share more of it, explain the how and why. Dang, the man had racked up huge bonus points with her. Taking a deep breath, she reached out and laid her hand palm down on Parker's. Looking up, she met his gaze. "I'm not going anywhere. In fact, I need to hear what you've got to share. Please go ahead."

Parker intertwined his fingers with hers and leaned forward. He raised their joined hands until they reached his lips. He pressed three kisses along her knuckles and lowered their hands.

"Thanks. I appreciate you hearing me out." Parker slipped his hand away from hers as he continued. "Being a hunk isn't easy. And yet you cherish the attention at some point. We're socialized to want it. Need it and almost beg for it."

"You're fine looking. I agree with you on that one." Angela hugged her knees and let go. "Is that the only reason?"

"No. I not as secure as people think. I'm country-born, country-bred and have country manners. A lot of country ethics and morals too."

"Being country does this?" Angela shook her head. "I don't get it."

"No, being country doesn't do this. It makes me different than a city gal like you. Suave, debonair, and sophisticated. That's what I first thought when I learned you were from California and San Francisco. You knocked some wind out of me when you said you have a BSN. I've got an associate degree." Parker hesitated. Angela wondered why. She kept quiet, waiting for him to finish.

"It took me three years to get it. I had to work my way through junior college. Going part-time wasn't easy either." Parker let out a sigh. "Making sure my youngest sister finished high school took priority. Being big brother and man of the house ate up a lot of my time."

"Damn," Angela whispered.

"Sometimes double damn. Women walked away because I was adamantly sure I didn't want kids. I'd done my share of raising them with my kid sister." Parker faced her. "Now I don't know. I'm getting older. Maybe there's a child or two in my future. I sure am not saying there has to be."

Angela leaned toward Parker with both of her hands out. "We've had our share of hard knocks. We survived. I've got something to tell you."

"Sure. What is it?" Parker clasped both of her hands.

"It took me five years to get my degree. Only reason I got my bachelor's was the money my great-grandpa left me. I had debt from my marriage, poor paying jobs, and biting off living in a city that costs more than the average paycheck to live in."

"Sounds like we both know the value of hard work. Why did your parents decide to live off-the-grid?" Parker tugged her toward him. "Please cuddle up again. I like holding you. It also calms me."

"Because they were tired of the idea money and things brought happiness. My dad used to tell us to use our imaginations and be creative.

Man, did that open our minds and thoughts. Got us thinking outside of the box." Angela moved into Parker's arms. "I like you holding me too."

Parker snuggled Angela to him. He kissed the top of her head. "Hope you're okay with me being affectionate. Again, words and actions backing each other up."

"It's fine. My parents are big on it too. Even now, we hug each other hello and goodbye when we're at family gatherings. It's unusual for us to not chat several times a month. My siblings get my need to be the farthest away. They call me Ms. Independence."

Parker chortled. "My mother refers to me as her long-distance child. I love my family but having them around constantly or butting into my life is more than I can take close up and overflowing."

"Same here. I guess we have more in common than we realize." Angela tilted her head back, adding. "I'd like to give you another kiss. This time on the lips, please."

"Sure. I'd like that too." He leaned down; lips puckered and pressed them to Angela's. She pressed hers firmer to his. Several moments passed as they held each other and shared a couple of chaste kisses.

Angela pulled back first. "My stomach is growling. I think I need to start cooking dinner. The biscuits are going to take about twenty minutes to bake. And the soup about that long to warm up too."

"I," Parker began, when a loud knock sounded at the front door. Sighing, he tossed the afghan aside and stood. "What does Matt need now?"

"Help shoveling snow? You offered." Angela responded, standing up too.

"Yeah, I did. Guess I best find my boots and put my coat on." Parker moved around the couch and walked toward the front door. "Can you handle fixing dinner if I help Matt?"

"Yes. Check what he needs and let me know. I'm gonna mix the biscuits." Angela entered the kitchen.

Parker looked out the front door peephole. Matt stood on the porch holding what looked like a bunch of envelopes. Had he made it to the complexes' mailboxes?

"Hi ,Matt," Parker said opening the front door. "What's up?"

"Mail truck got through. Henry gave me yours and mine. Your box is too full to put more in." Matt held out the stack of envelopes as he continued speaking. "Roads are partially plowed. County is asking people to not go out for another day. Henry gave me a message for you from Doc Stillwell. Don't head to the clinic for a couple more days."

"Thanks, Matt. You need help with shoveling? I'm available." Parker opened the door more.

"The Henderson boys from two buildings over pitched in. They're doing the last two buildings' walks and a few driveways. Patches of ice out here. Not worth taking a risk. Thanks for offering. Maybe you can help with clearing a few drives midmorning tomorrow."

"Sounds good. I'll be ready around eleven. Come get me." Parker took the stack of envelopes.

"I sure will. The Henderson boys will help out too. See you in the morning. Have a good evening." Matt turned and walked down the three steps to the front walk. He waved one more time before walking away.

Parker watched Matt carefully make his way down the walk, carrying a wad of mail in one hand and his shovel in the other.

As Parker closed the door, Angela entered the living room. "Everything okay?"

"Yes and no." Parker faced her.

"Yes and no? What's wrong?" Angela laid her hand on Parker's arm.

"Roads are partially plowed. Matt reports the county is asking people to not go out for another day." Parker placed his empty hand on hers and turned. "Bad part is Doc Stillwell sent a message via our mail carrier to not report to the clinic for a couple of more days."

"That is strange. After I get dinner cooking, let's see if we can get any cell phone reception. Maybe we can get through to Doc." Angela started back toward the kitchen.

"Yeah, we can do that. Just seems odd he'd send a message via the mail carrier." Parker followed her into the kitchen and sat down at the table. He laid the mail on the table. "Is it a bit warmer in here? Feels like it."

"Floor isn't as cold. I think the coils may be working. The water coming out of the faucet isn't as cold." Angela picked up the spoon she'd gotten out to stir the biscuit mix.

"I'll check on the thermostat reading after I've sorted the mail." Parker began flipping through the pile. He divided the stack into two smaller piles.

He picked up one envelope twice, shook his head and opened it. "Shit! How could I forget Elise's engagement party?"

"Elise?" Angela sat down next to Parker, stirring the batter.

Parker looked up and grinned. "No competition, sweetie. My sister. Youngest one. Her fiancée is military. Charla signed up right out of high school. She and Elise dated off and on."

"I wasn't asking about competition. Just wondered who Elise was." Angela got up and set the bowl on the counter. She tore several sheets of aluminum foil off the roll and double-layered them. She spooned batter into each one as she spoke. "Is your family okay with same sex marriage?"

Parker snorted. "Took Mom a while to come around until her great-aunt and sister both admitted their lifelong involvements with same-sex partners. Mom believes love is colorblind and is a proud parent partner of the local PFLAG chapter."

"Awesome. My eldest brother and his husband brought my grandparents into the twentieth century, to quote my dad. Even my maternal grandparents embraced things so much so that when my uncle came out they threw him and his life partner a wedding party." Angela folded the foil packets closed. "These are ready to put in the oven and nestled in the red coals. Soup is ready to put in the Dutch oven and begin heating."

"Great, my stomach is gnawing at my backbone." Parker laid the envelope he held on the table. "I've got a question."

Angela turned. "Now what?" she asked, grinning. "Dinner is almost ready to cook."

"Not about that." Parker took a plate out of the cabinet and put the biscuit packets on it. "I need a date for the engagement party. I'd like you to be my date. How about it?"

"I don't know. How you're going to explain us? I mean we're not. . ." Angela shrugged and turned back to emptying the soup container into the ditch oven.

"We're not what?" Parker handed her the plate. "I'll carry the Dutch oven in. You can decide where I need to place the biscuits to bake."

She took the plate. "We're not a couple. At least not. . . ." She stopped talking again. They hadn't said they weren't a couple nor had they said they were more than friends. Lord was this the friends with benefits talk? She wasn't sure that worked well. Last time she agreed to that the guy got super possessive and ditched her when she said she didn't need his permission to be. She wasn't going there *ever* again. Yet, she wanted more than just a casual fling. Affairs tugged on the heart and often caused more heartache than joy.

Parker faced her as she approached the wood stove. "First, I need to bank the fire to get the coals closer to the front. Second, we deal with getting the food cooking. Then I'm going to answer your unsaid questions."

"All right. It would have to be even if I didn't agree." Angela leaned down as Parker stirred the fire, noting where she saw hot red coals. "Place the packets tight to the coals. We'll turn them in about ten minutes."

Parker placed the packets in two rows tight to the glowing coals he'd raked forward. As he closed the door and straightened, he reached for the empty plate. "There's a few questions floating about that neither of us is voicing. I think it's time to drop these last barriers and say what we're feeling here." He touched his chest close to his heart and added as he entered the kitchen, "And in our gut. If we're going to make this work, we've got to be truthful with ourselves and each other."

CHAPTER FIFTEEN

Angela swallowed, trying to take a deep breath. Her throat went dry every time she inhaled. So much for catching her breath. Talk about knocking it out of her. Parker had once again cut the chase out of what he was getting at. His straightforward style didn't completely surprise her. He had to get answers quickly and clearly from patients or their family. She dealt with same thing doing intake and deciphering answers. Clarity mattered. She licked her lips, rolled her shoulders, and entered the kitchen.

Parker stood at the counter, with his back to her. His hands were on the counter. He appeared to be watching something out the window. He didn't look at her as she moved up beside him. He nodded and pointed. "Squirrel running from tree to tree. He's looking for where he buried a nut or root. Is that what we're doing? Trying to find a comfort zone to wallow in? Not move out of?"

Angela covered Parker's hand with hers. "I think we're ignoring what's in front of us. We get each other. We like each other and. . ." She deliberately shut up. If Parker missed this lead, then she'd have to guide him back into the conversation. He'd pointed out the squirrel in the room. Some people preferred to call it the elephant. Watching the squirrel running helter-skelter from tree to tree and partway up and down a couple of them outlined where their conversations had gone. Partway into the fire and flames like the fire when they added larger chunks of wood to it. The pellets had served to keep the flames burning. They were the safe places within the heat of the different topics that littered the air between them. Clearing it and the barriers they kept running into was going to take effort, partnership and commitment on both their parts. How did either of them call the other on their slip-ups and escape attempts? There were no ceramic ducks lined up neatly in a row. Nope, they had drunk, chilly squirrels ready to run up and down inserting themselves as they saw fit unless she and Parker agreed to call each other out when that happened.

Parker glanced at her. He waited until her gaze met his. Neither of them looked away. He leaned toward her, his lips puckered and partly open. She could hold up a hand, verbally ask what he wanted or she could go with what her gut and heart urged. Kiss him. Show him what she wanted. The passion and affection each of them had shown in bits and pieces.

Angela slipped her hand out from under his. Parker paused; glad he kept his eyes open. Was she withdrawing again? Leading him on came to mind. She hadn't done that or given him reason to surmise she was playing games with him. He turned facing her, one arm flung back. Would she pick up on his silent message?

She moved tight to him, slipped an arm around his waist and looped her other arm around his neck. Angela tilted her head, leaned toward him, lips puckered. She stopped a hair's breadth from his lips, nodded and inclined toward him until her lips met his. There was no mistaking what either of them wanted. This kiss wasn't going to be the chaste one they'd shared earlier or the brief closed-lip ones.

Parker wrapped his arm around Angela, splaying his fingers along her waist as he cupped her face with his other hand. He tentatively traced her lips with the tip of his tongue. Tasting and sipping more of her. Their earlier kisses left him wanting, needing and aching for more. They'd gotten here by mutual consent. Mutual want and reciprocated desire. Also, an underlying understanding and connection that they were finally acknowledging. Maybe even verbalizing. Right now, no words were needed. Only action and—-Angela parted her lips and tagged his tongue with hers. Their lips parted more, opening barriers and gates, letting pent-up emotions and feelings out.

He pulled back. She gave chase. They dueled, twisted and tasted each other until he couldn't remember anything other than the woman he held in his arms. She tasted of mint toothpaste, coffee, and bits of honey. Pulling her tighter to him, he pressed against her. Angela fit him in all the right places. Sliding his hand lower, he cupped her ass, enjoying the fullness of her filling his hand and then some. She had curves. Womanly curves that left no guessing as to where each part of her flowed and composed who she was. Angela murmured something and continued the chase as he withdrew his tongue from hers.

Parker, warm and tight within her arms. A dream she never thought would come true. This was better than any kiss her imagination came up with. He tasted of coffee, strong black coffee with a subtle hint of honey.

And his smell. Talk about divine. Soap and water smelled good on most people. The scented soap Parker used reminded her of the homemade soap her grandma taught her to make. Natural scents like clover, mint, and a touch of pine. Masculine without being overbearing. She wasn't letting him get away. She gave chase, boldly following him into his mouth. Tasting him as intimately as she could given their clothed state and the townhouse's inside temperature.

Back and forth, lips pressed tightly to each other. Hands cupping asses and fondling with light caresses adding to the passion their kiss fueled. Parker pulled back, one hand resting between her hip and ass cheek. His other lay close to the underside of her breast. Heat rolled off him and over her. Her swollen nipples ached, tingled with a growing need to be touched, suckled and. . .Angela pressed her lips together. Parker rocked toward her, his hips and groin brushing against her. He was hard. Very hard. There was no mistaking the want evidenced there. Were they ready to go to the next level? Become lovers. . .or was this a fling that ended when the snow melted?

Parker rested his forehead against Angela's. If he pressed any tighter to her, he'd. . .he'd given up fully clothed sex his first year of junior college. Having his own place presented freedom living at home didn't offer. He remembered the first time he sank deep into his lover, feeling her warmth surround him, clutching him deep within her and almost knowing what the pure ecstasy was his married friends talked about. Condoms prevented a lot of things. Unwanted kids, STDs and a few other things he'd since learned about. Taking chances with health and making babies wasn't a risk he needed or wanted. Taking care of himself and his partner meant discussing what mattered. Lovemaking preferences would—damn, he used the word *love* again. Slowly inhaling, he stepped back from Angela, creating a space between them that he hoped didn't dissipate the heat they'd already ignited.

"Biscuits," he said, sliding his hand upward until he reached Angela's waist. "Dinner has a priority. Part of it's cooking. Is the soup ready to heat?"

Angela's sigh caressed his cheeks and spirited away the lingering bits of warmth rising between them. Parker rubbed his lips together, wondering what he could say or do that would keep things from cooling more.

"You're right. Unless we want smoked bread and cold soup, we need to pay attention to what we're doing." Angela stepped back. "Sor—"

Parker pressed his fingers on Angela's lips. "No apology needed. We both want this. Need this and yes its attention grabbing."

"Sure is. Soup is ready to heat. I'll check on the biscuits." Angela picked up the plate she'd set on the counter earlier and exited the kitchen.

Parker carried the Dutch oven into the living room. As he sat it on the stove, Angela opened the stove door. Fragrant aromas rushed out, moving upward until each breath he took reminded him of another reason Angela caught his attention. She could cook. Not just put a meal together from processed items. She cooked from scratch. A feat not many women could do or chose to.

"That is heavenly scent filling this room." Parker stepped back from the stove. "Baked bread. God, I miss those scents. Lady, you're a gem. I'm so glad I found you."

Angela looked up, grinned and went back to checking the biscuits. "Glad to be found. What makes me such a gem?"

"We match in a lot of areas. Small ones that could otherwise make or break a relationship." Parker sat on the couch, turned so he faced Angela.

"Small things? Like what?" Angela closed the stove door and straightened. "I turned the packets. Biscuits will be done in about another ten to fifteen minutes."

"Yes, small things. Like food prep, cooking choices, attraction and work." Parker turned again as she dropped into the chair across from the couch.

"Is working together a small thing or a bigger issue? I've known couples that couldn't take the stress and strain of being together twenty-four seven." Angela laid the plate on the end table next to the chair.

"High stress and pressure can do that to a relationship. We work together and yet there are hours and shifts often apart. We *get and understand* each other's jobs."

"True. There's an unspoken trust that . . ." Angela went silent and shrugged.

"That what?" Parker leaned forward, resting his hands on his knees.

"You sure you want to hear this?" Angela slumped in the chair, wiped her sweaty palms down her leggings, and wrapped her arms around herself.

"Yes, I do. I could say you worry too much. That isn't fair. I worry too about letting people get next to me, sharing my thoughts. There comes a time you gotta trust. Trust you, your gut and—" He pointed at his heart. "Your heart. Second-guessing you makes you less important and not a priority. Not a good thing to do to yourself."

Parker held up one hand. "What I'm about to do isn't meant for you. It's meant for that jackass Doug."

He flipped his middle finger up and said. "Frig him and his dumbass selfish ways. You're more than that. You know that. Or you wouldn't have walked out and divorced him."

Angela smirked and heaved a deep sigh. She lowered her arms and sat up. "Very true. I got tired of being burned or chastised for what others call my old-fashioned values. I can plan a meal, figure out prep and cooking time faster from scratch than spending time reading boxes and doing mental calisthenics about what comes first."

"Exactly. It works for us. I had to learn how to cook that way due to Elise's allergies and my older sister Stacey's, too. Only way all of us could sit down to a family meal without worrying who was going to get sick. I don't like most packaged food taste. Though you'll find a few frozen pizzas in my freezer from time to time. Local health food store ones. Or a few packaged dinners from there too."

"All right. That's one thing I agree can mess up a relationship. What about our education differences?" Angela raised her arms and stretched.

Parker grinned. "Love the way you fill out that top."

Angela glared at him.

"Okay, I just said a male sexist thing. I like your curves. I like the way you think on many things. I like your work ethic. I can rattle off more. I'm a hetero male who likes women. I think about sex, even do it from time to time. I bet you do too."

Angela nodded. "Ingrained habit. Doug would do that to deflect things when he'd piss me off."

"Understood. I got a few of those too from my last live-in relationship, Sonya. She believed in defined set roles. One person dominated all the time and the other person was submissive. Partnering with her happened very little. We lasted eight months. She even tried dictating how our breakup and post-interactions should go. Another reason why I moved to Peyton Corners."

"How long ago was this?" Angela stood and moved over to the couch, sitting on the opposite end. She pulled part of the afghan over her.

"Three years ago. Still stings from time to time. My batting average is in the zilch column for success. A big reason why I held back with you. You asked about our education differences."

"And?"

Parker laid his arm on the back of the couch and settled into the corner more. He propped his elbow and forearm on the armrest. "Honey, we got what we need to do our jobs. You and I both had other things we had to deal with or we'd gone further. I'd like to get my bachelor's but I'm not sure in what. It's one of those bucket list things. I'm not jealous. You?"

"No jealousy either. You appear to like what you do. I like putting my nursing skills to work along with the business stuff I learned. Our jobs complement each other in many ways."

"Another way we get along in small ways. We're talking and working through some of the larger ones. Do you agree?"

"To a point, yes. How do we know if this will work out for the long haul?" Angela glanced at her watch.

"We don't. Life doesn't come with guarantees. If you need them, then maybe I was wrong about us." Parker stood. "I think the soup needs stirring."

He patted Angela's arm as he passed her. "I think taking a risk on us is worth it. I'm not saying make a leap into living together based on these past few hours. I'm asking you to date me, go to my sister's engagement party with me, take a trip to meet my family as a friend and be introduced as my new girlfriend. No real big risks in that."

"Isn't meeting your family taking this a step further than dating and tagging along as a friend? I mean your new girlfriend is a lot more than just pals." Angela tossed the afghan off her and rose.

"After last night, today and our mini make out session in the kitchen, do you think we're still just pals? I'm looking for more than friends with benefits. I think you are too." Parker laid the oven lid on the stove and stirred the soup.

Angela opened the stove door. "Can you hand me the tongs, please?"

"Sure. I think the soup is about ready. Biscuits?"

"Foil is blackened on both sides. Usually indicates they're done. Won't know until I open a packet." Angela took the tongs from Parker. She carefully grasped the packet closest to her with them. She glanced at the others further back close to the flames. They were very black. She carefully set the packet on top of the stove and closed the door. "I think the others are done. I'll know as soon as I open this one."

Pealing back the edges of the foil, she inhaled. Bread fresh out of the oven aromas greeted her. "Biscuits are ready."

"Great. Soup is hot. I'll get bowls and spoons, then I'll refill the kettle." Parker walked past her, turned around and came back. He walked up to her, looped his arms around her neck, and brushed his lips across hers. "I'd like to continue our discussion while we eat, if you're game. I also want you to know I'm not angry. Perplexed, yes."

"I'm good with continuing our discussion." Angela retrieved the rest of the biscuits from the stove while Parker got the bowls and spoons. She put them on the plate and set it on the coffee table. She walked to the edge of the kitchen and leaned against the wall. "I think I'm letting fear override concern and caution. Does that make sense?"

"Yes, it does. Mine's been kicking and screaming every time I voice my wants and concerns. I'm laying it all out there with the potential I'm going to get rejected. Not an easy thing to do. Question is, are we going to let that continue or do we take charge? Who's driving? Us or fear?"

Angela took a hold of Parker's arm as he started past her. He stopped. She kissed his cheek. "I'll let you know once we've served dinner. My stomach is demanding food."

CHAPTER SIXTEEN

Parker put the bowls and spoons on the coffee table next to the biscuits. He picked up the kettle and faced Angela. "There's something I need to add."

Angela frowned. "Not scowling at you. Just thinking about how we're skirting around things. It feels funny. Not right, if you get my meaning."

"That's part of what I'm getting at. Are we so fearful that we won't take a risk? A risk that might be one of the best things we've ever done. At least gained ourselves someone we're closer to than others." Parker started back toward the kitchen. "Let me get the soup ladle. We can talk as we eat, all right?"

"Sounds good. Don't forget the honey. Biscuits are better with a drizzle of honey."

Parker chortled. "A lot of things are better with honey. Of course, there is a *lot* of things that we could put honey on."

"I got a feeling I should be yelling *TMI* instead sitting here grinning and squirming." Angela looked up. Parker did an about-face and winked.

She put her hand over her mouth. Laughter still leaked out around and over her palm and fingers. Parker did a quick mini-bow and started whistling. Angela wrapped both arms around her middle, slid down deeper into the chair and started howling with laughter. Parker came back whistling louder and very off key. She hugged her stomach tighter, crossed her legs as tears rolled. Short eeks sounded as peals of laughter followed. She gasped for breath and looked up. Parker stood next to the chair holding his hand out.

"Are you okay?" He began to squat down.

Angela unwrapped her arms, trying to sit up. She wiped her eyes with the hem of her shirt. "Oh, yeah. I'm great. I haven't laughed that hard in a while. Absurd and ironic satire is a good take on what we've skirted around."

Parker took her hand, squatted down and placed his other on top of hers. "Can we make the leap from here to the next level?"

Angela slid her hand out from between Parker's. "I suspect we're partway there. I think I just signaled I'm interested in what this level has to offer."

Parker's stomach loudly growled. "I think food is the first line. How much soup you want?"

"Half-bowl for now. I can get more if I want more." Angela stood, moved over to the couch and sat down. She opened another of the foil packets. "These are a bit underdone. Just the way I like them. Soft and crumbly."

"Makes 'em easier to tear up into the soup like a dumpling. Like a soft warm cracker." Parker handed her a bowl. "Go ahead and start. I'm not big on waiting until everyone is at the table."

"I'd rather wait until you've got yours. Habit, and I *do* want to talk while we eat." She took the bowl from Parker, wrapping her hands around it as the warmth seeped into her fingers and palms. "Hot soup on a cold snowy day. This smells delicious too. We've gotta get Mrs. Pescalli's recipe."

Parker nodded as he sat down. "If she'll share it. She'd rather make it and give you a batch. At least that's what she told me when I tried to get her cookie recipe."

"Like my Grandma Fiona. She loves to cook and show you how to make things. Encourages you to write down the recipe as you go along. She wanted my sisters and I to carry on the family tradition of making each recipe our own."

"Nice touch. I wish I'd had that time with my grandparents. They died before Mom moved us back to the states. Did you get any of your grandmother's recipes written down?" Parker toasted her with a spoon of soup.

Angela returned the gesture, blew on the hot liquid and emptied the spoon into her mouth. Bits of bacon and meat slid across her taste buds, mixing with the onion and sage, giving it a bit of a kick and bite. "Oh my, that's good. I know what else would add an extra hint of heat and more punch."

"What?" Parker asked, his spoon partway to his mouth.

"Louisiana red hot sauce."

"That is a bit over my threshold. Too much zing. Guess I overdid it while I was living in New Orleans." Parker shrugged. "You ready to continue our main topic?"

Angela ate more of her soup and set the bowl down. She handed Parker one of the biscuits. She picked up another and tore it in half twice, placing the four pieces in her bowl. Leaning back, she glanced at Parker. He watched her as he drizzled honey on the biscuit. She wet her lips and spoke. "Main topic being us and where do we go from here. Right?"

"Part of it. There's also an intimate side to it, too. Not that I expect us to jump into that immediately. We've been dancing around it since last night and most of today." He grinned and added. "I don't know about you. I have no use for elephant manure in my living room or any garden to put it to use."

Angela snorted. She sat up and picked up her bowl. She stirred the biscuit bits into the liquid. "Good point on the fertilizer. I'll admit I'm interested in seeing where this all goes. Part of me is wondering if we've been on this level and not noticed it."

Parker grabbed his napkin and wiped his mouth. "Damn, you said a mouthful, hon!"

Angela wet her index finger and drew a line in the air. "Wondered if I could catch you off guard. Truth is we've come to a point where we're more relaxed with each other. Possibly, because we know we're going to take the risk. Maybe we already are."

Parker cleaned his hands with another napkin. "With that, let me get the kettle and mugs. I need to get my thoughts together before I say more. Give me a moment, please."

Angela didn't respond. She kept eating. If she let her mind speak, she'd apologize repeatedly. Another part encouraged her to be real and say what she needed. Issue was she wasn't quite sure. She learned she and Parker clicked on many levels since last night and today. Sure, they'd talked about some of this stuff before. Very little of it was from before. Since this morning, even probably well before their midnight snack, she'd felt different. Calmer, more centered and at peace. It was like she'd come home. Wait—no it was more like she'd found another part of herself. The other half of her ying was a male yang named Parker Jones. Her Grandma Fiona talked about angels and deities watching over the family. Maybe this was the sign that they were throwing at her with a rock attached to it. A rock called a snowstorm that forced her and Parker to search their hearts. Finally, acknowledge their hearts' desire? She sighed and set her empty bowl on the table. Letting Parker have some space made sense. He needed to figure out what was going on, too.

Parker set the kettle in the sink and turned the water on more. Air spattered water on the kettle and the bottom of the sink. Then water mixed with a few more blasts until it ran as normal. He tested the temperature of the water. Much warmer than last night and earlier today. He leaned down checking the angle of the sun as he glanced at his watch. Another hour and a half of daylight might give them enough time to grab a quick warm wash. Was Angela saying yes to them? Yes to intimacy when they were both ready? Hell, he was a guy and most of them wanted it without preamble. Parker didn't like the way he felt afterwards when that happened. Connecting with someone emotionally and intimately brought joy and added so much more to his pleasure. Could he verbalize that? He wasn't waiting until marriage like a past girlfriend had demanded. Man, he was glad he hadn't gone that route. Knowing if you got along on the intimate plane mattered too. Jumping into bed on the first date didn't always mean sex. He and Angela had jumped into bed. Well next to wrapping themselves around the stove or in a tight ball like a cat or dog would, the sleeping bags and air mattress were the warmest spots.

He cut the water back to its original trickle. He picked up the two mugs he'd put tea bags in while the kettle filled and the kettle. As he made his way to the living room, he knew one thing. Somewhere in the midst of his and Angela's banter along with the scattered heavier parts of their ongoing discussion, they'd grown and moved to another level. Did Angela agree?

"Thanks for giving me a few to gather my thoughts. I've got an off-topic item first. Water is warmer. If you want a quick shower, best get it right after dinner. I'm gonna grab one." Parker put the mugs on the coffee table. As he placed the kettle on the stove, he added. "Risking means saying what we're feeling and thinking without holding back."

"You're right to a point. I think you mean without getting vulgar or hurting feelings. We've each got limits." Angela handed him his bowl of soup.

"I think you're on to something with limitations. I'm going to go first, okay?"

"I'm good with that." Angela put her empty bowl on the table, picked up a biscuit, and tore a piece off.

Parker held up his bowl. "I like good food. I like you. I'm enjoying our time together. You get me hot. I want you."

Angela opened her mouth. Nothing came out. She coughed, cleared her throat and said, "I what?"

"You get me hot. Turn me on." Parker moved closer to her.

Angela tossed the remnants of her biscuit in her bowl. "Where's the limitation in that?"

"I said what I'm thinking without limiting myself. I put it out there. I took a risk." Parker stacked her bowl with his. "I'd offer to shower with you. But that is pushing limits. Your turn."

Angela inhaled sharply, glanced at Parker, and sighed. "You have a knack for doing away with the chase to use one of my grandma's favorite phrases."

"Just because I said it doesn't mean I'm acting on it without your input. You matter to me. Guess the best way to put it is I care about you."

Angela swallowed twice, licked her lips and faced Parker. "All right. My turn."

"Sure."

She looked down and back at Parker. " First, thanks for the offer to save water by showering with me. Not happening yet. Second, thanks for the compliment. You get me hot too. Yes, we're having a good time getting to know each other better."

"Oh, come on. Is that really what you want to say? Aren't you still straining things through a good manners filter?" Parker slid closer to her. "Say what you feel. Please."

She nodded. "You're right. Moving out of my comfort zone isn't easy."

"I promise you this." Parker held up one hand, put his other over his heart. "I am not going to hurt you. Doing that hurts me. I don't want to lose what we're embarking on here. Trust me some more, and trust you too."

Angela closed her eyes, heaved a sigh, and opened her eyes. She reached for Parker's hand. He entwined his fingers with hers.

"Sharing a shower sounds hot. Maybe when there's hot water and lots of it. You turn me on. Get me juicy in all the right places." She ducked her head and added, "Kissing you is awesome. Sexy awesome. And I wonder. . . " Her voice trailed off. What she said next might stall things. Still, she needed to get it out in the open.

Parker squeezed her hand. "Go ahead. I'm fine with hearing you out."

"I wonder if it's too soon to tell your family I'm your girlfriend. The idea of meeting them unnerves me some. I know if things work out I will meet them, but so soon?"

Parker lifted they hands to his lips. He pressed a kiss on each of Angela's fingers, rubbed his cheek against them and lowered their hands. "I like you took a chance saying what you're feeling and thinking. Meeting either of our families for the first time is going to be risky. But..." He waited until Angela looked straight at him. "If we're confident and secure in us, meeting them is going to be a breeze. We'll have each other 's back."

"It might not go as well as you think. Depends on the circumstances." Angela held up her other hand. "I'm not borrowing trouble. Just being cautious. Too optimistic or too cautious isn't good either."

"Right. How about we focus on here and now? I want you to come to Elise's party with me either way, friend or girlfriend. I think you'll like my family." Parker untwined his fingers from Angela's. "Kettle's starting to boil. Let's continue the discussion while we clean up the kitchen. Maybe washing dishes is best way to use what warm water we've got."

Angela laughed. "'I can't think of a better way to use soap and water. We're sharing the warm water together."

"Good come back."

Neither spoke as they carried their dishes and leftovers into the kitchen. Parker put the soup back into its container. He placed the biscuits into a large plastic storage bag. He leaned on the counter close to Angela. She had partly filled one of the double sinks with detergent and water. Their ease at doing things together, mixed with neither of them needing to continue talking, scored with him. He liked the quieter side of life too. Loud obnoxious noise ruled most of his workday. Non-stop go and do with a constant refrain left him wrung out and at odds many days. Being and doing together in the quiet of the moment felt very right to him. Maybe this was why others hadn't attracted him the way she did. Angela even got being quiet at work. Often she would bring him a cup of coffee and a few cookies as he and Mitch sat waiting for their next call or took a half-hour break to catch their breath on busier nights. She would check on them and pull the door of the break room partway closed, giving them a few minutes of quiet and relaxation. She got it. It wasn't something he could put into words, but she got it.

"You wash? I'll dry?" Parker offered, sliding his arm around Angela's waist and gave her a quick hug. "I appreciate all you've done to help out and pitch in. Thank you." He kissed her cheek and moved away.

Angela glanced at him, shrugged and started putting dishes in the soapy water. "You're welcome. Least I can do. I do this even when I'm at a friend's place or visiting my family. You help make the mess. You help clean it up. Fair and equal is how my parents taught us. You take care of you and others at the same time. It comes back around when you need it."

"Yup. Paying it forward without expecting it back is how my Mom called it. It has benefited me numerous times. How about you?" He reached for the first dish Angela rinsed.

"Me too. Especially in college. Money could be tight. Getting invited to a friend's or roommates' family dinners sure helped stretch tight budget moments." She handed him another bowl. "I've been thinking about what you said earlier about fear ruling."

"Okay." Parker started putting the dried dishes away.

"I'm willing to go to your sister's party with you. I've got one hesitation." Angela handed him the Dutch oven to dry.

"What is it?" Parker sat the oven and its lid on the counter.

"I prefer to go as your date. It keeps things low-key. No expectations laid on us by them said or unsaid. Make sense?"

"Sorta. Either way, you're there with me. Date or girlfriend doesn't change that. If you feel better using date, I'm game. I'm not going to argue semantics." Parker faced Angela. "Your comfort and well-being are important. Elise and Charla will welcome you with open arms. They're big on accepting people where they're at with identity and labels."

Angela brushed her lips over his, pulled back and gave him a half-smile. "Thank you. I'm sure they'll figure out there's more to it than what we've said at first. It's about expectations and people reading more into things than there really is. Been burned too many times by those."

"Not an easy place to heal from, I'm sure. I think we're all burned at some point by things that matter to us. One of my largest burns was when my ex-fiancée blabbed the reason we broke the engagement. I had so many people telling me what I should've done that I ended friendships, told relatives to mind their own damn business and didn't talk to my immediate family for almost six months." Parker hung the damp towel on the towel rack near the sink. "Sorry for the tirade."

"No issue. You said what you felt. You shared without worrying. That is trust at work. Thank you for trusting me with that." Angela rinsed her hands and dried them on the towel he'd hung up.

"You trusted me too. Thank you for doing that. I think we've moved into a new level. A level of deeper trust and mental intimacy." Parker dropped down on the couch.

"I suspect you're right. Question is, where do we go from here?" Angela sat down next to him.

"Oh, I got an idea or two. Main question is, are you willing to let me lead?" Parker kicked off his moccasins and sat crossed-legged, tucking the afghan around his feet.

CHAPTER SEVENTEEN

Angela slumped into the corner of the couch, pulling part of the afghan over her legs. She wrapped her arms around her knees, hugging them tight to her. Would Parker think she was taking a defensive posture? Was she afraid to let him lead? How much did she trust him? After Doug and helping Tricia escape a verbally abusive relationship, Angela doubted she'd ever trust anyone a hundred percent again. Trouble was she'd begun doubting herself until Parker pointed it out in their earlier conversation. "I guess it depends on where you're leading, too."

"Guess? That's pretty vague. Can you define your boundaries more definitely?" Parker rested his elbows on his knees, cupping his chin in his hand. "My strategy is to determine where hard core lines are. The stop areas. Another thing I value thanks to Charla and Elise's relationship. Took them some verbal processing and out loud thinking to get these understood."

"I hadn't thought about it that way. You make a good point." She loosely laid her arms on top of her knees. She took a breath, exhaled and repeated. Pointing at Parker, she added, "Boundaries are I trust you some. It'll probably grow as our relationship grows. I trust me most."

"Nice. I like how you put your trust first. Being your utmost importance is a big dynamic in self-care. Also being able to verbalize it to me matters too. I'm able to get where you're coming from. Reading minds doesn't work well."

Angela snickered. "Lost in translation rings loud and clear on that for sure."

"Back to the question, do you trust me to lead? Or are you willing to follow?" Parker rocked back, laying his hands on his legs. "Or different view, do we both lead, going in side-by-side?'

Angela stretched her legs out, leaning toward Parker. "Ooh, I like that. Let's us each lead without overwhelming the other. Nice touch. Where are you thinking about going?"

Parker rubbed his lips together, smoothed his sweaty palms down his jeans, and slowly inhaled. How did he say *sex*?

Well, the same way you always do, his smartass psyche chided. *Ain't like you're a virgin. This isn't a screw you, thank you, good evening, get out fast.*

127

He worried his bottom lip between his teeth. As he exhaled, he turned his palms up. "How do you feel about physical intimacy? Not strip off your clothes and go for it right here right now. We've both said we're attracted to the other. Even got the hots for each other."

Angela held out a hand to him. "I'm not afraid of it. I believe it's part of our chemistry and also what draws us to each other. I look at the whole person. Emotions, physical traits, how they act and treat others, etc. I need connection."

Parker nodded. "We're very close on that. I've screwed in the past and walked away. It wasn't pleasant looking myself in the mirror that night or even several days afterward. Learned I prefer to make love. Whole person connection like you described."

Angela took his hand as she spoke. "I've screwed too. The hollowness and empty feeling haunted me for a long time. Doug loved to get me hot and bothered then get off often leaving me with a quick orgasm when the fires were very stoked. I dated a few more guys who thought quickies was the way a woman loved it, to quote them."

Parker snorted. "Damn fucking fools. Guys and women can be multi-orgasmic. It takes someone who gets that to be that kind of lover. Glad I studied and learned about human sexuality."

"Did your homework well, eh?" Angela teased.

"How about I show you sometime how well I learned?" he bantered back.

"Might take you up on that. Sooner than you think. Up to it?" Angela laid both of her hands palms down on his. "Not right now. I'd feel like you and I were just doing it to do it. Maybe later. Work up to it if the feeling is mutual."

"Deal. What do you want to do with the remaining daylight we've got left?" He pulled his hands out from under Angela's.

"Charge my cell phone. Work dry shampoo through my hair and listen to the radio. Catch the news and weather. Maybe later we can read to each other." Angela stood up.

"Let me check the power level in the panels. If there's enough you can plug into the wall. If not, I'll crank the radio while we listen to it and charge your phone at the same time. Great way to work off any angst I got after your maybe later statement." Parker grinned and walked by her.

"Ain't promising something I can't keep. Also said mutual feelings. So we'll see where the evening goes." She followed Parker into the kitchen. "The dry shampoo needs to set for a while before I brush it out. Can is in my duffel."

Angela walked up behind Parker, slid her arms around his waist, hugged him tightly, and let go. He flashed her a wide smile, picked up the radio, and held his hand out. "Where's your cell phone? I can plug it in for you."

"In my fanny pack. I'll get it out in a moment."

"All right. See you in the living room." He kissed her cheek and walked out of the kitchen.

Angela stared after him. Wow. He gave her room to be. To do as she saw fit. He earned quite a few points for that. The more they openly talked, the more she felt at ease. This wasn't Doug prying out facts to toss in her face later or belittle her with. No, this was Parker who understood being strong. Got she needed space to be and hold up her end of things. How would he deal with her asking for help? Would he ask for help when he needed it? Being strong and dominant only got a person so far. There were times when teamwork got the job done because someone asked for and got the help they needed.

She grabbed her fanny pack and entered the living room. "I've got a question for you."

"Hang on a minute." Parker called out, but he wasn't in the living room.

Angela tossed her fanny pack on the couch, calling out as she picked up a flashlight off the end table near the stove. "Where are you? You okay?"

"Yeah." Parker's voice boomed out of the utility closet. "Checking how charged the solar panels are. On a clear day with a few hours of direct sun light, they charge a hundred percent and hold an extra ten percent in reserve. We've got about two hours of electric. Maybe four if we ration how much we use."

"I get you. Can we charge both our cells at the same time?" Angela clicked on the flashlight she held, shining it on the wall where Parker already had his aimed.

"Thanks." Parker glanced at her. "We could. Might be better if we did them separately. Plug yours in for twenty minutes. I'll crank the radio and charge mine while we listen to the top-of-the-hour news."

"Then you'll plug yours in and I'll finish charging mine by cranking the radio for a while." Angela stepped out of the closet.

"Radio needs some cranking. Not endless. I'll crank it while you work your dry shampoo through your hair. Then you can while I make our tea?"

Angela nodded. "I wondered how you would handle either of us asking for help. We've watched and pitched in without asking if the other needed help."

"I'll share a piece of advice my granddad gave me. Ask for what you need. Be prepared to do it on your own. Offer help. Be observant and know when to hold your tongue."

"Solid advice. I learned some of that from the school of hard knocks. Though my dad often said I was the most hardheaded of the kids." Angela grinned as Parker held out his flashlight to her.

"Tenacity works when it's combined with clear-headedness. Charging ahead without preamble can backfire. Of course, sometimes you got to make that leap of faith. Trust your gut, your heart and not second-guess yourself. Like I'm trusting mine now." Parker closed the gap between them.

He stopped when he stood toe-to-toe with her. He pulled the flashlight out of her hand, tossed it on the couch and slipped his arm around her waist. He moved tighter to her. He tangled his other hand in her hair, cradling her head. He leaned forward until his forehead rested against hers. "How does it feel being this close? Do you feel the heat rising between us? Enveloping us in its embrace waiting to scald us as it mixes with . . ."

"Our internal flames of desire," Angela whispered. She tilted her head forward until his lips touched hers. Their mouths opened at the same time. Tongues met. Over and around, lazily caressing each other as they sipped and tasted the others' essences until one didn't know where they stopped and the other began.

Parker slowly loosened his fingers from Angela's hair, careful to not pull or tug any strands loose. Pulling her closer to him would bring their bodies tight as if they were making love. Ready to take things to the next level that would create a bond of intimacy that there was no turning back from.

His cock ached with need. His balls swelled, demanding more room in his jeans. And his thoughts flew from sinking deep into Angela as she cuddled him deep into her warmth. He could name all the anatomical parts correctly and even call them the slang terms guys used. What did he care? Sex joined two people in an intimate way that made them part of each other until orgasm rocked them back to reality. His hand slid down Angela's hip until he cupped her ass. That fleshy part that drew his thoughts to what positions and pleasure areas each woman had. Learning Angela's was going to be fun. Fun that took two people to engage in. He pulled back, lowering his hands until air raced up between them, cooling his face and thoughts.

Cool air felt good at times. This wasn't one of them. He wished they could take this to the next level. A level that brought them past where they danced back and forth. Moving over the line into consensual want and desire along with realization they were meant for each other. No other woman had put him at ease the way Angela did. Even in the moments they'd semi-argued, he hadn't doubted the outcome. Friends, tight and close even when they were apart on viewpoints. Yeah, they had more to talk about but hell it was like granddad said when he and grandma celebrated their fiftieth anniversary, politics, personal likes and dislikes along with day in and day out doings couldn't take away from the core that bonded them—love. Love and caring that allowed each of them to be who they were at any given moment. Mom had talked about some yelling matches between them that had their six kids thinking the end was in sight. One of them usually saw the absurdity of what they were arguing about and took things back to a calmer discussion. Parker felt that was where he and Angela were. Learning about each other, and yet—ready to let their boundaries be permeable to letting the other in. He wasn't ready to bet they'd be together fifty years from now. He believed they had a great start to a wonderful future. No wonder he kept coming back to Angela when he thought of who he wanted to share things with. Maybe building their friendship first had brought them to this point.

"Is something wrong?" Angela asked, fanning her face.

"No. Enjoying the moment. The feelings. And you." Parker smiled, reaching for her hand. "Great kiss."

"Oh ,yeah. Smokin' great kiss." Angela grinned. "Why did you stop?"

"Truth?"

"Well, yeah." Angela cupped Parker's face. "I hope and believe we've gotten to that point."

"Oh, we have. Still better to ask than assume." Parker covered her hand with his, leaning more into it. "Seriously, we've got other things going on. It's about what we both want and need. Taking only gets you so far. After while the person giving gets to feeling used and wrung dry."

'Honey," Angela began, slowly removing her hand away. "I get where you're coming from. Thanks for being conscious of that. Being in the moment ain't bad either."

"Agreed. How about let's take care of those *chores* and we can see about getting back into this moment?" Parker winked, blew her a kiss, and dropped his hand.

"Sounds like a plan I wholeheartedly endorse." Angela started toward the kitchen, adding, "I'll get the radio and dry shampoo. My cell phone is in the outer pocket of my fanny pack. My spare charger is in there too. Go ahead and get them out."

Parker was surprised his mouth wasn't hanging open. It took a *lot* for a woman to say go into her personal bag aka purse or tote. Wow, he'd crossed into trusted territory for sure. If it were anyone else, he'd ask if she was sure. He wasn't though. She trusted him to get her phone and charger out. That's all he'd take out or even touch for now. The rest of her belongings were private and hers to share when and if she wanted to.

"Got 'em," Parker called out, zipping the outer pocket closed and putting Angela's fanny pack on the coffee table.

"Thanks," Angela replied, entering the living room with the crank radio in one hand. Her dry shampoo can and hair brush in her other. She handed him the radio and sat on the couch. "It looks like there's melting going on. Water is dripping from the icicles. And I could see patches of grass."

"I noticed bare patches on the parking lot when Matt dropped off the mail. Large amount of snow and clear sunny sky next day say icy and dicey out there come morning." Parker plugged Angela's charger into the wall socket closest to them and attached her cell phone. He laid the phone on the arm of the chair. "Be careful heading for the bathroom. Cord is in the way."

"Sure will. You too." Angela shook the dry shampoo can and leaned forward until her head was between her knees. She combed her fingers through each section as she sprayed. She sat up, capped the can and set it on the coffee table. Parker watched her as he cranked the radio. "Never seen anyone use dry shampoo before?"

"A few times. I'm watching you. Seeing you as you. There's comfort in that. Neither of us has been fake in the last day and half. Right?" Parker stopped cranking the radio.

"Yeah. Your sleepwear hasn't sent me running. Nor has that orange t-shirt. You've seen all my bulges and abundant curves. I work out to keep toned. Our jobs demand it." Angela picked up her hairbrush. "I guess we see each other for who we really are."

Parker sat next to her. "Given some of what we've worked through and dealt with, we have to. We've seen each other covered with blood and guts and without. I wouldn't trade knowing both sides of you as well as I do."

Angela covered Parker's hand with hers and squeezed. "We've saved a few lives. Seen the good and bad of life. Here we are ready to risk our hearts because we know love is a necessary part of life. Together we're stronger than alone."

Parker raised their hands, turned them over and slid his beneath hers. He brought her hand up to his lips and whispered, "Here's to us. I think I'm falling in love."

He pressed a kiss into her palm and closed her fingers around it. Angela swallowed hard, licked her lips and sighed. "Maybe we already have. Now we're ready to admit it."

Parker smiled, kissed her fist and lowered their hands. "Could be. I think basking in the moment holding you as we listen to the news is a good foundation piece to build on."

Angela moved tight to Parker as he clicked on the radio. He leaned back as the newscast began, looping his arm around her shoulders. War, strife and unrest continued on, peace and tranquility happened in small patches and in their corner of Peyton Corners. The newscaster paused for a commercial. Parker kissed the top of her head, blew in her ear and kissed her cheek. As he pulled back, he said, "After hearing that, being snowed in isn't so bad."

"No, it makes what we're going through shrink in the light and dark of the world at large. I think that's one reason why I went into nursing. To help someone have moments like these they could cherish with their loved ones.

And I cherish the ones we've had and are having." She tilted her head, leaned toward Parker with her lips parted.

Parker gave Angela a quick kiss. "I'll take a rain check for the moment on another kiss for after the news and weather finishes."

Angela stared at him quizzically. He grinned. "If there's more bad news, I don't want it to ruin a damn fine kiss. I like savoring those especially with you, darlin.'"

"I'm enjoying yours too." Angela reached for her brush. "I might as well make the time count."

Parker took his arm off the back of the couch and held out his hand. "I'd like to do that for you. Turn around with your back to me. I brushed Elise's hair every morning until she was old enough to do it on her own."

"Comforting taking care of someone you love?" Angela handed him the brush.

He laid his hand on Angela's shoulder as she started to turn around. "That and someone I'm falling in love with."

CHAPTER EIGHTEEN

"Falling in love with?" Angela stared at Parker, opened her mouth to say more when the newscaster began speaking. Parker pressed his fingers against her lips, motioned for her to turn around with his other hand. She nodded and complied.

Falling in love. . .a phrase that baffled many a mind, started a few clashes down through history and set many a heart fluttering like hers was. L-O-V-E, a four-lettered word that a while back she cursed, cried over and even swore wouldn't happen again. She snorted. Like emotions could be turned on and off like a light switch. She'd fallen in love with Tricia's black cat Midnight. The small kitten hadn't wormed her way into either her or Tricia's heart. No, Midnight leaped in, purring and curling up from the moment she clawed her way up each of their pant legs the day they volunteered at the shelter. Now Parker. . .he hadn't clawed his way into her heart. He hadn't even tried to take her clothes off. Not that that was a problem, given how damn cold it had gotten inside. They were headed in that direction. One that she bet he had in mind with each stroke of the brush through her hair. Had she fallen in love or was she still skirting along the edge? Was she ready to risk her heart again?

Parker counted each brush stroke like he had with Elise who wanted her hair brushed one hundred times each night based on some story their mother had read them. Touching Angela felt so right and good. Helping her work the dry shampoo out of her hair by brushing it gave him reason to do something for her, touch her and nurture the flame of love igniting in his heart—and mind. Were they ready to admit those feelings out loud and use the word *love*? He stopped counting as the weather report came on.

"All right folks. I know many of us are wondering how much longer this freeze will last. I won't keep you waiting. National Weather Service maps show the storm blew out of here this afternoon. Some places have temps in the thirties already. It's gonna be a few days before the white stuff is fully melted. The city and county are asking folks to stay off the roads for another day while crews clear them. Stay tuned as we begin our evening program of music."

Parker worked the brush through Angela's hair for several more strokes as the first bars of music sounded. He leaned forward, resting his arm on Angela's shoulder. "Jazz piece. I believe the group is Blue Ridge Jazz."

Angela took a hold of the brush. "They were a local group until two years ago. Played at an international jazz festival in Memphis and the rest is history. Their third CD releases next month."

"I went to school with Karl, their base player. He's from Charleston. He's part of the reason I moved to Tennessee." Parker stood up and stretched.

"So music and your friend Karl incited your move?" Angela asked, laying her brush on the coffee table.

"Not really. More like my Mom and sisters ragging on me to move closer. Or back in with Mom. Even my relatives kept checking up on me. A guy needs space." Parker walked over to the end table and picked up her phone. "Almost fully charged. You good with that or want a full phone?"

Angela snickered. "That is a loaded question. Now, let me see. . ."

Parker burst out laughing. "Yeah, a little pun and innuendo there. Oops?"

"Nah. It's all good. I've got a wicked wit when it comes to sarcasm and also to a good naughty joke. We know intimacy is going to happen at some point."

"Oh, we do?" Parker walked away from her, stopping before he entered the kitchen.

"I'm not commenting further for now. What you after in there now?" Angela followed Parker into the kitchen.

"Cookies! I got a sweet tooth attack happening. There's tea to make too. I need something to dunk in it." Parker grinned at her and winked.

She shook her head, grinning too. "Okay, I'll have a couple too, please."

"Sure. Sharing these is great. You might figure out the recipe before I have to bug Mrs. Pescalli for it." Parker grabbed the bag of cookies off the counter. He glanced out the window as he turned to her. "Shit. The sun is hitting the patio full-on."

"Best bring the ice chest in?" Angela took the bag of cookies from Parker.

"Yeah. Let's hope it ain't blowing and in the twenties out there."

"I'll be in the living room. Holler if you need me." Angela started moving quickly across the kitchen.

"Halt right there, Angela Sewald!" Parker called out. "I need you here to take the chest out of my hands. I am not handling that cold thing on my own."

'Oh come on, you can handle a bit of cold air and snow. You're a big strong dude. I know you can do it." Angela stayed right where she stood.

Parker pointed at her. "Nope. Need help or I warm my cold hands and feet on you when I'm done bringing the chest in."

"Parker Jones, that ain't fair." Angela tightened her grip on the bag of cookies. "I might not tell you the recipe if I did figure it out. Mrs. Pescalli might like me better than you and give me the recipe."

"Honey," Parker began, moving toward her slowly. "Cookies and recipe aren't going to stop me from warming my hands and feet if you don't help. Of course, there's always making out, too."

Angela ducked her head, glancing up as she backed up a step. "Now you're gonna make me blush."

Parker kept advancing, taking bigger steps the closer he got. "I'll have to check and see if you blush all over later on. Now give me the cookies and let's get that chest in before it warms up too much."

Angela moved to her left. Parker followed suit, keeping up with her until she backed up against the chair he'd pulled out from the kitchen table earlier. "Damn, I forgot about the chair." She tossed the bag of cookies on the table. "I call truce. I'll help with the chest. You leave the cookies be until we're back in the living room."

Parker grinned, nodding. "Dang straight I'm bobbleheading. 'Cuz I get to smooch you afterwards. Warms lips up real nice."

Angela sighed. "You know we still need to discuss this love thing you mentioned earlier."

Parker shrugged. "Talk okay. Right now, I've got an ice chest to rescue. Operation Rescue begins now."

He groaned as he completed two tugs on the slatted blinds covering the patio doors. He let another exaggerated moan and groan loose as he pulled the patio door open. Wind rushed in, blowing bits of wet snow and ice in, too. "Chilly but not super nasty."

"It's still cold. Hurry up." Angela stood next to him, arms out. "Get the chest and close the door."

Parker leaned out, glanced back over his shoulder and said. "Too bad it's icy out too. Otherwise I'd challenge you to a snowball fight."

Angela grabbed the chest from him and stuck her tongue out. "PFFFTTT. Iceball fight is what that would be. Remember when the James twins came in after their incident? Bruised arms and a couple of chapped hands."

Parker snorted as he slid the patio door shut and locked it. "Oh, it took me and their mom twenty minutes to get them settled down before I let them out of my truck. Rambunctious duo. I don't want or need those kind of bruises for sure."

"Neither do I." Angela set the chest on the counter. "I think this should go in the fridge."

"Me and the cookies will be in the living room." Parker untied the cookie bag, took one out and took a bite. "I might leave you a few."

Angela opened her mouth, ready to fling a comeback. Instead, she shut her mouth and put the ice chest in the fridge. Warming her hands on Parker might get her the bag of cookies before he could eat too many of them.

Parker dropped the bag of cookies on the coffee table. Steam poured out the kettle's spout. He pulled his sweatshirt sleeve down over his hand, took a hold of the kettle handle, and lifted it. As he moved around the couch, Angela entered the living room. Her grin reminded him of the ones Saturday morning cartoon characters wore to show their devious planning. Not that Angela looked like a cartoon. Far from it. She looked good with her hair down. Her usual work ponytail defined her work approach, simple-easy and ready to get on with looking after patients. Much the same reason he was clean-shaven and wore short hair. Patients came first. Another area where he and Angela meshed.

He filled the mugs sitting on the coffee table, straightened, walked over to Angela and stuck out his tongue. She leaned forward and began French kissing him. Talk about a fast, furious, first-class distraction! Parker gripped the kettle handle tighter lest he drop it and splash scalding water everywhere. He didn't move. He closed his eyes and stood still, savoring the kiss. Angela tasted of soup—spices, sage, pepper, and onion mixed with hints of beef. She kept kissing him and yet....she kept moving around. Almost squirming. He opened one eye intently watching her. Damn if she wasn't—"Angela, if you want cookies, say so. I'm holding a hot kettle."

Angela pulled back. There was no mistaking the 'who me?' look that dashed across her face. Parker stepped back, holding the kettle at arm's length away from them. Angela winked, moved back as well and leaned down. "Well, yes, I want cookies. Thanks for making the tea."

Parker shook his head, sighed and put the kettle back on the stove. "You're welcome. How about a dance? You know, something to do while our tea brews. Of course, finish your cookie first."

Angela looked up, popping the last piece of the cookie she'd taken out of the bag into her mouth. She chewed, smiling and nodding. Parker walked back over to the small open area between the couch and where the kitchen started. He faced Angela, held his arms wide open and began humming. Another of Blue Ridge Jazz's slow pieces rolled out of the radio like water cascading over rocks and into a pool that called out wanting attention. He swayed back and forth, humming louder, and staring at Angela. Would she get lost in the words and melody too? Wrap herself tightly to him like they had during the one lights-out dance at last year's Christmas party? God, he hoped so. The feel of her in his arms was so right and at times he lost sense of time and place with her there.

Angela quickly wiped her hands on the towel she'd tossed over her shoulder after she'd washed and dried her hands. She tossed it on the couch and closed the distance between her and Parker. He swayed right, smiling at her. She tried to copy his move. Except getting close when she couldn't see where his feet were made it almost impossible. "Can you stand still for a moment? I'd like to ..."

"Like to get on board? Snuggle your delicious self tight to me? Oh, yes, come on darlin'." Parker stepped toward her, still swaying from side to side.

She swallowed, wet her lips and reached out, hoping she landed on board Parker's moving boat. One step, then another found her moving and swaying with him as he slipped his arms around her waist, hugging her tight to him. "Just listen. Feel the music wash over you and lap back up your body until it submerges you in it. Let the lyrics sink into your soul, baby."

Angela looped her arms around Parker's neck and leaned into him, letting him direct which way they moved around the small area. The singer sang about heartbreaks that left a mark that burned deeper than anyone understood. His deep, sultry voice left nothing out. The tears, the pain and the healing that came with putting one foot in front of the other. She wasn't sure when the singer hushed and the chords of piano, saxophone and guitar penetrated deep into her gut, mind and yes soul. She and Parker swayed, slowly stepping around in a circle at times, others sideways and back across the space until on their last pass they bumped up against the couch.

"That was nice," Angela murmured, her head resting on Parker's chest.

"Been a while since I heard that particular cut. Karl wrote it during a difficult time in a friend's life. Beth lost her husband right around the same time my dad committed suicide. She was a young military spouse." Parker perched on the arm of the couch.

"Then the song doesn't bring back good memories." Angela laid a hand on Parker's chest.

"Actually, it does. It reminds me of the support and strength the three of us gave each other. Karl's parents split up then too. It forced us to reach outside ourselves and grow. We learned about caring and loving ourselves. Karl found solace in his music. Beth went back to school and became a teacher. I latched on to first aid and EMT training." Parker leaned against her.

"So your friendships helped you heal and find peace." Angela kissed Parker's forehead.

"Yeah. Also taught me I could survive. I had it in me to thrive when I thought I didn't." Parker hugged her tightly. "Thanks for getting it. Some people don't."

"Don't sweat it. There's a part where you accept who you are, what you are, and you let go. It's about faith and a deep conviction that you can be vulnerable and take risks."

Parker looked up at her. "I'm taking one right now. I want you so bad I hurt. Ache and yet I'm not going to go there without you wanting to be there too. Do you want to be there too?"

Angela licked her lips. Parker's gaze never left hers. He watched her intently waiting for some signal, maybe a sign. What each of them needed was mutual agreement to move forward. Become lovers. Take another big step toward becoming a couple. She rubbed her lips together, wet them again, and said, "I want you too. Safe sex is a mandate for me along with birth control. Talk to me about your sexual health. How safe are you? You got condoms?"

Parker cupped her face, brushed his lips over hers and pulled back. "I'm asking the same questions. See, I think neither of us wants to hurt or shame the other. So I'm going to answer your first question very succinctly. I get tested every three months. Local health code requirement. Keeps tabs on my overall health. My last tests and physical were last month. All normal. No STDs."

Angela kissed Parker's cheek. She took his hand. "I get tested twice a year. No relationship for the last three years. Still keeping on top of health matters makes sense. All normal too. No STDS. I got condoms and I'm on the pill."

"Good. I've got condoms. Not that I planned on seducing you. Precaution just the same. So where do we go from here?"

Angela pointed at the couch. "We've got tea to sip and a couple more cookies to nibble while we talk about what you mean by falling in love."

Parker sighed. "You're right. I need a few moments to shift gears. Let me refill the kettle."

He trotted around the couch and picked up the kettle. "Don't get me wrong. I'm filling it so it continues to humidify the place. Can you check on the fire? Being ready for when the temp changes makes sense."

Angela walked past him. She didn't say anything nor did she look at him. Had he messed up? Putting words together didn't always come easy for him. Like telling his balls to stop sending lava hot signals to his groin and brain that sex was happening. What was it Karl said one time? Oh yeah, a stiff dick was like driving a stick shift with your feet on the brake and clutch at the same time. Gears ground to a halt after you stripped 'em. Parker grimaced. That wasn't happening. Would Angela get his analogy if he explained it to her? He doubted it.

CHAPTER NINETEEN

Parker watched the kettle fill. What did falling in love mean? Were there expectations? Limitations? Inclusions? He leaned on the counter as more words and questions flooded his mind. Did they need a solid answer before they moved forward? What were Angela's thoughts?

"Angela," he called out, putting the lid on the kettle and taking it out of the sink.

"Yes?"

"Does my falling in love with you bother you?" He winced at his question. Damn, he sounded like he expected her to be fine with it. "Sorry, let me rephrase that."

Angela met him at the stove. "Fire's fine. I added more wood. About your question, you're fine."

"Thanks. Can you explain why you asked what I meant?" Parker dropped down on the couch. "I'm trying to understand."

"Falling in love is different things for each person. Some guys say it to score. Some women use it to gain a ring, a piece of paper, and think it's going to guarantee marital success. I don't want us to read more into things than we're ready for." As Angela sat down next to him, she added. "Unsaid expectations create messes."

Parker nodded. "I think I get where you're coming from. I know I care deeply for you. I want to spend time with you. When I'm around you, I get a sense of peace and calmness. Best I can say. Make sense?"

"It does. I feel joy when you're around. I like talking with you. Hearing about your trips. I care deeply for you too. You're a friend and more. I believe what you're saying is coming from here." Angela laid her hand over his heart. "I like that you speak from your heart. Am I capturing what you're saying?"

"You are. Let me see if I can paraphrase what you're saying." Parker propped his feet up on the coffee table. "You like talking with me. You're interested in me inside and out. You want to hear what I've got to say. I get you hot and horny like you do me. Caring and friendship helps solidify those feelings. How'd I do?"

"Pretty good. We're picking up on each other's unsaid things too. Nice. I like that. Feels good that joint acceptance is going on." Angela turned, leaned toward him and whispered. "I want you. Whose condoms are closer?"

Parker coughed, shook his head and sat straight up. "Wow. There's no mistaking that message. Umm, I'm not into sex just for the sake of doing it. Are you?"

Angela smiled, shaking her head. "No. But—I don't want to stop once we get in the mood again. And, well. . ."

Parker stood up. "I got the hint. How about you work some of that energy off by cranking the radio to charge my phone while I get what you asked about?"

He moved around the couch at a fast pace, slowing as he got partway up the stairs. "Um, are you allergic to latex?"

"Yes. Thank you for asking. One reason I have condoms with me." Angela unplugged her phone from the wall.

"I've got non-latex ones too. Don't like ruining things with allergic reactions. We'll make sure we got both yours and mine handy." Parker added as he continued up the steps, "I'm gonna grab a shower. I'll be down in ten minutes."

"Okay. Leave me some hot water too, please." Angela plugged Parker's cell phone charger cord into the outlet on the radio and began cranking. Fifteen cranks later, she paused, checked the phone's battery level and began humming along with the easy listening piece playing. As the music's rhythm changed pace, she cranked faster. Keeping pace until the song finished. She glanced at her watch. Parker had seven minutes left to shower and dry.

Parker shucked his clothes, tossing them on his bed. Wincing at the floor's chill, he slipped his moccasins back on and grabbed his robe off the back of the bedroom door. As he headed for the bathroom, he called out. "Angela, I'm getting in the shower. There's a robe on the back of the guest room door you can use after you shower. Come on up and get ready to get in after I get out. I'll leave the water on."

He didn't wait for her answer. He shut the bathroom door, grabbed the towel and washcloth off the curtain rod and tossed them on the counter. He snatched the soap off the counter, turned the hot water on full-blast, and took off his robe. The battle between warm and cold water furiously began.

Parker ducked under the spray, lathered the soap and washed his underarms, groin, chest and face. As he rinsed, a blast of ice-cold water doused him. "Frack, that's cold!" He stepped out of the shower, trying to keep from splashing water on the floor. He wrapped the towel around him, cracked open the door and yelled, "Next!"

Angela had barely made it to the top of the stairs when Parker yelled next. She raced into the guestroom, pulling her shirt and sports bra over her head. She tossed them on the bed. Stepped out of her moccasins, shoved her leggings and underpants down her legs until they refused to come out of her socks.

"WTF!" She bent over, trying to pull one foot out of a sock and cursing under her breath. "Damn socks. Now you decide you want to stay on. Ah, shit. "

"Got a problem?" Parker asked from behind her.

Not sure her ass could blush as much as her face and neck probably were, Angela turned, hoping her smile looked real and said, "Nah. Close the door please."

"Why? I like the view. Nice to know you can bend over and touch your toes easily. And your. . ." Parker winked at her and patted her bare ass.

"Touché. We're even now, I believe." Angela straightened. "Going to stand there and gawk?"

"Not gawking. Admiring the view, darlin'. And an awesome view it is." Parker's grinned deepened. "Why you blushing?"

"One of us has to!" Angela grabbed for the door, ready to shove it closed.

"Honey, you're only a little more dressed than how I plan to have us in a short while." Parker turned, started whistling again and made his way down the stairs. "I'd hurry up or what warm water there is will be gone."

Angela flipped her middle finger up, sighed and sat on the bed. She jerked her socks off, then her leggings and underwear. She pulled the robe off the back of the door and trotted into the bathroom. Wetting and soaping went faster than she thought she could move. Underarms, breasts and mons, and between her legs. She quickly wet her face and soaped it. The water got colder as she rinsed. As she toweled off, she called out. "Parker, I'm going to warm my cold parts on you."

"Oh, please, do. In fact, I'll help you warm them up. Hurry on down so we can get started." Parker walked over to the patio doors. He shivered as he drew the blinds. The sun was just setting. If the chilly air by the doors was any indication of what the air temp outside was, they were in for another very cold night.

He rubbed his arms as he entered the living room. They had enough pellets to get them through the night. It might be chillier than this morning. The larger chunks of wood would burn low and hot for most of the night. He wouldn't use them unless it got so cold inside they could see their breath fog. Passing the night naked in the sleeping bags worked if the outside temp didn't drop below fifty. Well, they had to be ready to layer on clothes as needed. Parker got to the bottom of the staircase as Angela started down. "Sorry to make you turn around but we're going to need sweatshirts and sweatpants if the temp drops too much. Bring your clothes down."

He waited until Angela got down the stairs before he started up them. "I'll be back down in a moment."

Angela tossed her clothes on the back of the couch. How were they going to rekindle the mood if other things kept distracting them? She heaved a deep sigh as she wrapped the afghan around her as she sat down. She inhaled, closed her eyes and counted to ten twice.

"I know that look. Frustration isn't easy to deal with. I'm sorry things aren't flowing smoothly. I'd like to cuddle while we drink our tea." Parker rubbed his knuckles against her cheek.

"Yeah, okay. I'm tired and cold. I think I need to put my sweatshirt on and crawl in the sleeping bag." Angela stood dropped her robe and pulled on the sweatshirt.

She tossed the afghan on to the air mattress and crawled in her sleeping bag. Parker joined her, still wearing his robe. He handed her her mug and pulled the blanket and afghan over them.

"Please talk to me about what's going on here and here." Parker touched her heart and head.

Angela swallowed a gulp of her cooled tea. "I'm wondering if we're really ready. I want to make love. We keep dancing up to it and something jumps in the way."

Parker reached for her mug. "I'm done with mine. You?"

"Done." She handed him her mug.

"What's happened is a quick change. A slow down. Desire's fires cooled down some. They're not out on my part." He pressed his lips to hers and pulled back a bit. Parker set the mugs on the coffee table.

Angela watched him for a few moments. Her mind wanted him. Her heart said he probably loved her. Her gut said go for it. The hair on the back of her neck wasn't standing up. All her usual warning signals were calmly saying, take the risk. "I'm ready to add fuel to the fire. You?"

Parker took off his robe, stood in front of her in all his nude glory, and pulled on his sweatshirt. His cock and balls jiggled as he walked toward her. She never really looked to see if her lovers were circumcised or not. Most of them were. Parker appeared to be. His head and pubic hair matched. Though why that observation ran through her mind she didn't know. Estimating a guy's length and width flashed amongst the mundane thoughts formatting the closer he got. She knew she could accommodate him because women stretched and lubricated. It wasn't like he sprouted a huge hard- on. She'd already seen him erect even if was brief. Heck, she'd dreamt about it too. Angela smiled as Parker kneeled down on the air mattress. His interest and desire were evident in his partial hard-on.

Parker dropped the hand full of condoms he held on the coffee table. Nonchalant wasn't any part of what was going on. Angela had openly stated she wanted him and was ready to move forward. Stroking their individual desires into a mutual flame that took them where pleasure and satisfaction combined was one goal. Another was eliminating guilt or expectations. Their first time might not bang-a-gong as some of his buddies described their ultimate sexual encounter. His pleasure and Angela's mattered more than earning some hash mark to brag about later. Not that he had or ever would. Their lovemaking was private, between the two of them. If some dude asked or hinted at wanting to know, Parker knew what to tell 'em: Ain't none of your business. Case closed.

"I'm ready, willing and able, hon." He tossed his sleeping bag open and crawled in. "If there's something you need or want, say so. No topic is off-limits. I'm not into kink, power play doesn't thrill me, and *your* pleasure is important. Your likes and dislikes matter. Let me know what is working and what isn't."

"Right now I want to kiss you. See where it goes. If I need you to slow down I'll let you know." Angela scooted closer to him.

"Sounds good," he said, slipping an arm around Angela's waist. "I like kissing you." Parker leaned closer, tilting his head to the left. Angela tilted hers to the right. Each puckered their lips, continuing to lean toward the other until they touched. Angela rested her hand on his chest balancing herself. He closed the gap between them. If they didn't have sweatshirts on, they'd be flesh-to-flesh.

Their lips met. Softly brushing and rubbing on each other like a cat tentatively getting used to a new person's touch and energy. Angela parted her lips some permitting him to sip and savor her taste. Mint toothpaste greeted him first, then hints of her essence followed—sage, onion, honey and a bit of Italian seasoning mix. As her lips parted more, she followed his retreat, giving chase with her tongue.

Angela cupped the back of Parker's head with one hand and the side of his face with her other. Touching him made the kiss feel more intimate. Heat sparked across her fingers, searing its way deep into her palm and further into her. Parker tasted of honey, molasses, butterscotch and a hint of chocolate. Did Mrs. Pescalli know her cookies were aphrodisiacs? Angela didn't care if Mrs. Pescalli did or didn't know, getting the recipe from her topped a priority list that lagged way behind the want and desire brimming closer to boiling over as Parker touched her. He looped his arm around her shoulders, tangling his fingers in her hair much like she had hers in his. He tugged a little, soothing with a light rub after each tug. His tongue met hers, touching and tasting until she couldn't tell who pursued or chased. It didn't matter. Parker pressed his lips tighter to hers. He slipped his hand down her neck, resting it lightly on her shoulder. His other hand slid upwards until he reached the underside of her breast. He pulled back, breaking off the kiss.

Parker rested his forehead against Angela's. He closed his lips, slowly inhaling and exhaling. Angela's breath warmed his face. Neither of them had shut their eyes as they kissed. Their silent communication kept going until their touches said what words weren't. The desire to move ahead was there. Did they take the next step together simultaneously or did one of them make the first move?

Angela slipped one hand, palm down, under the hem of his sweatshirt, resting it on his abdomen. She leaned back some, tilting to her left. She inclined toward him, her other hand on his shoulder. Warmth coursed over him, reaching deep into his core. His eyes closed, surrendering, placing himself in Angela's care.

Angela watched Parker's eyes close. In that moment, she knew he'd let go and placed his trust in her. A trust that not many men had dared to give her. Those that had had taught her to believe in herself and how to read the silent communication that flowed when mutual pleasure occurred. *Thank you Anthony,* flashed across her mind as she kissed Parker's neck. Nip, kiss, nip and kiss again marked her path up to Parker's earlobe. She suckled the lobe between her lips, worrying it lightly with her teeth.

Parker arched toward her, tilting his head closer to her. "Hmm, that feels good," he murmured.

She nipped and nibbled a bit more and let go. "I like touching you. You're soft and warm. I hope my hands aren't chafing you."

Parker smiled, slipping his right arm out of the sleeve and placing his hand on Angela's. "Not at all."

He slid his left arm out of its sleeve. He reached down and under his sweatshirt, laid his hand on Angela's, and asked, "Are you ready for me to get nude?"

He waited, counting his breaths slowly. If Angela raised her hand, she'd feel the fast and steady beat of his heart. Her touch set more on fire, his heart racing. Beating with anticipation and eagerness. His cock was wet. Wet due to excitement mixed with want and desire. The more he tuned into his feelings and the energy simmering around them, the wetter he got.

Angela licked her lips. Was she into oral sex? He wanted inside her. Feel her warmth engulf him. Wrap around him and take him deep into her, letting their consciousness and energies blend until orgasms pounded through them.

Angela slid her hand out from underneath his. She reached up, taking a hold of one of her sweatshirt sleeves. She slowly worked it off her right arm. Then off her left until the shirt covered all of her. Hiding her from his sight. What was she doing?

She tugged the shirt partway up, grinned and asked, "Are *you* ready for *us* to be nude?"

CHAPTER TWENTY

Parker tried to speak. His lips moved. Nothing came out. He swallowed twice, ready to respond. His throat went dry again as Angela started pulling her sweatshirt up more. He'd seen her bare ass along with parts of her mons and labia. Some men in the medical profession lost interest in a nude female body after seeing them as part of their daily routine. He hadn't when he connected with the woman. Cared on an emotional level as well as an attraction one. Angela hit on all his levels. Seeing her totally nude for the few moments when she took her robe off and put on her sweatshirt let him put aside his fantasies and see the real her. Breasts that still had some perk left. Misty pink areolas topped off by suckable nipples. All a definite plus. Her waist nipped in close to her navel. Some would go so far to say a non-flat stomach was a deal-breaker. Not him. He liked his woman curvy. At a healthy weight for them. Once Angela took her sweatshirt off, he'd get to enjoy her full effect. See and enjoy all of her loveliness as a total person. He reached out, touching her hand closest to him. Wetting his lips again, he was finally able to speak. "Yes, *I'm ready for us to get nude.*"

Angela gripped more of her sweatshirt in her hands and started to shove it up further. Words failed her at Parker's declaration. Not because she wasn't ready to get and be nude with him. His emphasis and throaty tone warped right into her ramping her confidence upward toward a peak she'd never felt before. Knowing that she knew she turned Parker on, and seeing his reaction as well as expressing it, turned her on in ways she lacked the ability to put in words. He positively wanted her. Saw her as a whole person and even partially nude he still wanted to go further. See her in all her glory without the trappings and covers most people hid behind. What a heady feeling it gave her. A rush that pumped into her very being, her essence, and blasting away any lingering doubts she had. They were here because they wanted to be. This cemented a link between them that backed up the words they'd alluded to and said with caution earlier. She knew she made the right decision. Angela quickly glanced down as she began working the sweatshirt up over her breasts. Parker was hard. His cock stuck out glistening with

150

pre-ejaculate. He was very turned on. Would he welcome her licking, sucking and tasting him?

She exhaled slowly, eased the sweatshirt over her head, tossing it aside. Parker's gaze roved lower. His smile deepened. A glow filled his eyes as his gaze lingered the lower he looked. Heat rolled off him, pooling around her as if a waterfall of desire, want and a bit of lust pulsed forth from deep inside him. The cool air settled around them as the sunset lowered, adding a layer of darkness to their area. Parker leaned toward her, whispering, "We can continue in the waning light or pause to find where I put the blasted battery lantern?"

Angela snorted. "Subdued light is great for making love. Total darkness. . .nah, let's find the lantern. Last I saw it, it was on the coffee table."

Parker scooted on his knees behind Angela until he reached the edge of the air mattress. He braced his hands on the chair arm and stood. Moving fast in the cooling air sent chills rushing over him. He remembered the lantern being there earlier in the day. Squinting, he moved around the end table, keeping the coffee table in view. The closer he got he could make out a large shadowy figure. Sighing as he reached the end of the coffee table close to the kitchen, he burst out laughing. "You'd think I'd notice where I put it."

"Umm, you were a tad distracted?" Angela offered.

"Oh darlin', very distracted and happily so." Parker picked up the lantern, clicked it on and set it back on the coffee table closer to the air mattress.

He hastily made his way between the couch and coffee table. Kneeling on the air mattress, he chafed his arms. "It's gotten cooler in here."

"Sure has." Angela wrapped the afghan around her. "Maybe we need to get dressed."

"Nope," Parker blurted out as he unzipped his sleeping bag. "Unzip your sleeping bag. Zipping the two together makes a double sleeping bag. Shared warmth is what we need."

He undid the zipper on his bag and reached for Angela's bag. She started to move the extra blanket they shared last night. "Hold on to it. We'll need it. Insert the end of my bag's zipper into the pull of yours and zip up and around."

Angela followed Parker's instructions smoothing her half of the now doublewide bag out. "I don't know about you. I'm getting in and warming up."

Sounds of a zipper moving up and down sounded as she worked the blanket and afghan over her. Parker snuggled close to her. "Warming each other up is great when the flame is ready to have more fuel added." He pressed his lips to her neck, nibbling and laving his way lower.

Flesh to flesh, nothing separated them now. Each caress, touch and nip added to her growing internal heat. She laid her hand on Parker's chest, stroking and dragging her short nails up and down. "I love touching you."

"And I you. " Parker turned on his side, facing her. His hand rested on her stomach below her navel. He captured her lips with his, pulling her tighter to him. He traced a path down to her mons and back each time his tongue touched hers. On his next pass down, he roved lower, dragging his fingers through her pubic hair and back up to the top of her mons. He pressed his hand against her, the warmth of his palm and fingers mingling with hers.

Parker broke off the kiss, tilting back until he could see Angela, but not separating their closeness otherwise. "I want to taste all of you. Feel you move against my face as I lick you."

Angela ducked her head and shivered. He felt every breath she took. She looked up, stroking lower on his cock as she did. She encircled him, lubricating her hand with his wetness and stroked downward. Parker jerked toward Angela, leaving not a hair's width between them. "I want to taste you too. Feel you shudder and pulse as I take you in my mouth, licking you all the way down to your testicles and back to the tip of you. Are you game?"

Parker groaned, thrusting in counter-movement to each of Angela's strokes. "Ahh. Yes, I-I'm game," he moaned. She didn't stroke back up. His shuddered breaths matched hers. "A-are we doing it together or . . ." He couldn't say more. On her upward stroke, Angela tightened her grip on him, enough sending his focus one place—his cock and testicles.

"One at a time this time. Tightness," she began, squeezing Parker as she slipped her hand partway back down him. "Limits our movements."

"Ye-s-s," Parker hissed, jerking toward her again. His hand covered hers. "You go first. Much more up and down and I'll come. Might take me a bit to recover if I do."

Angela let go, raised her hand and licked her palm and fingers. "Hmmm. Nice sweet taste. Just a hint of salt. Lie on your back, please."

Parker undid part of the zipper and turned on his back. "Easy on the touch. Tasting too much and I'm done."

Angela tucked her hair behind her ears, knelt beside Parker and gripped him close to the base of his cock. She pushed the covers down until his bare torso and groin were exposed. "Don't worry. I prefer you come inside me. I'm sipping and licking some."

She puckered her lips, parted them and leaned down, brushing them slightly over and around him twice. Parker lifted his hips off the mattress. She held him steady, opening her lips more, taking the head of him into her mouth. Flicking her tongue gently over, around and back put his taste where she wanted it, on her taste buds. A quick up-and-down elicited more groans and moans. Angela opened her mouth, let go and lowered Parker's cock. "Wonderful. Sweet and salty. You taste delicious."

Parker propped up on his elbows, shot Angela a weak grin and reached for her. "My turn now. Are you multiorgasmic? Some women like many brief orgasms. Others one maybe two larger ones at best."

"Depends on my lover. Connection. And their interest in shared orgasms. Most of the time, gentle ones leading up to a larger one during intercourse happen." Angela sat on her knees beside him.

"Thanks for sharing, hon. For tonight, gentle and satisfying okay?" Parker rolled on to his side, patting the space next to him. "Lie down, please."

Angela stretched out beside him under the covers. He kissed her, cupping her breasts in his hands, working her nipples like a corkscrew between his thumb and forefinger. Soft moans emanated from her. She arched her shoulders, lifting her partway off the mattress as he tugged more. He let go of one nipple, licked his fingertip and rubbed it across her nipple tip. Angela groaned. "Oh, man, you know how to get me hot."

Parker slipped his hand beneath Angela's breast, lifting it up to meet his lips as he bent down. He suckled the nipple, worrying it with his teeth as he sucked. He let go and captured her other, giving it a similar treatment. He let go of it, moving far enough away so he could blow on each nipple. Angela tried to sit up. He laid a hand on her stomach. "Relax. I'm not done yet."

He didn't move. Angela looked at him, blinked and nodded. She lay back, stuffing her pillow under her head. He straddled her, slowly lowering until he brushed against her. His cock grazed over and against her mons as he worked backwards. He moved one leg, then his other over hers until he was lying on her without penetration happening. Rising up on his hands, Parker pushed up, gaining his balance so he knelt between Angela's thighs.

Angela's gaze raked over him slowly as if she memorized every aspect she could see. He'd done the same as she took off her sweatshirt. Some men got off on breast sizes. A few criticized their women on their breast size. He found them fascinating no matter their size and shape. A woman who accepted her body and figure turned him on more than those who worried about that did. Evidence of Angela's workouts showed on her well-toned arms. She helped lift patients off and on gurneys. Her calves and thighs were firm. She wasn't runway model size. She admitted she enjoyed serving a well-prepared meal. Keeping healthy topped her list of priorities.

Angela's gaze met his again. She smiled and blew him a kiss. No matter where their relationship went from here, he'd always cherish this moment. The moment intimacy and trust mixed with the strong friendship, camaraderie and bond they had. Strengthening the love he'd finally acknowledged even if it was still new.

Parker scooted back more until he easily sat back on his heels. Noting how Angela laid, he leaned forward, resting on one hand, reaching for her with his other. The soft downy wisps of her pubic hair brushed his fingers. Soon he'd bury his face in their softness as he licked and tasted her. Parting her labia, he noticed how wet she was. There was no mistaking the orgasmic traces coating her clitoris and flowing out of her. He stretched his legs out behind him, dropping onto his stomach, putting him inches from her deliciousness. He looked up again. Angela spread her legs wider. He slipped one arm under each leg right behind her upper thigh, laid his hands on her inner thighs and bent forward.

Angela closed her eyes as Parker's tongue slid across her clitoris. Around, up and down, over and back. Twinges and tingles exploded. Her clitoris and nipples swelled in tandem with each lick. Blips of color erupted behind her closed eyes. Blues, yellows and the pinks of spring she loved so much came and went. Parker picked up his pace, sucking her between his lips like he held an ice cube there. Faster the flares and bursts of color came. Building in frequency and intensity until—she cupped Parker's head with her hands and held him still. He kept licking and sucking. Yellows mixed with reds and crimsons like fireworks filling the night sky. She jerked, rubbing up against Parker's face, riding him in short jerks as one orgasmic wave after another crashed over and through her. She let go as she took a deep breath, opened her eyes and glanced down over her body toward Parker. He grinned at her, wiping his face on his arm.

She licked her lips, rubbed them together, and exhaled. "Wow," she managed to get out. Her clitoris still pulsed as more short waves of orgasm poured out of her.

"I agree. Wow." Parker sat up, grabbed part of his robe and wiped his face and arm off. "Need a breather?"

Angela snickered. "Not sure. First time I came like that. That's some connection we got."

Parker shoved his robe off the coffee table, picked up one of the foil condom packets off it. "I can soak inside of you while you recover."

He tore the packet open, laid it on the table and glanced at Angela. He wasn't moving forward without her buy-in. They'd gotten this far together. They were going the rest of the way together too. He sat up with his legs under him.

Angela propped herself up on her forearms and elbows, fanning herself. "I'm hungry."

"You really want food right now?" Parker touched his chin, making sure his mouth didn't hang open. If Angela wanted food, okay. Lovemaking used up a lot of calories.

"Not that kind of hungry. Hungry to have you inside me. To experience together what just happened with you inside me." Angela pointed at the table. "Don't want to waste the condom either."

Parker grinned at Angela's wink as she lay back. He took the condom out of the packet, worked it down and over him, knelt between Angela's legs and guided himself home with her help.

Heat grew the more he slid inside. Angela tensed around him, enveloping him in a hug that rippled up and down him, setting off earthquake vibrations deep in his groin. "Wonderful. So wonderful to be joined." He tipped his head back, slowly sinking all the way into Angela. Bracing himself on his hands, he pulled back some and set the rhythm for their mutual ride to pleasure. In and out, whispers of endearment, kisses, and moans of pleasure filled the air around them. He reached between them, finding Angela's clitoris, stroking it, he increased the rhythm. His testicles tightened to him. Angela wrapped her legs around him, holding on to his shoulders. Their gazes locked until he couldn't keep his eyes open. His slammed closed. Flashes of bright light, crescendos of pleasure poured out each other, playing a rhapsody that spiraled him higher until blackness engulfed him. Parker went rigid.

"It's okay." Angela touched him. "Lower yourself on to me. Let's enjoy the afterglow."

Angela cradled him against her. He felt the blankets cover him. He lay with his head on her chest, pillowed by her lovely breasts. If he could catch his breath, he would open his eyes and thank her.

Angela cuddled Parker to her, stroking his head. Talk about a double wow. Her second orgasm slammed into her, ricocheting back to Parker setting his off and finishing out in mutual pleasure. How was he doing? "Parker," she said.

Quiet. No response. Then it sounded. A soft snore. She smiled. His pleasure rocked him like hers had her. Another snore sounded. Angela kissed the top of Parker's head as she shook him. "Can you roll on your side? Makes it easier to breathe, you know."

Parker raised his head, looked at her and nodded. "Sorry. I need to use the bathroom. Be right back." He rolled off her and stood. He blew her a kiss before sauntering to the bathroom.

She straightened the sleeping bag and blankets out, flipped Parker's side open and stood. Chilled air rushed over her causing goose bumps to rise over her arms and legs. Angela quickly pulled her sweatshirt on and crawled back under the sleeping bag and blankets.

Parker yawned and stretched as he rejoined her. "Too tired to talk. Kiss me and I go zzzz."

Angela laughed. "Put on your sweatshirt it's on the coffee table. Then I'll kiss you after I tuck you in. ZZZZ sounds wonderful."

Parker flopped down on the air mattress, bouncing them tightly to each other. Parker kissed her cheek, managed to get his sweatshirt on in between yawning and trying to kiss her again. He laid down on his side, pulled the covers over him, patted her cheek and closed his eyes. Angela curled up on her side tight to Parker. As she closed her eyes and her breathing slowed, a thought flashed through her mind—*you really love each other.* "Yes," she murmured as sleep claimed her.

CHAPTER TWENTY-ONE

Parker blinked, yawned and sat up. He quickly held up his hand shading his eyes. The sun was up and. . .he was sweating. Crap, what had he caught? He hoped he hadn't given it to Angela. He scooted to the end of the mattress and stood. Hot air blew across his head, swirled down and over him, kicking up dust particles that glowed and danced in the breeze coming from. . .he looked up. Warm air met him as he tilted his head back more. A loud tick sounded followed by three bongs. Turning around, he watched the second hand on the wall clock move, ticking off seconds. "Damn, the electric is back on!"

He glanced down. Angela watched him, grinning from ear to ear. She sat up. "I think it came on an hour ago. I heard this click, then the ticking of the clock and drifted back off."

"Solar panels clicked on by themselves. Regular electric came back on since heater is on." Parker stood up. "Kidneys call. Be back in a min."

Angela heard the bathroom door click. She glanced at the clock. The hour read wrong. The tick-tick wasn't. Did she tell him she found the condom on the sink last night? Or the slight tear partway down the side? Her period wasn't due for another four to six weeks. She'd only missed taking the pill two nights since she hadn't picked up her refill at the hospital. The few times she missed taking them with Doug she hadn't gotten pregnant. She wasn't worrying now. False alarms did nothing but cause angst. They'd have to talk about it. Kids weren't a topic either of them had said much about during the last two days. She closed her eyes, counted to ten and let go a deep sigh. She'd tell Parker over breakfast.

The bathroom door clicked open. Parker came out whistling. He stopped at the edge of the mattress, leaned down and thoroughly French kissed her. "A repeat of last night would be nice. But. . ."

Her breath caught in her throat. She bunched the blanket in her hands, steadying herself for the worst. Parker rocked back and forth, grinning much like she had a few minutes ago.

"We've got hot water," he blurted out. "You want dibs on the shower?"

Angela tossed back the covers, stretched and stood. She put her hand over her stomach as she stood. Could she act nonchalant and hold her tongue a while longer? Popping Parker's happiness bubble didn't feel right. If she were pregnant, she wouldn't know for a few more weeks. Sometimes she had skipped a period before going on the pill. How did she bring up the topic? Just blurting it out felt odd and inconsiderate...inconsiderate of who? She took a deep breath and let it go. Right now a hot shower sounded absolutely wonderful. Maybe she'd figure things out after she shifted into normal again. Was her norm her normal reality any longer?

"Thanks for dibs on the shower. I'll take you up on that offer. Let me get a set of clean clothes out of my duffel." She trotted into the kitchen, trying to not hold or rub her stomach. Her parents figured out when she tried to hide things or cover something up as a kid. They said her poker face was great, however her other actions weren't. Frack, she didn't even know if her worry had any basis. She was raising a false alarm for sure. Adding fuel to a possible non-existent fire. Angela shook her hands and reached for her duffel bag.

"Is something wrong?" Parker asked. Damn, did he have to be right behind her? Watching her like a hawk? Guilt and angst bubbled up, ready to sabotage her with a hard punch, shattering her confidence when she'd first woke up with Parker cuddled to her, his arm around her waist.

Angela gripped the back of the chair holding her duffel. Counting every breath she took, she tried to click off the pros and cons of what she needed to say. If she didn't it could send a signal she didn't trust Parker. Damn it, she did. Would he still after she told him what they might be facing? She let go of the chair and faced Parker.

"Depends on how you look at things." Angela held a hand out to Parker. "Sit down for a moment, please."

Parker put her duffle on the floor and pulled out the chair next to him. He perched on the edge of the seat. "It's cool. Sitting on it might chill certain anatomy."

"This won't take long." Angela took Parker's hand between both of hers. "Do you remember what you did with the used condom last night?"

"Vaguely. Why?" Parker looked at her quizzically and looked away like he was trying to remember.

"Well," Angela began, cupping Parker's chin to ensure his gaze met hers. "I found it on the sink later. Picked it up to toss in the trash and . . . er...well..."

"What? You can say it. Tell me." Parker leaned toward her with his lips puckered.

Angela dropped her hand. "How do you feel about kids?"

"Are you saying you're pregnant just from last night? We used birth control." Parker stared at her. "How could this have happened?"

Angela caught her tongue between her teeth, stifling her smartass comeback. She squeezed Parker's hand and let go. "Facts of life we both know. What did happen is part of the condom tore along the side. Don't know if any semen leaked out. I ran out of birth control pills two days ago. I should be covered since my period isn't due for four to six weeks."

"Yeah, but skipping them can also mess up your cycle. How are you feeling about this?" Parker rose and engulfed her in a big hug.

"I know. Won't know for sure for at least two to three weeks if I am. I figured I'd have kids someday. Just hadn't found someone I cared to parent with." Angela moved out of the hug and started pacing.

"I accept full responsibility for my part in this. You can count on me to be present in our child's life. I'm not going to be an absentee parent." Parker touched her shoulder.

"Thanks. I'm more comfortable now that we've talked. I hate false alarms and unsaid expectations. Sorry." Angela set her duffel on the chair.

"Nothing to be sorry for. Condoms do break. No birth control is a hundred percent effective. Only one I ever heard of was holding an aspirin between your knees all night and screaming no." Parker grinned at her.

Angela snorted. "Can't say our child wasn't conceived out of mutual participation."

Parker laughed. "Oh, I admit being there. I know you were there."

Angela nodded. "Sure was. For now, we'll see what happens. I need to shower. Then I'll fix breakfast."

Parker took a hold of her hand as she pulled clothes out of her duffel. "Let's make breakfast together. I can cook too, you know."

"Okay. We'll work on that after you shower." Angela walked out of the room, not waiting for Parker's response. Her stomach was already topsy-turvy. She couldn't be morning-sick already.

Parker waited until he heard Angela's footsteps across the upstairs floor. He sank back into the chair he'd been sitting in. *A father*. That took a moment longer to sink in. Was he prepared? Could you prepare for fatherhood? Parenting took focus, time and dedication. He'd learned that first-hand from his mother and also his eldest sister. His nieces and nephew could be a handful from time to time. His child would probably be the same. He and Angela hadn't talked much about wanting children or their views on starting families at their age. Mid-thirties wasn't old nor was it virginal territory. He shrugged. Life handed you things, you flexed, learned and grew. Maybe this was the thing Mitch mentioned when he found out his wife was pregnant again. Planning takes you so far, then you wing it. Parker stood up, shivered and raced for the stairs. Heat was great; having a cold ass wasn't.

He stopped at the top of the stairs, just outside of his bedroom. Which one of the bedrooms would work for a nursery? He shook his head. Angela might want them to move into her place. Again, planning took two, his conscience chided him. It took two of them to get Angela pregnant. Parker inhaled, shook his hands and exhaled. He nodded. He wanted kids. If Angela was pregnant, he was in. Even if she wasn't, he was in. She was very special.

He heard the water cut off and the shower curtain pull back. He tiptoed up to the partially open door and listened. Angela was humming. A happy tune. He couldn't put words to the melody. She appeared at peace with things. Parker quickly back away, entered his bedroom and tossed clean clothes on the bed. Their next moves depended on the two of them. The two of them—that had a nice feeling to it. One he definitely liked.

Angela toweled off and hung the towel on the rack close to the shower. It'd been a while since she'd actively partnered with anyone. Co-workers, yes. Relationship partner, no. How did the last forty-eight hours change her and Parker's work relationship? Did it? He contracted with the center via the county. She worked for the center directly. Their paths crossed some nights. Some they didn't. What would Doc Stillwell do? She leaned on her hands on the counter, looked in the mirror, and smiled. Worrying decided nothing. Changed nothing and sure the hell didn't stop her and Parker from being sweeties. Nor parents if that came to pass. As she pulled on her clothes, she started humming a childhood tune. One that talked about being happy and knowing it. Her happiness ran from the top of her head to the soles of her feet, looping back up to the top of her head and on down to her arms and hands. The idea of a child intrigued her and inspired her to accept where she was—falling in love with Parker.

She grabbed her moccasins and opened the bathroom door. Parker lounged against his bedroom door. She knew that look. He was trying to act casual. Look like nothing bothered him. His work face. Mitch called it the extreme poker face. She walked over to Parker, squeezed his hand, and kissed his cheek. "Stop trying to read my mind. It's not nice. And I haven't had coffee yet. I probably don't make sense."

She continued, humming and headed down the stairs.

Parker shucked his sweatshirt, threw it on the bed, and walked to the bathroom. Nothing like being ignored standing half-naked with a semi-hard on eyeing your gal. Ah, well. She'd said the magic word. . .coffee. He turned the shower on and pulled the curtain closed. Maybe after coffee and food, he'd wise up and ask what Angela thought instead of trying to figure things out based on a ten-minute conversation.

Angela put her dirty clothes in her duffel along with her toiletries. She located a pair of socks and her hikers. She glanced around the room as she sat on the couch putting them on. There was safety in the bubble they'd created in the last forty-eight hours. Survival and growth came about. Now new things, changes and perspectives loomed right outside the door. She pushed off the couch, wiped her sweaty palms on her jeans and entered the kitchen. Food and coffee came next.

In the fridge, she checked the ice chest contents. They were cold and partly frozen. The egg carton date showed they needed used up. Cheese and the few ham slices could be added to the eggs. High protein omelet. A container on the counter held the powdered remnants of the honey pancake mix she'd put together yesterday. Decent side dish. Maybe even some toast if Parker had more bread. They'd eaten all the drop biscuits. She'd wait to begin cooking like Parker asked. She enjoyed making a meal together. She filled the automatic coffee maker, measured coffee into the basket, and filled the carfare with water. Soon smells of fresh coffee filled the kitchen. Angela sat down at the table, nibbling a cookie. She definitely had to get Mrs. Pescalli's recipe.

Parker hastily soaped, shampooed and rinsed even though the hot water called for him to linger. He tossed his towel over the shower curtain rod. "Are leisurely showers a thing of my past?" he asked, pulling on his t-shirt and briefs. "Sleep and eat. Run by the market and try to fix a meal before I drop into the bed. Damn, I do need a relationship. I gotta slow down and enjoy life."

"Nice to know I count for something," Angela quipped, opening the bathroom door, and setting a cup of black coffee on the counter. "Coffee's hot. Omelet and honey pancakes? You're out of bread."

"Sounds good. Yeah, I usually bake a couple of loafs on my day off. Haven't been any this week. Also no chance to get to the farmer's market either." Parker saluted Angela with the coffee cup and sipped. "Oh, man, that is nectar from heaven."

Angela chuckled. "Echoes my sentiments. I'll get the omelet started. You can do the pancakes, okay?"

"Sure. Be down in five minutes." Parker sipped more of his coffee and set the mug down. As he pulled on his shirt and jeans, one thought took hold. The bond they'd began continued. Looked like things were working out.

He reached the bottom of the stairs, drinking the last of the coffee in his cup. He looked around the living room. Vestiges of their last two days together remained. Angela had folded the afghan and blanket. The air mattress wasn't quite flat. And the sleeping bag. . .now two separate ones again lay on the couch. Parker smiled and nodded as he reached the kitchen. A solid bond had formed.

Another few minutes passed before they sat down at the table, ready to eat. Parker waited until they were halfway through the meal before he broached the idea he had percolating. "How soon can you be ready to leave?"

Angela sputtered, set her utensils down and pushed back from the table. "Right now. I thought we were getting along good."

Parker held up both hands. "Man, I messed that up. Please sit back down."

Angela waited several moments. What the hell was going on? Parker better clear things up or one hell of a fight was brewing. "I'll sit back down after you explain what the frack is going on."

"Seriously, my bad. I got in the zone and didn't verbalize everything. Sorry." He got up and walked over to her, offering his hands palms up. "Please sit back down. I'll explain everything."

She took a breath, raced through a five count, exhaled and sat down. "You explain. I'll finish eating."

"Okay. We're going to Charla and Elise's party, right?" Parker sat down. He picked up his coffee cup, sipped and continued explaining. "Why not go now? The party is next weekend. Center is closed. I'm sure Doc will approve the time off."

Angela laid her knife and fork on her empty plate. She toyed with her coffee cup, spinning it around in circles a few times before she looked up at Parker. "First, apology accepted. We're still learning each other's quirks. Second, I can't drop and go just like that."

"What do you mean?" Parker put their dishes in the sink.

"I need to check on the house and the SUV. Also, I need more clothes than a spare uniform and my gym clothes." Angela started washing dishes.

"True things. What if we run by the center and your place on our way out of town? If we can get your vehicle out, I'll follow you to your place. You can check on the house and pack what you need."

"Plausible *if* it's thawed enough and my drive is plowed. Otherwise it doesn't work." Angela handed Parker their plates to dry.

"Or I could take you shopping on our way to Charleston. There's quite a few malls on the way." Parker put away the dried dishes and utensils.

Angela drummed her fingers on the counter as the sink drained. She had plenty of clothes. Work clothes more than anything else. The two or three dressier outfits she owned next to her several pairs of jeans and t-shirts hadn't been out of the closet since the holiday party. "I'm game, but. . ."

She waited until Parker faced her before adding. "I'm paying for my stuff. I'm not broke."

Parker handed her the dishtowel. "Fine by me. I need a new suit too."

Angela smirked, shaking her head. "We're going to a party, not a funeral."

Parker stuck his hands in his jeans pocket as he exited the kitchen, "My sister added a PS in the invitation. Jeans aren't allowed. I gotta wear dress pants, a shirt and tie at least."

Angela rolled her eyes and followed Parker out of the kitchen. Sounded like they were going to be out of their element. At least they would be doing it together.

CHAPTER TWENTY-TWO

Angela looked at her watch. They'd found the center's parking lot iced over. It had taken careful driving and maneuvering to get her SUV and Parker's truck back out on the main road. After checking in with Doc Stillwell and getting the okay for four to five days leave, they'd driven to her house. The upper portion of her drive had started to thaw and expose pavement. Between the first part of the slope and the last section where the drive flattened out close to the house, snow and ice remained. The eastern stand of trees blocked enough of the morning and afternoon sun that only small patches of snow on the western side of the drive had melted any. For now, her SUV sat in Parker's garage at his townhouse. Six hours ago, they crossed the Tennessee state line into North Carolina on their way to Charleston.

"You know I think good luck shined on us," she said turning slightly in her seat. "You easily found your shirt and tie. The pullover sweater you found on the markdown rack was a stroke of luck."

"For sure. If I hadn't been looking for my suitcase, I wouldn't have found those two pairs of pants. You lucked out too. A couple of tops, dress slacks and undergarments along with a sleep shirt for under a hundred dollars. Nice shopping." Parker pulled the visor down blocking the sun's direct beam into the truck. "Normally I'd drive straight through."

"With daylight savings time, we've got four more hours of daylight. How much farther to the state line?"

"Only two more hours. We've had a lot happen the last few days. How about a quiet night at a nice hotel, room service, and a solid eight hours sleep? Maybe an in-room movie too?" Parker changed lanes and glanced at the GPS sitting on the dashboard.

"Have you told your mom you're bringing a guest? You said you hadn't RSVP'd yet." Angela tilted her head and stared at Parker.

He shrugged. "I said I'd be there. I hadn't officially done the 'count me in with a date' thing either."

Angela cleared her throat. "Isn't that going to blow our plan?"

Parker glanced at her as he changed lanes. "Hon, our plan is to show up. Present as a couple and deflect questions as much as possible."

166

"You have a knack for cutting away the chaff." Angela patted Parker's arm.

"Helps when you can't be wordy." Parker glanced in the rearview mirror. "I made a reservation at a hotel forty-five minutes from my Mom's place."

"Why haven't you shown me pictures of your family?"

"Wasn't time before we left. I'll show you the ones on my phone when we get to the hotel. What questions do you have about them?" Parker slowed down, taking the next exit.

"How old is Elise? How did she and Charla meet?" Angela squirmed in her seat.

"Need a bathroom break?" Parker tapped the windshield and pointed at the sign they were coming up to. "Rest stop is a quarter-mile down the road."

"Numb butt. Sitting too much gets me antsy. One reason I like working at the center."

Parker grinned. "Same for me most shifts. Stay busy and keep active. Slow nights aren't bad. It's nice when folks aren't needing us."

"For sure. Talk to me about Elise and Charla."

"Elise is four years younger than me. Dad was ready to deploy when Mom found out she was pregnant with her. She never got to know him well. His suicide hit her hard. Freshman year of high school isn't easy by itself. Dealing with crap about your Dad killing himself compounds things." Parker slowed for a stop light.

"You were in college when that happened. Wow."

"No, I hadn't moved out yet or gone. Good thing, too. We had each other for support." Parker pulled into the intersection, looking both ways. "Hotel is to our left. Restaurant row is to our right. You hungry?"

"Not really. You mentioned room service." Angela cracked her window. "No snow since we got south of Charlotte."

"Winters are warm in Charleston compared to Tennessee and northern North Carolina. Room service it is. The steak house attached to the hotel has awesome half-chicken platters with huge baked potatoes and a chocolate cake that is famous around here."

"Goodness, the way we talk about food, you'd think all we did was eat and eat." Angela chuckled. "I guess we're part foodie too."

"Nothing wrong with that. I figure cooking is my hobby. Doesn't hurt that I eat most of what I make.

"Most?" Angela snickered. "Dare I ask about the stuff you don't eat?"

"Mitch and Matt take stuff from time to time. I brought stuff in to work a few times too." Parker turned left at the next intersection. "Back to Elise and Charla."

"Right. So how did they meet?"

"They both attended South Carolina University. Elise had a full-ride scholarship whereas Charla was ROTC. Both started out as early childhood education majors. Charla joined the Army after she decided engineering held more interest for her. Elise works at a nearby school."

"Here's our hotel. I'll explain more after we check in." Parker parked close to the entrance. "I'm glad we've got one suitcase. Last time I was here the elevator was out of order."

Angela slipped on her coat, leaving it unzipped. "I'm glad I got a lightweight cardigan to wear instead of the pullover I looked at. Does it stay this warm at night?"

"Temps bounce in between cold and cool until mid-May. Then spring hits the area full force. You'll want your coat in the evening." Parker held the door for her. She slung the strap of her fanny pack over her shoulder like a purse and entered the hotel lobby.

Angela hesitated partway across the lobby. A three-tiered fountain took up the middle of the lobby. In the ceiling over it was a skylight. Sunlight streamed down onto the gray and moss colored stones flowing onto the water, creating a rainbow cascade out across the lobby floor. The soft sounds of running water gave an ethereal feeling to the setting like they'd passed through a portal to another phase in their burgeoning relationship. Parker came up beside her and stopped as well. He slipped his hand into hers. Neither of them spoke for moments. The quiet and warmth seemed to soak into her. Calming her fears, lulling her pounding heart into a slower beat and giving her confidence she'd made the right choice coming with Parker. Her comfort doing things on the fly ranked somewhere among 'oh hell no' and 'maybe I'll try it sometime' thanks to Doug and his compulsive and impulsive antics. With Parker, it was different. Definitely different. They'd discussed options, weighed pros and cons together. They'd made the final decision to be here together. Tomorrow would be their first outing as a couple.

"Good evening, Parker. Good to see you again," the desk clerk said as she and Parker approached.

"Hi, Carolyn. Elevator working this time?" Parker asked, as he reached the desk.

Carolyn laughed. "Yes. Elise stopped by this afternoon. She dropped off more party favors. Charla's plane is due in late tonight. I bet your Mom will be surprised when you walk in tomorrow."

Angela elbowed Parker. He glanced at her, winked and reached for the pen Carolyn laid on the counter. "She probably will. Carolyn, this is my girlfriend Angela Sewald. Angela, Carolyn Greers. Mom's next door neighbor and best friend."

"Pleasure to meet you, Carolyn." Angela held out her hand.

Carolyn briefly shook hands. "Nice to meet you too. I won't see your Mom, Parker, until tomorrow at the party. I ain't spilling the beans you're here with your girl."

"Thanks, Carolyn. I appreciate your help keeping the secret. Surprising everyone is part of our plan." Parker signed the credit card receipt and registration card.

He picked up their room keys and started toward the elevator. Angela caught his hand as he pushed the call button. He entwined his fingers with hers, raised their joined hands, and kissed both of them. Once inside the elevator, he tugged on her hand. She moved toward him. He slid an arm around her waist, pulled her closer and pressed his lips to hers. Tongues met, dueling fleetingly thanks to the bell chime announcing they'd arrived at their floor.

"Room 383," Parker read out loud, glancing at the envelope holding their room keys. "Carolyn whispered something about a soaker-hot tub in the room."

Angela snorted. "Love bird special, eh?"

"Carolyn is a romantic at heart. For all I know, we got the honeymoon suite." Parker stopped in front of the next door they came too. "Not that I'm rushing there or even said anything of the like."

"Maybe she hoped we'd slip Charla and Elise the keys and stay at your mom's?"

Parker slid the key card through the electronic lock. The lock clicked as a green light flashed. He opened the door, reached inside and flipped the light switch. He entered the room, saying, "Let me check things out, okay? You keep an eye out too."

"Right behind you." Angela stayed near the door, keeping Parker in her sight.

Parker turned around as he reached the center of the room. "Looks okay. I'm going to check under the bed." He lay on the bed on his stomach, reached down grabbed the edge of the duvet and yanked it up. Dust particles filled the air, dancing toward and away from him.

"AAHHCHOO." Parker sniffled. "Come on out, you sneaky dust bunnies!"

He sneezed again, dropped the duvet, and rolled over punching both fists in the air. "I fought the dust bunnies and I won."

"Oh? Your nose and eyes say you didn't." Angela set the suitcase on the luggage rack near the TV stand. "Maybe it's a draw."

"Nah. We each put up a good fight." Parker sniffled again. "Think a truce is in order."

Angela sat next to him. She laid her hand on his chest. "Your heart is full of courage. Even if it's only dust bunnies you slay so well."

Parker covered Angela's hand with his. "Thank you, my love. My heart is full of joy knowing you appreciate my valor and slaying skills so much," he said in an over dramatized voice.

Angela snickered, snorted and tried to cover her mouth as first one eek then another of laughter started. Parker crossed his eyes, stuck out his tongue and fell out laughing too. Several minutes passed before either of them could look at the other without laughing more.

Parker sat up, sitting sideways on the bed. "When do you want to eat?"

Angela looked at her watch. "Maybe in an hour. I'd like to take a walk. Been cooped up too much. No offense."

"None taken. I like the idea. There's a park about a mile from here if we follow the trail through the woods at the back of the parking lot. I love it's not getting dark for another three hours."

"Me too. Let's go." Angela slipped her jacket on and zipped it.

Parker pulled his on as he exited the room. Angela followed him. Neither of them spoke as they walked to the elevator, rode down to the lobby, and crossed the parking lot.

Parker took a hold of Angela's hand as they stepped on to the trail. "How do you feel about interracial couples?"

Angela stared at him for a moment and stopped. "That's an odd question. Though one that matters or you wouldn't have asked it. I do my best to judge people by the content of their heart and their deeds. Why do you ask?""

"Charla is African-American. I figured it was better to ask and know, than spring it on you when I introduce you at the party." Parker squeezed her hand and continued walking.

"As long as they're happy, that's all that matters. Love knows no boundaries."

"It took Elise and Charla a while to come out. Mom and I thought Elise was a late bloomer since she didn't date much. And most of the guys she hung out with were as geeky as she and Charla." Parker hesitated as they came to a vee in the path.

"Sounds like my older brother. He got married two years ago to his college roommate's twin sister. Dillon didn't date much during school and college. He said education came first. Terrie is a computer programmer and extrovert. The opposite of Dillon, who is content to sit in a lab all day by himself."

"Then there's us. The do it on our own ones." Parker chuckled. "Guess that's why we're a good match. We're strong enough to go it alone. Know how to partner well and are team players."

"A great foundation to build on." Angela sat on the bench near the vee in the path. "We've been walking for twenty minutes. Do you want to go on to the park or start back?"

Parker sat next to her, looped his arm around her shoulders and hugged her. "I'm fine with starting back. You okay?"

"Yes. Getting hungry. Puzzled by something too." She moved to the end of the bench and stood.

"Talk to me. What's up?" Parker rose and faced her.

"Are there other things I need to know about your family before I meet them tomorrow? Things that might shock me." Angela slipped her arm through Parker's, matching his pace.

"I've got a few screwball cousins as well as some nosy relatives who won't ask outright what's up with us, but they will hang on every word we say. I think every family has them. You having second thoughts about going to the party?"

"No. Hate being caught off-guard. Don't want trouble for you."

Parker kissed her cheek as they exited the woods. "Don't worry, sweetums. My relatives know better than to openly cause chaotic trouble. Mom cleared the list with Charla and Elise. Charla's immediate family will be there. Only about forty people at best. Neither Charla nor Elise like crowds and lippy gossips."

Angela heaved a sigh. "First impressions are nerve wracking. I'll be fine with you by my side."

"Same here, darlin'. Mom will be busy keeping the vultures at bay and being the hostess with the mostest. She loves presiding over parties. Comes from being a military commander's wife. I'll field her questions at another point." Parker held the hotel door open. "Room service or eat in the restaurant?"

"Room service. While you were checking in, I leafed through the movie guide on the counter. There's a romantic comedy I'd like to watch."

"Is that the one where the guy can't find where he hid the engagement ring?"

"Yeah. His family keeps putting it in plain sight and he stashes it somewhere else 'cuz he keeps getting cold feet with them around waiting to hear him propose."

"Mitch saw it. Says it's a hoot. Okay, romantic comedy and two chicken dinners. Sounds like a fun-filled night." Parker handed her one of the room keys. "Go on up. I'll get the dinners and be up in a few. I need to call my mom and let her know I'm here."

Angela kissed Parker's cheek. "Good luck with the call."

Parker waited until the elevator doors closed before he walked to the counter where Carolyn stood. He leaned on it as Carolyn moved closer. "How many times did you call Mom?"

"Parker Jones, do you honestly think I'd do that?" Carolyn scowled at him.

"Yes I do, *Aunt* Carolyn. What did you tell her?"

"That you arrived safely and checked in. Nothing about Angela. One call, that's all. Elise called me. Told her the same thing I told your mom." Carolyn crossed her arms tightly to her.

Parker let go a deep sigh. "All right. Let me handle it from here, okay?"

Carolyn nodded. He took a deep breath, let it go and walked into the restaurant. He loved his family, but some days their caring got to be overwhelming and meddlesome.

Angela zipped the suitcase shut. Their party clothes hung in the closet. Toiletries lined the bathroom counter. She'd even turned the bed down. They'd packed condoms and her refilled birth control pill prescription. A lot of good the latter was going to do. The pharmacist said she might be covered but she might not. She couldn't resume taking birth control until she had her period. That could be a few days from now or weeks depending on how much residual was still in her system. Only time would tell. Parker had reassured her he was in for the long haul. He was a gem for sure. Would he want to make love tonight?

Parker ended the call with his mom as the waitress set the bag with the dinners in it on the table. He could see right through his mother's feigned aloofness. At least, she hadn't tried guilting him. Guilt trips quit working on him his freshman year of high school. There'd be questions tomorrow. Some they couldn't avoid. Some they'd answer. Others. . .well, walking away and ignoring the super nosy would take some finesse. Finesse he and Angela possessed plenty of.

As he walked across the lobby to the elevator, he caught a glimpse of the ballroom where Charla and Elise's party would be tomorrow night as a hotel worker exited. Burgundy and teal decorations stood out amongst the streamers and banner he saw. Another image flashed across his mind and vanished. His and Angela's names on a similar banner. How could he be so sure she was *the one* this soon?

Parker set the bag holding their dinner debris and empty water bottles out in the hall. As he closed the door, he noticed how quiet it was. Angela was showering. They'd laughed so hard during the movie their sides ached. The hero's family reminded him of his own. Angela had pointed out things that reminded her of hers. The final scene had them applauding. The proposal happened because the hero's grandmother slipped him a ring and then locked the couple in a closet, refusing to let them out until he'd done the deed. Angela mentioned, in between hoots of laughter, she could see her grandma Fiona doing something similar.

The bathroom door opened. Angela came out wearing a mauve nightshirt and yawning. He patted the bed as he got in. "Come on. We're both ready for a decent night's sleep."

Angela nodded and got in. She blinked twice, yawned and blinked again. She put her glasses on the nightstand and turned out the light. Darkness embraced them. Parker spooned to her, his arm around her waist. His breathing matched hers, slowing as sleep claimed them.

CHAPTER TWENTY-THREE

Parker tugged at his tie. Why he tied it so tight every time he wore one he didn't get. "I don't need this choking me for the next five hours."

"Here, let me do it." Angela undid his tie. "I learned how to do one loosely for one of my waitressing stints. Manager taught every waitperson how to make a slip knot that allowed for comfort and also kept the top button of shirt undone without showing it."

"And here I thought maybe your dad had taught you so you could help out with your younger brothers." He undid the shirt's top button. "This is another reason I chose a profession that wears simple uniforms to work."

Angela slipped his tie off, put it around her own neck, and faced the bathroom mirror. "My dad wears clip-on ties. My youngest brother learned to tie a tie from our grandfather. Dillon refused to wear a tie and still does."

"You make wrapping that thing around itself look simple. *Not!*" Parker slipped the loosely tied tie over his head and down over the shirt's collar. He fumbled the collar.

"It took me a bit until I could remember if it was over-under-over or the other way. I left that job and kept the tie-tying ability." She reached up and straightened his collar. "Now go sit down so I can finish dressing."

Parker kissed Angela's cheek and exited the bathroom. They'd dressed and undressed in shared space like they'd done this for some time. He shook his head as he sat in the desk chair. Part of him worried that this bubble would burst and he'd misread everything. Messed up again. He drummed his fingers on the desk, counting slowly to ten forwards and backwards. One step at a time, live in the here and now, and stop overthinking this, he could hear his granddad saying. One last count and Parker rose. "You about ready?"

Angela stepped out of the bathroom. "Yes. How do I look?"

Parker motioned for her to turn around. She'd braided her hair and coiled it into a loose bun at the back of her head. She liked the look the red short-sleeved shirt, black pants and matching open-front cardigan made. This outfit worked nicely. The pants covered the tops of her hikers enough they looked like laced up oxfords. She nodded as she faced Parker again.

"Nice. Very nice. Shall we go join the party?" Parker offered her his arm. "Short cocktail hour, sit-down dinner, and some dancing. Not a bad way to spend the next few hours."

"Part of me believes it'll all turn out okay. Then the experienced part of me keeps asking are you so sure." Angela took Parker's arm.

"My family doesn't bite. If they nibble, don't worry. They've had their shots. Besides, I already nibbled you lots." Parker brushed his lips across hers as they waited for the elevator.

Angela hoped the smile on her face reached her eyes and convinced herself and others she was happy to be here with Parker. Meeting his family previously might have been a big step they discussed and planned better. Here she was jumping in and hoping her past nasty experience with Doug and his family wasn't lurking and waiting to trip her up.

Parker glanced at Angela as the elevator doors closed. He'd seen that smile before. The one where she acted and sounded nice, but something else was going on inside. He knew because he witnessed the dork and his wife who jumped all over Angela on a busy night at the center. They felt their illness ranked over the single parent with two puking kids and her tossing her cookies herself. He'd bit his tongue and hovered in the background that night, ready to assist her if needed. She'd held her own, took care of the pains in the ass by letting them cool their heels in an examination room while Doc Stillwell took care of the mother and kids. Yes, Angela could handle pains and do it well. He'd keep his eye on things and step in if needed.

As the elevator reached the lobby, he squeezed Angela's hand and whispered, "We've got this covered."

Angela's gaze met his, her smile deepened as she nodded. "I'm sure we do."

Parker looked to his left and right as they exited the elevator. Carolyn stood outside the ballroom door, clipboard in hand, checking names off as people entered. His mother stood next to her, chatting with people. To her left were Charla's parents and two of her siblings. He hesitated halfway across the lobby. "My mom is in the green dress next to Carolyn. The people to mom's left are Charla's parents and two of her siblings."

"Names, please." Angela gripped his hand harder. "It makes introductions easier you know."

Parker snorted. "It sure does. Charla's parents are Harold and Tisa Lewis. That's her brother Mike and sister Sheila. My mom, well. . ."

"Parker I can't call her Mom." Angela tittered.

"Not yet. Most of my friends do at some point. Any who, she's Beth Andrews. My stepdad is probably around here somewhere." Parker moved forward. "Don't be surprised if she insists you call her Beth."

"Got it. Let's get the introductions started." Angela picked up her pace. "Then we can get the partying started."

Parker lagged behind her. She glanced back waiting until he was beside her. "Is there a problem?"

"Nah. Just wondering how much Mom is going to chew my ass out later for not telling her about you or officially RSVP'ing." Parker shrugged. "It's one of those 'damn I'm a kid again' moments."

"Had 'em too. I think all of us have. Even your mom," Angela said.

"Right. Let's go in." Parker raised their joined hands. "Together we'll dazzle 'em. Individually we'll dazzle 'em too."

"We sure will." Angela closed the distance between her and the people standing at the entrance. Seeing Parker squirm a bit lightened her angst and anxiety. Parents wanted the best for their children. Even after they grew up. She'd seen it with her parents and siblings. Even with the grandkids.

Carolyn nudged Beth. "Parker approaches. That's his girlfriend Angela. The one I told you about."

Beth nudged Carolyn back. "You said he wasn't alone. Not much more. I appreciate you letting him break the news."

Carolyn snickered. "Well, at least make the introduction."

"Parker, glad you made it," Beth said, stepping away from Carolyn and Charla's family.

"Me too, Mom." Parker hugged her. "Wouldn't miss Elise and Charla's party and wedding."

"Would be nice to know sooner than right now." Beth slipped her arm around Parker's waist.

"Unless snow stopped us." Angela held out her hand. "I'm Angela Sewald. Pleasure to meet you."

Beth looked at Parker, nodded and took Angela's hand. "Nice to meet you too. I'm Beth Andrews. In case this one," she nudged Parker, 'forgot to tell you."

"He did until we walked up. Nothing that we haven't corrected." Angela let go of her hand.

"Parker, I like this one. Strong, independent and apparently knows you well. Good choice." Beth turned to Charla's family, motioning them to her.

"Angela, this is Harold and Tisa. Charla's parents. Her brother Mike and sister Sheila."

"Pleasure to meet you both." Angela shook hands with Charla's family.

Parker bumped fists with Mike. "Dude, good to see you. How goes med school?"

"Residency is kicking my butt. Rounds and lots of actual putting things in real time." Mike grinned. "You?"

"Loving life. Working lots and saving lives from time to time."

"Nice." Mike patted Parker's shoulder. "My fiancée is inside. I'll introduce you later." Mike entered the ballroom.

Sheila faced them. "I'm Sheila. Pleasure to meet you, Angela. Parker, good to see you."

Parker laid his hand on Sheila's arm. "Sheila, it's great to see you. How goes the internship?"

"It's going good. Moving to Denver from Atlanta is taking some getting used to. Cooler temperatures and *snow*." Sheila smiled and nodded as Angela spoke.

"Snow a four lettered word that can be naughty or nice." Angela offered Sheila her hand.

Sheila took her hand, shaking it as she replied. "Colorado State University is an awesome school. So far, I'm enjoying teaching undergrad physics courses."

"Wow," Angela said, glancing at Parker. "Sounds like she and my youngest niece need to meet. Carol loves science, especially hard-core science. Takes after her dad, my younger brother. He's a Nuclear Physicist."

"Happy to talk with her. Parker has my email address. Have her email me. Having contacts with women in STEM jobs and universities with STEM programs is awesome networking." Sheila turned around, adding. "See you inside."

"My youngest niece is quiet and introverted.. Doesn't say much until she gets to know you. I'm the one she talks to the most next to her mom, my sister," Angela quietly said to Parker.

"Sheila understands. Have your brother email Sheila too. I bet once Sheila breaks the ice with Carol, you'll see her bloom." Parker offered Angela his arm. "Shall we join the others?"

Parker entered the ballroom. Angela moved up beside him. "This place looks *awesome*."

Teal and burgundy streamers hung from the ceiling in loops with bows wrapped around bouquets of gold-colored daisies, white chrysanthemums, and baby's breath. Center of the room was a champagne fountain. Across the room, a string quartet played vintage love songs. Tables with place settings for six dotted sections of the room. Parker pointed toward the front where a microphone and a long table were. "Carolyn told me last night we were close to the front. We've got name cards. Hope you don't mind being Parker's guest."

"Not at all." Angela hugged Parker's arm. "We could cross it out and add girlfriend. But why be obvious?"

Parker laughed. "I think we've been that from the moment we walked in. Holding hands and hugging."

Parker looped his arm around Angela's shoulders. "My sister Stacey couldn't make it tonight. She and her kids are flying to Germany to see my brother-in-law who's in the military."

"Military runs deep in your family. I kinda stand out. I'm not military affiliated." Angela leaned into his embrace.

"Nothing to worry about. Stacey and Brett were high school sweethearts. College separated them for a few years until they accidently met up on UCLA's campus. Brett enlisted during the first Gulf War. He's ready to come home and stay stateside after this tour. He's a plane doc, keeps 'em running and healthy." Parker pointed to a table near them. "Mom said we were first table on the left back from the main one."

Angela stopped near the table and faced him. "I think I did well on first impressions."

Parker leaned closer and kissed Angela's cheek. "Honey, you're awesome. I suck at small talk. You do it at work so no problems here either. I'm glad you're with me. You?"

Angela let go a sigh. "As long as you're okay and we're solid, I'm good. I don't want issues for you with your family."

Parker snorted. "They're down-to-earth country folk. In a way, you are, too. We're very accepting of people. Believe me; Mom will have you calling her mom after a couple more visits. All my friends do. Even Elise's and Stacey's. Mom looks out for everyone. It's her nature. One reason she made a good command wife."

Angela pulled out a chair and sat down. Parker sat next to her. "I see you are city enough to let me seat myself."

He stuck out his tongue. "I got manners. City and country ones. I also know you would have waited if you wanted me to pull out the chair."

Angela ducked her head, looked up and nodded. "True. Sometimes my very formal manners come out. Too many Beverly Hills functions."

Parker laid his hand on hers. "I do own a tux. Even know how to tie a bow tie with a bit of practice. Those stuffy shirt parties are all about show and brag. You show and brag about your latest conquests. Or gossip about people who aren't there or in different cliques. Not my idea of fun."

"They're not. That's one main reason Mom attended a medium-sized rural college. Get out of the city and the false games." Angela pointed at the place card next to her. "Looks like your mom is sitting with us."

"Yes, she and my stepdad Randy. The other couple is Elise's godparents. I'll get quizzed and scolded about not visiting more. You'll get grilled on you."

Angela laughed. "I know me pretty damn well. We'll use work as an excuse. Different shifts, overtime, and also getting to know each other better."

"Sounds good. I've got fishing and camping stories to share that will take my stepdad's mind off things some. I'm here if you need me." Parker squeezed her hand.

"Me too." Angela squeezed back. "Did Carolyn do the centerpieces?"

"Mom, Carolyn, Elise and Charla did them. Kept Elise busy while Charla was deployed. Front-line duty wracks even those that aren't there."

"*Parker*!" a female voice called out from the other side of the room. Footsteps sounded. Parker stood and turned just as a woman launched herself at him. Parker caught the short blonde-haired woman who wrapped her arms around him like he was her life preserver.

"Elise, please." Parker managed to get out. "I thought you gave up making loud showy entrances."

"Not when my big brother sneaks into the room and I see him being affectionate with a woman." Elise laughed as she let go of Parker.

Angela started to stand up. She noticed the tall slender woman with russet, reddish-brown skin watching them. Her short-cropped red hair framed her face. She moved around the table, coming toward them.

"Elise make quiet entrances? I doubt it." The woman stopped next to Angela. "I'm Charla."

"I'm Angela. Pleasure to meet you." Angela smiled. "Nice to know this is normal. I won't be caught off-guard next time."

Charla grinned. "Took me a while to get used to it. Of course, family gatherings and greetings can be noisy."

"I've got five brothers and sisters. I understand. My mom used to say quiet meant something was wrong."

Parker sat down again. "Elise, this is Angela."

"Nice to meet you. You're Parker's new girlfriend, aren't you?" Elise grinned from ear to ear, sort of bouncing up and down with giddy energy.

"Yes. I look forward to getting to know both of you better." Angela sat down.

Elise leaned down, hugged her and let go. "Me too. Charla, Mom said they're ready for announcements and to serve dinner."

"We'll talk more I'm sure," Charla said laying her hand on Angela's shoulder. "Thank you for coming."

"You bet. Congratulations." Angela laid her hand on Charla's.

"Thank you and you're welcome." Charla withdrew her hand and followed Elise to where their name cards were on the long table.

A bell chimed. Several wait staff began filling water glasses and placing breadbaskets on tables. Other couples joined Elise and Charla at the main table. Parker nudged Angela. "On Elise's right is her maid of honor and her husband. To Charla's left is her best man and his husband."

"Thanks. It helps to know who is who." Angela bit into her buttered roll.

"I don't remember everyone's name. Before the night is done, I might remember who is who. Too many names and unfamiliar faces." Parker sighed. "Gentleman in the clerics is Reverend Bailey from the local community church."

"Church weddings can be nice. I hope he isn't long-winded." Angela sipped her water.

"Me too," Parker said.

Someone tapped on their glass and a hush fell over the room. Reverend Bailey said a few opening remarks about joyous occasions and how good it was to see so many friends and family members present to help Elise and Charla celebrate. He walked to the center of the room, opening the small book he pulled from his pocket. "Charla and Elise, if you're ready to exchange vows, please join me."

Charla came around one side of the long table, pausing at her parents' table. She briefly hugged them and made her way to where Reverend Bailey stood.

Elise made her way around the opposite side of the table, crossing the room until she was at her mother's table. She hugged her and Parker, then went to stand by Charla.

Reverend Bailey spoke about the joy of two people joining in matrimony. "Elise and Charla wrote their own vows. This is their time to exchange them."

Elise spoke first. "Charla, you've been my best friend, confidant and partner in so many things. I came out to you first. You encouraged me to accept who I am and to allow others to know the authentic me. Falling in love with you is one of the best things that's happened to me. Now you're going to be my wife, life partner and that tops my list of the best things in my life."

Charla turned toward Elise, speaking next. "Elise, you're my diamond in the rough. The person I grew up with, befriended, and told my deepest heart felt secrets too. I fell in love with you before you came out. I found my courage to come out supporting you through your time of self-discovery. As our friendship deepened, so did my love for you. Today I can freely say I love you. I'm joyously happy I get to spend the rest of our lives together with you as my wife and I yours."

Elise's Maid of Honor stood next to her. Charla's Best Man stood next to her. Each attendant held out a small opened box. Elise took the band out of hers, took Charla's hand and slipped the ring on her finger. Charla took a similar band out of hers, took Elise's and slipped the ring on her finger.

Reverend Bailey laid his hand on theirs and spoke. "What these two hearts have joined, let no put asunder. Charla and Elise have come together with those of you present to declare their love and join together in marriage." Reverend Bailey dropped his hand, stepped behind Charla and Elise as he said, "Congratulations Charla and Elise. May your marriage be long and prosperous!"

Reverend Bailey blessed the food as the servers set up the buffet. Food and wine occupied the next forty-five minutes. Angela glanced at Parker from time to time. He smiled, blew her a kiss and went back to talking with Charla's godfather. Parker's parents regaled her with stories about Parker's youth and teen years while asking about her and her family too. None of the questions were intrusive. Neither were they overt small talk. Parker's parents apparently wanted to get to know her and were protective of him at the same time. Angela put her hand on Parker's leg, enjoying the warmth and how relaxed his muscles were. Definitely a good sign. They'd made it through the first half of the party. The night was still young. What would the second half bring?

CHAPTER TWENTY-FOUR

More glass tapping sounded. Charla's father rose and walked to where the fountain was. He held up a champagne flute. "Twenty-nine years ago on a stormy spring night, my eldest daughter made her entrance into my world. My wife and I knew nothing about raising kids, a few things about what worked and didn't, and prayed the books and advice our families gave us made sense. Fast forward fifteen years, my baby was homecoming queen and making straight As. I thought I had this parenting thing down pretty good. We had a lot to learn. College years happened and we watched our daughter bloom even more. Charla, you're a remarkable woman. Strong, determined and know yourself very well. Now you're engaged and getting married soon. Elise is someone we've gotten to know and love. May your years together be filled with joy, much happiness and solid love filled with strength to get you and Elise through good times and bad ones when they arise." Harold filled his flute, raised it and spoke again. "To Charla and Elise."

Tisa joined Harold at the fountain. She filled her glass, raised it, and said, "To Charla and Elise, may joy and love always be yours."

Beth and Randy made their way to the fountain, filled their flutes and faced Charla and Elise. Beth spoke first. "Elise, you're not a baby anymore. Lord knows you weren't like your sister and brother. You walked early, loved emptying my kitchen cabinets, and playing tag with our dog Keely. Your inquisitive mind helped you excel in school. Here you are a teacher, engaged and ready to begin the next phase of your life. Much love to you and Charla." Beth raised her flute. "To Elise and Charla."

Randy cleared his throat. "Elise, I came on the scene after you went on to college. Your mom regaled me with stories until I felt I knew you almost as if I helped raise you. Being your step-dad has brought me a lot of joy and laughter. I know you're going to succeed at passing your love of learning on to your students. It shows in their smiles as you interact with them. As you and Charla start your life together, remember stay inquisitive, communicate and keep on doing it, and most of all be in conscious relationship with each other because it takes both of you to keep the joy and love growing and going." Randy raised his flute. "To Elise and Charla."

Other family members, guests and the brides' attendants made their way to the fountain, filled their flutes and in unison called out, "To Elise and Charla."

Elise and Charla picked up their flutes off the table, walked hand-in-hand to the fountain and filled their flutes. They faced the semi-circle of their parents, family and friends. Elise spoke first. "Thank you, everyone, for sharing this time with us. Charla, I'm so blessed to have you in my life and as my wife. I didn't think I'd find someone who understands me as well as you do. I love you."

Charla beamed. "I love you, Elise. We've been through a lot together. Good and bad. Our friendship grew into best friends and now wives. Having someone who gets you, understands your silence, and knows how to read you is awesome. Here's to our marriage filled with love, joy and happiness."

Several cheers broke out in between drinks of champagne. A drum roll sounded. "Folks, the dancing is going to begin in a bit. Cake and other desserts are available at the front of the room along with coffee, tea and more water. Please see the front desk at the end of the party for your room key and your overnight bag if you haven't already done so. We ask that no one drive under the influence," the DJ announced.

"What if we didn't bring an overnight bag?" someone called out.

"Double XL t-shirts and an assortment of undergarments along with toiletries are available at the gift shop. And as Ms. Carolyn pointed out earlier, the valet has your keys and if you can't pass the breathalyzer test, you aren't getting your keys," the DJ responded.

"Besides," Elise said in a loud voice, "Sheriff Coffey is my godfather and he deserves a night off, don't you all think?"

A gray-haired gentleman moved up near Elise, waved and stepped back. Laughter sounded.

"Let's get the dancing going. Here's an Eighties hit that has a beat to move your feet." The opening chords of a popular dance song resounded. Couples lined the dance area as the servers moved the champagne fountain out of the room.

Parker reached for Angela's glass. "Dance?"

"Love to." Angela handed him her glass. He set both of theirs on a nearby table. He took her hand and led her out to the dance floor. They joined the third line of people dancing to the line dance lyrics of the song.

More music followed. Slow delicious couple tight to each other dances, fast energetic ones and a few more hold each other and sway around the floor topped out the night. Elise and Charla made their way around the dance floor, hugging their guests and family good night. Both hugged Parker and Angela twice before hugging their parents last as they left.

Parker glanced at his watch. Midnight. Pressing his lips together he stifled a yawn. Angela leaned against him as he wrapped his arms around her. The evening was a success. More than once his mom and Randy said they wanted to see more of Angela. They even invited her to their anniversary party in a few months. Yes, the night had gone extremely well. He wondered how Angela felt. She tilted her head back, reached up and patted his cheek. "I'm tired. So sleepy. Glad we get to sleep in tomorrow."

Parker smiled. "Me, too. Let's go to bed."

Hand-in-hand they exited the ballroom after bidding his mom and Randy and Charla's parents good night. As they waited for the elevator, Parker couldn't stop smiling. A deep sense of contentment and happiness filled him. He couldn't think of another person he would have had as much fun attending with. Angela garnered huge points with him tonight.

Inside the elevator, he pulled her into his arms, hugging her to him. "I enjoyed tonight. Thanks for coming with me."

"You're welcome. Your family's nice. I like Charla. I talked with her parents for a few moments before we left. They asked us to get in touch with them next time we're in town. They want to have us over for dinner." Angela put her hands on his chest and pushed back. "No offense. Just need a little space. Noise and people overwhelm me after a while."

"None taken." Parker faced the front of the elevator, yawning. "Hope you don't mind a bit of cuddling as we settle into sleep."

"That's welcome. Just need a few to wash my face and brush teeth. Then I am in bed." Angela yawned as the elevator doors opened.

Parker followed her out and trotted down the hall ahead of her to their room. He quickly unlocked the door and waited for her. As they entered, he took a hold of her hand. "Dibs on bathroom long enough to piss and brush my teeth. "

"Go for it." Angela said passing Parker as he locked the door. "Want my nightshirt and sleep very soon."

Neither spoke as they prepared for bed. Lingering looks and touches happened as they passed in the bathroom. Angela washed her face, brushed her teeth and peed. She turned off the light as she exited the bathroom. Parker laid on his back under the covers, his hands behind his head, watching her as she undressed.

"Is this a preoccupation of yours?" Angela tossed her clothes on the chair close to her side of the bed. "Watching me is kind of obsessive."

Parker laughed. "Yeah, I'm watching. Not obsessed with you. Making sure you're okay. One gripe many of my buddies say is their wives have is not paying attention or going to sleep while she's getting ready for bed."

Angela pulled on her nightshirt. "If we're going to bed at the same time, it might be an issue if you went right to sleep without saying something. If sleep times differ due to work hours, not a biggie if we're aware of it. It means communicating. We're pretty good at that."

Parker rolled toward Angela as she got into bed. "I agree our communication is good. I hope it stays this good and even gets stronger and better."

Angela scooted closer to him. "I don't read minds. Got enough going on with my own. You best speak your piece even if it's something I may not like. Being lied to is a big no-no for me."

"Hon, open honest communication is the best. Sometimes we may not understand each other. Questions will arise. Hell, even Mom and Randy bicker from time to time. Lying isn't an honorable thing. I try not to do it. Situations may necessitate it. I hope those never happen with us." Parker moved closer to Angela, putting his arm around her waist.

Angela sighed. "I hope we never lie to each other. Confidential aspects of our work aside. My parents admit they fib to each other at times. Like about surprise parties or gifts. Unforgiveable lies...there's been a few times. They worked it out. Took a lot of yelling and talking. Us kids thought a divorce was coming."

"We may have those moments too. Let's not worry about that. We'll figure it out together. We trust each other enough to put those touchy issues out there." He kissed Angela and hugged her. Parker rolled on to his other side. He glanced over his shoulder as he added. "Sweetie, we've got a good foundation. I'm happy with what we've got. I strongly believe in us and that we're going to build our future together."

Angela cuddled to him. Her arm across his waist. She kissed his neck and whispered in between yawns. "I agree. Good night."

In that moment, he would have turned over and initiated lovemaking if his mind and hormones agreed. And if he could stop yawning. He could feel Angela's breathing deepen, indicating she slept. Parker blinked twice and ...sleep claimed him. Neither noticed the lamp still lit on the desk.

Ring! Ring!

Parker squinted against the bright light as he opened his eyes.

Ring! Ring!

He reached for his cell phone as the ring sounded again, louder than the prior ones. Shielding his eyes with his hand, he blinked, trying to focus. The bedside clock partially came into view. Ten A.M. Damn, they'd slept deep. He remembered turning over twice and a trip to the bathroom. He'd never looked at the clock. The ringing volume increased more. He sat partway up. It wasn't his phone. It was Angela's.

Parker sat all the way up. "Angela, your phone's ringing."

"Huh?" Angela sleepily asked.

"Your phone is ringing." Parker put his hand on Angela's shoulder and shook her slightly. "You might want to answer it before the ring goes full volume."

Angela sat up, combed her fingers through her hair, and tossed off the covers. "Yeah. It can be loud." She fumbled for her phone. On her second grab, she got a hold of it and read the caller ID. "It's my mom."

"Hey, Mom. Sorry it took me so long to answer." Angela put her hand over the mouth section of the phone, hoping she muffled her yawn. "No, you didn't wake me."

Parker patted her shoulder. Angela shrugged. "I'm sorry I didn't hear you."

Angela put the phone on speaker. "Mom, are you crying?"

Sobs rolled out the speaker. "Yes. Here, talk to your dad."

Angela's dad spoke next. "Baby, I hope you're sitting down."

"I am, Dad."

Her Dad's ragged sigh rippled out of the phone. "Grandma Fiona passed in her sleep last night."

Angela knuckled a tear off her cheek. "What happened?"

"Tyra and Rich went to bring her down for a visit for her birthday. When they went to get her up this morning, she was gone. A smile on her face. Grandpa Will's photo was next to her on the bed."

Angela swallowed hard, trying to quell the tears running down her cheeks. Parker slipped the phone out of her hand holding it out so she could speak and still hear her parents. "I-I don't know what to say. I talked to her a week ago."

"We all did. She was laughing and joking about reaching a hundred. Damn, we all thought she'd make it. Even her doctor."

"Okay, Dad. When's the funeral?"

"We're not sure. Autopsy and medical papers are needed before we can do that. How soon can you be here? Your mom needs all of you here right now. Me too."

Angela turned to Parker. He mouthed something. She couldn't make it out. Tears blurred her vision. "Let me check on flights and I'll call you back."

She took the phone from Parker and ended the call. He engulfed her in his arms and held her tight. Tears and sobs mixed with anguished sighs for several moments. She sniffled, leaned back and waited until Parker came into focus to speak. "Thanks. I hate to rush us back but I need to get more clothes and see when I can get a flight out."

"You're not going alone." Parker followed her into the bathroom.

"What?"

"You're not going alone. This isn't a time when you're strong for everyone but you. You and *I* are going. Mom and Elise will understand and even tell me go with you. We're in this together. Got it?" Parker hugged her again.

"After all, babe, your family is gonna meet me at some point. Might as well be now when I'm with you supporting you."

Angela sniffled again. "Yes, you're right. Let me shower. You call your mom."

Forty minutes later, they pulled out of the hotel parking lot with Elise and Beth waving goodbye. Neither had disagreed with Parker. Beth had been adamant that Parker was doing the right thing. Elise agreed as well. What a way to end her first meeting of Parker's family. Hell, what a way he was going to meet her family for the first time. Besides Doug, Parker was the only other boyfriend she'd brought home to meet her family. How would it all play out?

Two hours into their return drive, Parker exited the highway. "We left in a hurry. I need coffee and food. What about you?"

"Me too. I needed time to cry. Thanks for giving me that. Your support is awesome. You held my hand while I got the edge of my grief out of my system. It's still a shock. Grandma Fiona turned the remaining family acres over to Mom and Dad before Caleb, my older brother, was born. She lived close by until she moved to the assisted care facility in San Francisco five years ago. Now she's gone."

"You lost a cornerstone of your life. Not an easy thing to deal with. When my great-aunt Nancy passed, it hit Mom and us kids hard. Aunt Nancy was our landing spot in between base changes and coming back from overseas. We lived with her after Dad's death. I get part of what you're feeling." Parker pulled into a small diner's parking lot and got out. He opened Angela's door.

"Thanks. Knowing I hadn't seen her in a while aches too. I feel bad for taking her presence for granted like that." Angela reached for his hand.

"Would she have wanted you to come back often? Or did she encourage independence? Send her the occasional letter or card?" Parker took Angela's hand.

"She told me and my sisters more than once to get out and build our own life. She loved hearing about our travels and jobs even wanted to know about college. Letters mattered. Arthritis crippled her hands so she couldn't write much. She'd send a card now and then." Angela pointed to an empty booth close to the door.

Parker picked up the thread of their conversation after they placed their order and had a few swallows of coffee. "Sounds like a strong, independent woman. I'm glad she was part of your life. Family's important. I'm glad you got to meet mine."

"Me too. Now you get to meet mine." Angela sipped her coffee. She liked the idea of having Parker there giving her support. Explaining why she hadn't mentioned him during the call from her parents. . .well, how did you say, 'oh by the way my new boyfriend is coming with me'? Timing wasn't there. Maybe a barrage of questions wouldn't happen. There'd be a few.

"It'll be okay. We'll be fine. Different topic..." Parker hesitated as the server placed their plates on the table. He refilled their coffee and left. Finishing his statement, Parker said, "I texted Doc Stilwell while you were showering. We've got a week or two total time off. If you need more, you call him."

"Good to know. I'll check on flights once we're back home. I might be able to use frequent flyer miles to offset the ticket costs." Angela cut into her sausage patty.

"Let's eat and get back on the road." Parker saluted her with his coffee. Angela saluted back with her fork. Talking coherently with her mouth full of scrambled eggs wasn't happening.

Forty-five minutes later, they were back on the road. Two hours out from Peyton Corners, she'd dozed, silently cried more and thought about the next leg of their trip. Finding decent airfares meant flying out of Nashville. More driving than she really wanted to do. Could she find them non-stop flights to San Francisco? The drive from San Francisco to Gilroy would take two to three hours. She had a numb ass from the three hours they'd been driving already. Five to six hours in the air and two to three more to Gilroy? Could she do it?

Angela glanced at Parker. He appeared intently focused on his driving. She cleared her throat. "I have a question."

"What is it?" Parker asked, changing lanes.

"Non-stop or connections? Last time I flew to San Francisco, I got a good fare out of Knoxville. But, I had two connections. I prefer non-stop. Especially since we've got at least a two hour drive to Gilroy."

"If this were a vacation, I'd say let's do Chattanooga. Take a day to enjoy the city. It's not. I say Nashville even if we pay more. Non-stop and no red eye flights or middle of the night." Parker glanced at her and added, "Nine is the earliest I can handle getting on a plane. Need coffee and food before I even think about zipping through the sky nowhere near the speed of light or sound."

"I'd like to leave out tomorrow." Angela started to pull out her phone.

"We may not be able to get out until the day after depending on how bad the storm hit the airport. I'm game with staying at your place since we haven't checked on it yet." Parker exited the highway.

Angela zipped her fanny pack outer pocket closed. She usually didn't get antsy about travel, seeing her family and . . .ah, shit, this wasn't a usual trip home. Nor could she rush through it either. How soon would the California leg of their travels begin?

CHAPTER TWENTY-FIVE

Angela inclined her seat and stared out the plane's window. Finding them tickets had been the easy part. Finding a flight that wasn't a week later was the hard part. Once they checked both their places, staying at an airport hotel made sense so they'd be available to check in early for their flight. Patches of ice and several snowdrifts along the runways kept the number of outbound flights to a minimum for an extra day and a half.

She and Parker sat in the last two first class seats on their flight out of Nashville. Between the two of them, they had enough points to get upgrades from economy plus to first class. The first two and a half hours, they'd sacked out sleeping in spurts until they leaned against each other sleeping deeply for ninety minutes. Even now, three and half hours into the flight, all she wanted to do was sleep more. The lull of dreamless sleep pulled at part of her. It was like Parker said, grief touched all parts: mind, body and soul. The thing that bothered her most was her mother's wish for her help picking out what to lay her grandma out in. Maybe the best thing was the fanciest dress Fiona had. Send her off in style.

Angela let go a deep sigh and faced Parker. He was engrossed in an article in the onboard magazine. "I'm still at odds over Mom's request. Why me?"

"Were you the closest to your grandma?"

"Not any more than her other grandkids. We shared a love of learning and discussed why she chose getting married instead of striking out on her own in Los Angeles or San Francisco."

Parker closed the magazine and put it back into the seatback pocket in front of him. "Maybe your Mom thinks you can handle it better because you're in the medical profession. Or she just doesn't want to deal with it."

"Probably both. Not that any of us are handling this well. My sisters' messages were so tearful I almost started bawling just because they were."

Parker covered her hand with his. "Sweetie, best I can suggest is make a choice once you look through Fiona's closet. Or go with the first thing you pull out."

Angela elbowed Parker. "Grandma Fiona would haunt me if I sent her on her way in an outfit as badly clashing as your PJ's do."

Parker coughed. "I don't think you'd do that. Why not the outfit she brought with her for her birthday celebration? You said something about a wake celebrating her life."

Angela grinned, nodding. "Thank you! That's an awesome idea. Saves Mom and me from having to hem and haw over this. Grandma Fiona made the choice for us."

"Good. That takes pressure off you and your mom." Parker raised their joined hands, kissed the back of hers and lowered them. "Your mom and your grandma were very close?"

"Yes, Grandma Fiona is my Mom's mother. I'm not sure how my Dad's handling it. He referred to Fiona as his second mom." Angela let go of Parker's hand.

"Men handle grief differently. Some of us let it out in private. Some in spurts. Others muffle it and act emotionless. I can't speak for your dad. I know I'd be pretty tore up and need cuddling like you have. I'm glad I'm with you." Parker stretched.

"Me too. Two hours until we land. Part of Mom's last text perplexes me." Angela reached for her fanny pack.

Parker stopped her. "Rereading it isn't going to change it. What about it baffles you?"

"Writing part of the eulogy. Grandma was spiritual. She didn't attend any particular church. So how am I supposed to eulogize her?"

"Hon, I suspect your mom wants you to talk about Fiona and share her life with those present. Tell a few stories; share your warmest memories and what her legacy to you is. That's what I did at a friend's funeral. The minister said part of the soul's immortality is the memories and influences the departed created or shared during their life. Makes sense to me."

Angela fished a pen out of her fanny pack and took the pad Parker held out to her. "Is this why you stuck two steno pads in my backpack?"

"Part of it. Sometimes writing helps jar loose the roadblocks we put up trying to get at what's bothering us. I've got a private journal I use when I need to hash things out. Nothing says you have to share what you write. Mine is password protected on my computer. Lost parts of it with a few hard drive crashes. Point is ,you put action and words together. Your mind starts percolating and it works for you or it doesn't." Parker inclined his seat. "I suggest write what comes to mind even if it seems off. Maybe start with your feelings on eulogizing Fiona."

Angela tapped the pad with the pen for a few moments. She folded back the top and began writing. Words, emotions and grief poured out in the first few pages. She stopped twice, skimming back over what she'd written. She glanced at Parker. He slept as if he knew all along she needed to vent, gather her thoughts, and know what she felt wasn't wrong or right. It just was. She dealt with life and death on a daily basis at work. This was the first it had touched—no, swamped—her in a quite a while. She reread the lines she'd written about taking things for granted. Could she have done anything to prevent this? Change the outcome? Or was acceptance also part of grieving? Accepting that life came with ups and downs, hard times along with good ones, and through it all you lived. Kept going with help from family, friends and loved ones. She'd used the word *lucky* a few times. Maybe luck wasn't part of it. Perhaps it was embracing life and seeing as well as knowing down deep inside all aspects, good and bad, added to living. Living a full and authentic life. Her mouth dropped open. That was the one thing Fiona talked about and taught each of them. Authentic living even when life hurt.

Angela flipped to a new page and started writing again. She wrote about learning to skin fresh-caught fish and learning about the cycle of life, burning her first home-cooked meal and sharing how Fiona taught her to time cooking, balancing what needed done with enjoying the task at hand, right down to the moments they sat sipping homemade peppermint tea with the leaves they'd picked from the herb pots Fiona had on her kitchen windowsill. Fiona had helped her mourn Doug. Not that Doug needed mourning. Instead, Angela learned about forgiving herself and taking stock of what she'd learned and how to move on. She laid her pen on the seat tray next to the pad. She'd edit things later. She leaned her seat back, clasped Parker's hand and slept. Slept knowing Fiona and her cherished gifts would be with her always.

"Babe, we're preparing to land. You need to sit up." Parker's voice cut through Angela's sleep-hazed thoughts. She blinked, opened her eyes more and yawned.

"Where is the pad and pen?" She brought her seat forward. "Did you put my seat tray up?"

"Yes I did. You hit it twice with your leg while you slept. The journal is in the seat pocket. No, I didn't read anything. Just flipped the pad closed and put the pen in the wire spiral on top. Your choice to share or not." Parker brought his seat upright.

Angela glanced at him, frowning. "Thanks. I'd rather you'd woken me up and let me put the journal away."

"Understood. Trust is earned. Sorry I acted without asking. I figured it was better than letting it fall on the floor as I got up to go to the restroom." Parker shrugged. "I'm being truthful."

Angela flexed her hands, wiped them on her jeans. "I believe you are. I do trust you in many areas. Privacy is one place I've got strong ethics on, given a few past experiences."

Parker held out his hand. "I'm not going to guess who violated it. I think we've all had that happen. It's what makes us leery and skeptical as we move forward. Truce, okay? Noted to ask you about private things before taking action. How's that?"

Angela took his hand and leaned into him. She kissed his cheek. "Truce for sure. I shouldn't have gone through your cabinets without asking. I owe you an apology."

Parker snorted. "Hon, kitchen, living room, and downstairs bath are open areas. No foul done. No harm either. Snooping in my private area like my bedroom or going through my mail would get me riled."

Angela leaned back, flashed him a smile, and said, "Sounds like a discussion for when we start spending more time at each other's place."

"Yup, sure does. Now I've got a question on a different topic."

"What?"

"Are we renting a car or is someone picking us up?"

Angela sighed. "My bad. I forgot to tell you, my brother Caleb is picking us up. He lives in San Francisco. A rental car would sit for most of the time we're here. We can borrow a car if we need one. He'll give us a ride back to the airport when we leave."

"Okay. Don't worry about it. We pulled things together fast. I'm glad more of the snow melted while we were in South Carolina. Made getting down your driveway a hell of a lot easier." Parker winked at Angela.

"It sure did. I'm glad my neighbor cleared the bottom section. The sun doesn't always reach the side shaded by the house. Not slipping and sliding on your first time there let me breathe easier." Angela squeezed his hand as she added. "Now we're in sunny California. Don't think it doesn't get chilly here. You'll be glad you brought your coat. Wind off the bay this time of year can be pretty cold at times."

Parker nodded, letting go of Angela's hand. "I'll let you in on a little secret. I hate landings. Jostling my ass, cock and balls around is bad enough but when a bounce and added jostle happens. . .ouch!"

Angela snickered. "Poor baby. Maybe I need to massage and make better later?"

"I don't think your parents would appreciate us doing that under their roof. That's one of my no-no areas." Parker gripped his seat's armrest as the two-bell warning sounded in the cabin indicating their final descent into San Francisco airport.

Fifteen minutes later, he unfastened his seatbelt. He leaned over to Angela and whispered, "Balls and cock ok. Didn't know I could clench my ass cheeks that tight. Or suck my stomach in that far. Not a bad landing."

Angela snickered as she unfastened her seat belt. "Good. You got a rain check on my massaging and making them feel better for now."

"Noted. Now let's get our stuff and go claim our baggage." Parker slipped his backpack on and started toward the open door. He made sure Angela followed him.

As they entered the jet bridge, he took a hold of Angela's hand. She intertwined her fingers with his and squeezed. He was on her home turf now. He hoped meeting her family went as well as hers had with his. Part of the outcome was up to him.

Parker pointed at the sign not far from their arrival gate as they entered the airport. "Looks like we go to the right and follow the baggage claim signs."

Angela nodded as she hesitated close to the gate's seating area. "Let me turn my phone on. Caleb or Mom may have texted."

"Yeah. I need to text my Mom we landed. She asked to let her know we made it okay." He pulled his phone out of his jean's pocket.

Each of them took the next few minutes to check messages, voice mail and send a couple of text messages.

"We're in luck. Caleb texted my cousin Sara is working today. She is waiting for us two gates down with a cart. She'll get us to baggage without having to make the hike." Angela looked up grinning. "Sara is a tall redhead. She could have been a model. Instead, she chose to major in business and organizational leadership. She's probably checking up on her staff and the airport. She's the assistant manager of operations."

Parker let out a low whistle as they began moving into the flow of walkers making their way through the corridor. "Where my family is military and associate degrees, yours is business and agriculture. With a few side folks like us in medical, your siblings in science and procurement. Also Elise in education."

"We're an independent bunch. Fiona and Will made sure of that." Angela pointed at the redhead sitting in a cart in the empty gate area ahead of them. "There's Sara."

Parker swallowed hard. The woman waving at them was a definite looker. Short curly red hair, a minimum of make-up he'd guess though he was bad at that, and a smile that would have knocked a few of his old high school chums over. As Sara got out of the cart and walked toward them, he swallowed hard again. There was a time when looks set his hormones off and ignited hard-ons that were difficult to hide. He wasn't that youngster anymore. He appreciated the eye-candy Sara offered. He'd enjoy it. He was with Angela and she was his top choice. His only choice. The more they were together and the more they went through even in this short amount of time, his heart and gut said he'd made the right choice. What he felt was growing and where his thoughts and dreams went over the last four days indicated what he'd recently begun pondering made sense.

"Hi Sara," Angela said moving into her cousin's embrace. "Keeping an eye on things?"

Sara laughed. "Yes. And helping out. An employee's wife went into labor this morning. Short staffed. You help out."

Angela stepped back. "Sara this is Parker. Parker, my cousin Sara."

"Pleasure to meet you." Parker shook Sara's hand.

'Like wise. I'm glad you're with Angela. Mom said Aunt Linnea wasn't handling Grandma's death well."

"I suspect quite a few aren't," Angela offered as she got in the cart.

"Some aren't going to make the funeral or wake. Fiona's attorney called yesterday concerning her will. About twenty of us are due at his office in three hours."

Parker got in next to Angela. "Large family all around?"

Sara chuckled. "Four and five kids is the norm with this branch of the family. Grandpa Will was Fiona's second husband. His kids from his first marriage are all out of state. His first wife died in childbirth. Grandpa Foster, Fiona's first husband, died in World War II."

Sara put the cart in gear and moved in and out of the flow of walkers heading toward baggage claim. "Caleb is parked on the first floor of the parking structure close to where the cabs are. Let him know I'll meet you at the attorney's office."

"Will do." Angela watched as Sara zoomed in between groups of people and around others looking at the departure and arrival boards. Better Sara driving than her. The tight maneuvers and sharp turns Sara made left Angela wondering how she'd ever got her driver's license given how brutal California traffic could be. 'Practice' a voice whispered in her ear. Angela knew that voice. Grandma Fiona's always encouraging and reminding any of them that practice brought experience which enhanced ability to do things.

"Here ya go," Sara sung out slowing as they entered the multi-carouseled baggage claim area.

"Thanks, Sara." Angela got out of the cart. "We've got it from here."

Parker turned toward Sara. "Awesome driving. You would make a great ambulance driver."

Sara smiled. "Thanks. I'll ask you about that later. Not that I'm interested in another job. Want to know why you think I could."

Parker laughed. "Maneuvering in and out of traffic. Tight twists and turns. Maybe we can share hair raising stories later."

"Might just take you up on that. Bye for now." Sara completed a neat four-cornered turn around and sped off back the way they came.

"I like Sara. She's got a sense of humor. And drives real good." Parker started toward the carousel holding their luggage.

"She does. She taught most of us how to parallel park and how to drive a stick shift. Not that I caught on too well." Angela grabbed her bag off the carousel. She faced Parker. "Ready?"

"Yes. Let's go find Caleb. My turn to meet more of your family."

Parker kept up with her as she made her way toward the closest exit. They darted through traffic as they made their way toward the parking structure and the lines of cabs waiting for passengers and fares. A tall dark haired man hovered near the entrance to the parking structure. He looked left and right, then down at his phone. The next time he looked up, he started waving and rushing toward them.

"Caleb, you dyed your hair again," Angela scolded. "You could have told me."

"And miss the look on your face that some dude with purple and red hair wasn't swooping down on you. Never. Besides shock value wore off after the first six months. Also better paying jobs require a more sedate look." Caleb hugged her tight and let go.

Caleb turned to Parker. "You must be Parker. Sara texted saying a guy was with my sister and to be nice."

"Yes, I'm Parker. You're doing great on the nice." Parker shook Caleb's hand.

Angela chortled. "Caleb felt it was his duty to check out his kid sister's dates before he let them in the house. Dad kept telling him the job was his and to let me decide who I wanted to date."

"Ah the big brother role, I get it. Elise got the same thing from me." Parker got in the backseat of Caleb's car. "Elise is my youngest sister."

Caleb got in and started the car. He looked at Angela. "See he gets it. You still got issues over me checking guys out back then?"

"No, Caleb. Maybe you do. Or you didn't get to check Parker out like you wished you had with Doug. Sorry, I get to make my own mistakes. That one I learned a lot from it."

Parker put his hand on Caleb's shoulder. "How about I tell you a bit about me and how Angela and I met?"

"*Yeah, I like the sound of that.*" Caleb exited the garage and moved into traffic. Angela glanced at her brother, then at Parker. This might be one of the longest drives home she'd ever made.

CHAPTER TWENTY-SIX

Angela spent the next fifty minutes listening to Parker highlight how they met. Caleb hadn't quizzed her on it or interrupted Parker. The next twenty minutes Parker talked about being an EMT and a bit about his family. Angela unclenched her hands. Twenty non-stop questions was Caleb's arsenal in the past. Not letting the guy answer until he pissed them off and then. . .Caleb was older and mature. Parker knew how to hold his own with inquisitive people. It appeared she didn't have to worry about a fight breaking out.

"Okay, so you work with my sister. Known her for two years and started dating a while back. How come she hasn't mentioned you before now?" Caleb glanced at her.

Angela stiffened. Caleb had a knack for asking loaded questions when you least expected it. She opened her mouth, ready to come to Parker's aid.

"We weren't sure what company policy was on employee relationships. I basically work for the county and your sister works for the center I'm assigned to. Fine print things some of us don't read until we need to." Parker leaned forward laying his hand on her shoulder. "When you work graveyard shift, your dating hours are when everyone else is at work."

Angela laughed as Caleb glanced at her again. The puzzled look on his face said more than if he'd spoken. "Come on, Caleb. You and Izzy worked out your dates around her class schedule and work. Why would it be different for Parker and me?"

Caleb shrugged. "Trying to figure out what kind of dates you'd have? Except maybe breakfast and a sleepover. Is that what you did?"

Angela fisted her hand and pulled her arm back, ready to sock her brother.

Parker squeezed her shoulder. "Our business. Sometimes we'd go to a matinee movie. Cheap tickets, lots of good popcorn and then an early dinner. You learn to be creative. In our jobs, we rack up plenty of overtime. Another reason it took us a while to decide if we were right for each other."

"Caleb, enough questions and suggestive innuendos. How's Izzy?" Angela lowered her hand.

"Doing good. She's interning at San Francisco General. Mom keeps asking when we're to going make things legal. I keep telling her, when we're ready." Caleb shook his head as he took the exit ramp for Highway 101. "Parker, sorry I grilled you, dude. Gotta look out for your kid sister. Hope you understand."

"I do. They also grow up. Mine told me unless I wanted to blush permanently, stop asking questions that could lead to TMI moments. Know I care for your sister a lot. And let us work out our relationship as we see fit. Saves you time and worry. Medical interns need care and TLC bunches. We know that first-hand." Parker leaned back in his seat.

Angela yawned. "Caleb, I love you. I care for Parker a lot, too. If I need you to beat 'em up I'll call you. Right now you need to focus on Izzy and getting her through med school. You also need to be sure your grad school grades stay up to keep your scholarship going. Dad loves the idea you're going to be a lawyer."

"There's no guarantee I'm going to law school. I've got another year of school. Going part-time slows this down. Izzy's residency is next. If she gets a West Coast hospital, I'm set to transfer to other schools within the Cal State system."

Parker leaned forward again. "I think what's best for you and Izzy comes first. Maybe you can go to work where she does her residency."

"We've discussed that. Maybe we'll get married this summer and see what next year brings. I agree with you, Parker. Angela, who knows? We might end up out your way." Caleb slowed as he exited the freeway.

Parker settled back again, rubbing his eyes. "I'm going to cat-nap for a while."

Angela started to yawn again. She covered her mouth. "Caleb, you and Izzy do what works for you. I'm behind you both whatever you decide."

"Thanks, sis," Caleb said, slowing for a stop light. "We've got another ninety minutes until we reach the lawyer's office. You might as well nap too."

"Yeah, time change is hitting me hard. By the way, Sara said she'd meet us at the lawyer's office." Angela slumped down in her seat, closed her eyes and let the lull of the moving car pull her into a light doze.

Caleb glanced in the rear view mirror. Parker leaned slightly to the right. The shoulder strap of his seatbelt kept him upright. Angela's did the same.

Caleb grinned. He liked his sister's boyfriend. Parker stood up and spoke his piece. Angela appeared happy and content. All the things he wanted for her. What was it Grandma Fiona had told him recently? Oh yeah, life brings what you need. Your job is to recognize it and use it wisely. He wouldn't have found Isabella Gutierrez if she hadn't missed her bus two years ago and jumped in his cab for a ride to the university.

Ninety Minutes Later, Lawyer's Office, Downtown Gilroy

Parker looked around the conference room. Only three chairs at the table were empty. Two rows of possibly ten more filled chairs lined the back wall of the room. People were standing in the corners chatting. He'd counted six people sitting at the table. The two hugging Angela must be her parents. He'd hesitated when he entered the room wondering, where he should sit.

"Parker," Angela called, motioning him to her. He made his way around the table, stopping close to her.

"Mom. Dad. This is Parker, my boyfriend." Angela sat down next to her parents.

"Sir. Ma'am. Pleasure to meet you." Parker offered the slightly gray-haired man his hand first.

"Bascombe Sewald. Call me Bass. Sit here with us." Bass pointed at the empty chair next to Angela's mother. "Linnea, move over, please."

Linnea rose, turned and held her hand out to Parker. "Parker, I'm Linnea Sewald. Nice to meet you. Bass sometimes gets his priorities mixed up."

Linnea shook Parker's hand and sat in the empty chair.

Bass shook his head. "Sometimes I do. After thirty years of marriage, you'd think you might let that quirk slide. It's good you catch my slipups." Bass sat next to Linnea. She kissed his cheek. "You caught quite a few of mine, dear."

Angela moved over next to her father, patting her empty chair. "Please sit down, Parker."

Parker sat, glancing around the room again as he did. He spotted Sara in the rear of the room next to Caleb. He bent toward Angela, whispering, "Who are the others at the table?"

"Mom's brothers and sisters. To Mom's right is my Aunt Willow. The man next to her is my Uncle Ned. Next to him is my Uncle Ralph. Last two are my Aunt Sabrina and Aunt Zelda." Angela glanced at him and winked. "Their spouses are sitting in the row directly behind us. Behind them are the grandkids and a few great-grandkids who could make it."

"How am I going to remember all these names?" Parker muttered.

Angela snickered. "You're not. Some of them I don't remember and they're my relatives. My brother Dillon and his spouse Drake are standing next to our sister Nancy. Candace is sitting with her youngest close to the door."

Parker clasped her hand and squeezed it. She took a deeper breath. Her earlier antsiness and anxiety dissipated each time he touched her. Knowing he was here helped more than she could have imagined. Fiona had told her she'd know when the right one came along. Parker was definitely pointing in that direction.

A tall, slender, bearded man followed by a woman carrying a chair with a pad under her arm entered the room carrying a large beige envelope and a manila folder. He laid both on the table. Pulled out the remaining empty chair and sat down. He took a pen out of his suit coat pocket and tapped on the table with it. The woman placed the chair she carried next to him and sat down.

"Good afternoon, everyone. I'm Randall Baker, Fiona Stewart's attorney. I asked you all here to make her last wishes known and to read her will. Many of you already know portions of her will. She made it a regular habit to discuss who was getting what in hopes to prevent bickering and contesting her will. Please wait until I finish reading both documents before you ask questions. My secretary will take notes for follow-up as needed." Mr. Baker pointed to the woman seated next to him.

Mr. Baker opened the manila folder and took out several sheets of paper. "Fiona disliked funerals. All the bickering and fighting simmering or that broke out bothered her. She wanted to preserve the peace and tranquility this time needs. Please hear her words as I read from her final letter to you all."

My dear family,

I'm with all of you here today. I believe the soul lives on even after the body stops functioning. I taught many of you about the gifts of memories and shared times along with the things I imparted to each of you. I asked my doctor to sign my death certificate as soon as possible after my death so the mortuary could claim my body for cremation. Will and I discussed this right before his death. Each of us didn't want any bickering over where we were laid to rest. I want the remainder of his ashes and mine mixed and scattered to the four winds. I'm sure there'll be some arguments from his children. They got part of him to bury with their mother. The rest of him belongs to me and is mine to disburse as I see fit. Please know these are my last wishes. I didn't discuss them with you because I didn't want you encumbered by them or overwrought due to them. I love each of you very much. Mr. Baker will explain what comes next.

Always with you each,

Grandma Fiona

Mr. Baker laid the top sheet on the table and looked up. "This is Fiona's death certificate. She died of natural causes. Her cremation took place yesterday afternoon."

Several gasps sounded. Mr. Baker placed the death certificate on top of Fiona's letter. He waited a few moments and continued speaking. "A brief ceremony tomorrow at the mortuary will mix her and Will's ashes. We're then driving to her favorite beach, Spanish Bay Beach near Monterey along the seventeen-mile drive, to allow each of you a chance to toss a small vial of their ashes into the ocean or open the vial and allow the wind to carry them off on their next journey. Are there any questions?"

A few asked about keeping the vials. Mr. Baker repeated Fiona's wishes. Many nodded and remained quiet. The reading of the will took longer spelling out who received what of the estate.

After a brief period of silence, Mr. Baker stood. "Fiona's wake takes place at Seaview Bistro in Carmel right after scattering her ashes. She deposited money with me to pay for the event. The last thing she wanted was for any of you to bear the burden of paying for her last expenses. Thank you all for coming. Please give my secretary your questions. I'll answer them as soon as the estate is settled."

Mr. Baker left the room. Many mingled and talked quietly amongst themselves. A few approached the secretary, voicing their concerns and questions.

Angela faced her parents. "Do we need to get a hotel?"

Linnea shrugged. "Your choice. Big house is rather empty with everyone moved out."

'I'd like a chance to get to know Parker some," Bass offered.

Parker laid his hand on Angela's shoulder. "I'm fine with staying with your parents." He faced Bass and added. "I ask you put us in the guest room. Not her bedroom."

Bass laughed. "That's my office now. We turned the big house into a Bed and Breakfast. We built a smaller place for us adjacent to it. You can stay in the guest room."

"Is this the big surprise you texted about while I was on the cruise with Tricia?" Angela shook her finger at her father. "You had me trying to call you ship to shore. Do you know how much that costs?"

Bass stuck his hand in his pants pocket. "You want cash or credit card reimbursement?"

Linnea cuffed her husband on the shoulder. "I don't think she is saying that. Are you, Angela?"

Angela sighed. "No, I'm not. I texted three times and tried to call several. Only got your voice mail. Dad, sometimes you're *bad*."

Parker tried hard to suppress his grin at the way Angela emphasized bad and drew it out. Her mom shook her head, patted Bass's cheek and muttered. "Like father, like daughter. I think I'll go talk to Caleb for a moment."

Bass managed to kiss the palm of his wife's hand before she pulled away. He turned to Angela, his arms wide open. "Ah, come on and give me a hug. One of those *I forgive you* ones, please."

Angela rolled her eyes, glanced at her dad, then Parker who shrugged. "Can't say I didn't warn you. You're in. Best put on your oxygen mask 'cuz the puns and innuendos are starting."

Angela walked into her dad's embrace, tightly hugging him. Bass pulled back, kissed her forehead and let go. "It's good to have you home, baby. We've got a long day tomorrow. I'm sure we all can use some extra sleep after a good dinner."

"Parker and I are running on East Coast time. We'll probably turn in early. Dinner sounds good. Are you expecting Mom to cook?"

Linnea rejoined them with Caleb following her. "Did I hear someone say cook and my name in the same sentence?"

"Linnea," Bass began. "You know it's been a while since Angela has had a home-cooked meal."

Parker coughed, lest he blurted out about them cooking and roughing it at his place. Linnea and Bass looked at him, silently waiting for him to say something. Angela waved her hand up and down between them, saying, "Dad, I can cook. I usually do. If you mean Mom's cooking or yours, it's been a long time. I think Mom has another idea in mind."

Parker cleared his throat and said, "How about I treat, and we go to the steak house I saw as we entered town?"

"That's the high end place," Bass remarked. "There's a smaller place across town that we like. Nice cuts of steak, all-you-can eat salad bar, and seafood. You can make a meal on their baked sweet potatoes. Dripping in cinnamon, brown sugar and fresh whipped butter."

"Sugar shock for days," Caleb said. "Langers is awesome for their grass-fed beef and organic ingredients. I'm in if we're going there. How about you, Sara?"

"Oh, yeah. Caleb, are you driving back to San Francisco tonight?" Sara asked.

"Crashing at Kelso and Amy's. They said to tell you you're welcome too," Caleb responded.

"I'm riding with you then." Sara stood next to Caleb.

"Sounds like Mama Lucia's in Peyton Corners. Home-cooked meals. Local produce and meat. I'm in. Angela, you wanna ride with your parents?" Parker faced Angela.

"Sure." Angela waited until her parents walked away before turning to Parker. "Are you ready for my Dad's interrogation? He's a sly one. Mom will tag-team with him if she thinks it's necessary."

Parker grimaced. "I'm going to tell them the same thing I told Caleb. If he gets too personal, I'm going to stand my ground that's between us. I doubt he's going to ask about our sex lives."

Angela snorted. "Mom will shut him up before that happens. I think you've got a good idea. I'll back you up. They don't want another Doug episode happening. AKA overly dominant and obsessive."

Parker took her hand as they exited the conference room. "I like your parents keeping an eye on things. Mom and Randy do that with my sisters and me. I want the best for us too. Even our kids, if we get to that point."

Angela nodded. Parker had a point. Knowing her parents kept an eye on her and her siblings added an extra layer of comfort that she hadn't been aware of before. Part of her thoughts focused on being grown and on her own. This new insight lowered much of her anxiety and anguish about this visit and Fiona's wake tomorrow. Everyone was coming together, supporting each other and caring about the outcomes. Her future took on a bright hue. One that glowed strong amongst the others she felt called, too. The outfit she'd packed for the wake made sense. Tomorrow possibly presented a new beginning.

Parker burst out laughing as they reached the lobby doors, pointing at the ocean-blue-colored SUV pulling up in front. "Please tell me your dad is a car aficionado. That is one pristine 2007 SUV."

"That and he loves to work on them too. He had to keep the farm equipment running. Cheaper to work on it yourself or at least know what needs done so you don't get conned." Angela pushed the lobby door open.

Parker exited first. "Same thing one of my neighbors taught me at sixteen with my first car. He owned the local body shop. I swept up, took out the trash and worked counter on weekends. He helped me rebuild the car's engine and replace a rusted muffler."

"That explains why you drive your pickup. Solidly built and you can keep it running. I buy used and save the difference between what it and a new car would cost." Angela reached for the back passenger door of her dad's SUV. Her mother got out of the front.

"Parker," Linnea said, taking a hold of Angela's arm. "You sit in the front with Bass. You boys have a good talk while Angela and I visit in the back."

Angela looked at Parker, shrugged and got in the back seat. The one move she hadn't thought her parents would do, divide and quiz them. Good thing she and Parker had sorta discussed their answers. How inquisitive would her parents be?

CHAPTER TWENTY-SEVEN

"Parker, you're an EMT," Bass, said, pulling out into traffic. "Tough job. Not great pay, I hear from ours here in California."

"Yes, sir, I'm an EMT. Pay varies from locale to locale. Peyton Corners and Tennessee pay good wages. The county contracts us to urgent care centers, hospitals, hospice care and nursing homes. We get paid hourly or by the nature of the run we make. I'm earning money if I am working or sitting still due to a quiet night on the job."

"Wow, that is nice. I like." Bass turned at the next side street. "You like my daughter?"

"Sir, that answer is obvious. I think you want to know do I care for her. Yes, I do. By the way, I own my own home. I've worked two years with Angela and we started dating more because there's no conflict of interest happening, nor are workplace relationships frowned on. I enjoy camping and fishing. That is my short bio. Do you have yours ready to share with me?" Parker glanced at Bass, grinning as he caught Angela gawking at him in the rear view mirror.

"Dear," Linnea said. "I think our cover's blown."

Angela gripped her mother's arm. "Mom. Dad. *Please*. Parker and I each have our own places. We make good money. Sometimes we work the same shift. Some days we don't. Like he said, until we knew workplace relationships were okay, we didn't make our interest known. Now can we stop with *the Doug inquisition*?"

"Sorry, Parker," Bass offered, pulling into a parking space. "Angela you're right. I apologize, baby."

Linnea patted Angela's hand. "Honey, ask Caleb. We did the same thing with Izzy when he brought her home the first time. You'd think we'd learn. We'll always be your parents wanting the best for you."

Parker held out his hand to Bass. "Angela's told me about Doug. I feel the same way you do about making sure she's safe and appreciated. I'm the same way with my sisters. Even when my mom remarried. No offense taken, sir."

Bass clasped Parker's hand, firmly shaking it. He turned so Linnea and Angela could see his face. "I like this one, Angela. He passes muster. Good pick."

"Thanks, Dad. Now can we go eat? I'm starving."

Ten minutes later they were seated and placing their orders. Large baskets of steaming fresh bread and butter sat middle of the table next to three large pitchers of lemonade. As the meal progressed, Bass regaled Parker with stories of fishing and hunting with his father. Linnea shared some of her favorite Fiona memories. Two hours passed, filled with good food and lots of different conversation topics.

Angela smiled as she sat next to Parker, holding hands on the ride back to her parents'. Having Parker with her felt so right. A sense of peace and calm enveloped her. She loved tonight. She'd—if she dared acknowledge what her gut and heart just murmured—fallen in love.

Angela covered her mouth almost at the same time Parker covered his. Neither of them was hiding their yawns very well. Even her dad and mom yawned. They'd come through a day of stress and grief mixed with joy and some laughter. Tomorrow would hold some of the same. Bidding Grandma Fiona good-bye hurt on many levels. Shared pain helped ease the passing. Remembering her joy and passions along with the wonderful loving memories they'd all share would help them start on their journey of healing and moving into the next phases of their lives. Angela knew Fiona would always be a part of hers every time she prepared one of the recipes they'd come up with together.

As Bass turned into the drive leading to the house, he glanced in the rearview mirror. He smiled. Parker had his arm around Angela, propping her against him as she slept. He rested his head on top of hers as he slept. Bass glanced at Linnea, winked and said, "I think those two are in love."

"You may be right. I noted how they looked at each other throughout dinner. There's a definite connection that goes pretty deep. I hope they work out." Linnea laid her hand on Bass's arm and squeezed.

Parker roused first, slowly uprighting Angela. "Sweetie, we're here."

Angela blinked, yawned and blinked again. "Oh, yeah. Damn, we forgot to get our luggage out of Caleb's car."

"No worries," Linnea said as she opened the front passenger door. "Caleb texted me he put them in the house on his and Sara's way to Kelso's."

"Glad Caleb did that," Parker said getting out and stretching. "I'm going to sleep sound tonight."

"Me too." Angela shut her door.

Twenty minutes later, silence ruled the house. Two couples, at different ends of the house, slept, knowing tomorrow required their focused attention and mutual support.

Twelve hours later-Spanish Bay Beach-17 Mile Drive

Six cars pulled into parking spaces along the parking area close to the beach walkway. The doors of the largest car opened and six people got out.

Angela smoothed her hands down her teal blazer. The multicolored skirt and top she wore were a gift from Fiona on one of their last shopping trips together into San Francisco's garment district. As they shopped for the fabrics to make the outfit, they'd talked about life, what brought each of them joy and courage mixed with the will to go on. Fiona had pointed out how dressing in rich vibrant colors helped lighten her mood even when things seemed the darkest. Angela had begun to appreciate the sentiment as they sat watching the sun set out over the bay. Life was filled with color that could represent an array of sentiments, emotions, and aspects in different ways depending on the person and where they were at in their life.

Parker stood next to her wearing a navy suit, blue-checkered shirt and navy tie. She'd complimented him as they dressed. His cheeks tinged slightly as he thanked her. He admitted he wasn't used to getting compliments on what he wore, adding most of the time he was in black or blue work uniforms. He stepped up next to her, taking her hand.

"Are you ready?" Parker asked.

"Are you ever ready to say good-bye? I think that's the hardest part of death. The saying good-bye and getting used to the empty space the person used to fill." Angela wet her lips and continued. "If you believe in a hereafter, you're never really alone. According to Fiona, your loved ones check on you and are there if you open your heart and mind to the still small voice within."

Parker nodded. "Spirituality teaches us to have faith and believe in the living essence of all things. Mom used to say that Dad was around when we needed him if we just took time to listen and talk with him. I learned that tapping into our memories and the things they taught us allows us to experience their presence again."

Linnea and Bass walked up beside them. "Reverend O'Neil asks that we lead the way down the walkway. Angela, you came here with Fiona more than any of us. What part of the beach was her favorite?"

"When there weren't a lot of people on it. She liked watching the waves and listening to them crash upon the beach. Often we'd find a place to sit and watch the sky, waves and people in general. She referred to this as her cleansing spot. The one place where air, water and sun washed over and through her." Angela pointed toward a rocky spot partway down the walk. "She often stopped there, adding a rock to the growing pile of balanced artwork folks made there. Saying if she could help someone add balance and order to their life with her anonymous addition, the day and time spent here was worth it."

"I think that's the place to spread our vial. I wish I could have met Fiona in person. She sounds like an awesome lady who cared about others, gave of herself without asking in return, accepted help when it came and graciously acknowledged those that graced her and Will's life with love, joy and acceptance," Parker offered.

Bass slipped his arm around Linnea's waist, hugging her close. "Honey, I think we're being told that's the spot." He pointed to the break in the clouds, the sun beamed down almost directly on the rock grouping. A group of seagulls flew over the rocks at the same time. Bass added, "Remember how she used to say seagulls were deity's signal to her all was heard and all right."

Linnea sniffled, wiping the tears off her cheek. "Yes, she did. I'm sure she's signaling that's the spot. Let's go."

Angela and Parker took the lead with her parents following. Behind them followed Caleb and her other siblings, along with the grandkids who understood the ritual they were part of. Fifteen people made their way down the walk, pausing to spread some of Fiona's ashes along the way. Reverend O'Neil led a brief prayer in Gaelic and English before emptying his vial into the surf licking the base of the rocks. Others shared a brief memory of their time with Fiona visiting the same beach. One last prayer was offered as they formed a semicircle around the rocks and, as if Fiona knew what they did, the sun beamed down on all of them, warming them.

Many tossed their vials into the ocean as a symbolic release of Will and Fiona wishing them well on the next phase of their eternal journey. Some kept the vial as a remembrance. Angela knew that tossing hers into the ocean her grandma loved to sit and watch signified a letting go that started the healing process. As she stepped off the walk one conversation in particular with Fiona came to mind. Fiona believed people came into your life for a reason and blessings often came with them. Angela knew Parker was one of those blessings. She was very glad he'd come into her life.

Thirty minutes passed as they made their way back to the cars and drove into Carmel-by-the-Sea. Seaview Bistro sat on Junipero Street close to the other main hotels. As they made their way into the dining room at the back of the restaurant, Angela noticed the artwork and decoupage mosaics lining the walls. Fiona's artist's talents mirrored the mosaics. Every art class they'd taken together opened doors to new thoughts and views. This was part of what had inspired Angela to move and find her own internal mosaic. One that she wouldn't finish designing until the day she entered the next phase of her existence. As she entered the room, Angela knew the time for sorrow ended. Time for remembering the joy, love, and happiness Fiona brought to all their lives began now.

Linnea and Bass spoke about how Fiona locked the two of them in a room shortly after they were married and arguing. She told them that shouting and hurling angry words at each other solved nothing. They could either talk it out quietly or stay in the room until they were done shouting. Laughter sounded as Linnea told about how they got very quiet and whispered angry words at each other until they started repeating each other. "Fiona unlocked the door, cracked it open and asked us if we'd run out of hot air or were gearing up for round two. Bass snorted. I clapped my hand over my mouth, unable to hold back my laughter. We learned a valuable lesson that day. Arguments happened. How we dealt with hearing each other out mattered. Fiona grinned as she opened the door completely. She later told us she heard us whispering and knew we had to really listen to each other to hear what was said."

Caleb talked about learning to cook. Fiona had insisted he help with meals when he visited, saying a man needs to know how to take care of himself and, later, his family after marriage. "I learned about budgeting and making lists so that I could afford the best ingredients my funds would buy to prepare nutritious meals without sacrificing taste and quality."

Angela smiled as her other siblings shared how Fiona touched their lives with lessons and time together that helped them with schoolwork, making important life decisions and finding joy in living a life well-lived. She stood as her youngest brother sat down.

"Figuring out how to remember Grandma Fiona was hard at first for me. Parker helped me figure out how to do that. Fiona taught me about balance. Life needs rebalancing at times, like when you make a bad choice. Getting up and moving forward takes focus and with that comes keeping your balance. Knowing when to let go, cuss or even stop to savor what life gives you. I learned about timing meal preparation, how vital that is to not burning all or part of a meal along with taking care of the food and items you're using. Not everything is replaceable. Knowing this prepared me for moving cross-country and starting a new life. One that brought change and choices. Thank you, Grandma Fiona, for showing me how to find my balance." Angela clasped Parker's hand as she sat down. He kissed her cheek and smiled. Rebalancing her life with Parker in and part of it was awesome.

Several others shared their memories as the servers brought in food. Fiona had provided the chef, a good friend of hers from high school, with several of her family's favorite recipes. For the next two hours, they ate and reminisced more. After the chef shared his Fiona memories, Reverend O'Neil and Mr. Baker stood, offering closing remarks, reminding them that either were available to answer questions or help as needed.

Caleb and Parker headed out first. Angela took a few moments to bid her nieces and nephews good-bye along with her siblings who were heading to their homes. She looked around wondering where Caleb and Parker were as she exited the restaurant. Bass and Linnea said the two of them were discussing something and pointing up and down the street before they walked off toward a section of shops two blocks down.

"Don't worry. Those two hit it off once baseball came up. Maybe they're window shopping and discussing the upcoming season," Sara said, holding up a set of car keys. "They either ride back with me or with your parents. I'm sure they'll be back soon."

"You're right. I'll wait here with Mom while Dad gets the car." Angela shaded her eyes, trying to make out where Parker and Caleb were.

"Thanks, Caleb," Parker said, exiting a shop. "I appreciate you covering for me with the baseball discussion."

Caleb laughed. "I don't know what you bought. Saying you needed a gift for my sister is reason enough. I bet she'll love whatever you got her."

Parker patted his suit coat pocket. "I hope so. too."

The antique dealer had cut him a deal when he explained what he wanted and why. The solitaire diamond sat center of two deep blue sapphires. A jewelry designer friend of his would take the stones and reset them in a new band making what was old new again. He watched Angela's reaction when Mr. Baker read the part of Fiona's will about what pieces of jewelry went to whom. Angela knuckled away a tear when she found out she was receiving the pieces that remained of the set Fiona's grandmother had bequeathed her. Angela had explained as they lay in bed how she had always worn the piece when she and her grandma Fiona had make-believe tea parties. A locket encrusted with blue sapphires and a small diamond bracelet were the secret identifiers that let the princess and her lady-in-waiting enter the tearoom incognito. Angela had gone on to share bits of the stories Fiona and she made up as they had sipped their lemonade from mismatched china cups and ate homemade shortbread. Parker patted his pocket one more time, knowing his heart hadn't told him wrong.

Caleb matched his pace as they trotted back down the street to where Angela and Linnea stood. Parker winked at Caleb and stood next to Angela. "Caleb mentioned the antique place down the street carried used baseball cards. My nephew Sean collects them. I went to see if they had a limited edition one for a player from the San Francisco Giants back in the Seventies. Sean turns seventeen this summer. That is a card he's been saving up for. "

"Did they have it?" Angela asked as Bass pulled up.

"No. The owner said he'd keep an eye out for it as he often goes to a collectibles flea market in Sacramento. He knows a guy who may have a way of getting one." Parker got in beside Angela. Sean would be surprised if the other purchase came through.

Parker quickly moved the box to his other pocket. Keeping it a surprise would take some effort. How long it would take his friend to design and make the new setting played into this. Hopefully, he could spring the surprise before Angela knew whether they were getting a bundle of joy nine months from now. For now he'd move forward with his plan once they were back in Peyton Corners.

Partway back to Gilroy, Parker's phone buzzed twice. He frowned as he looked at it. He nudged Angela, showing her the message.

"Doc's *what*?" Angela gasped.

CHAPTER TWENTY-EIGHT

"Getting hitched. Giving married life another try, to quote him. He's off on his honeymoon." Parker scrolled through two more messages. "Repairs on our clinic are on hold. Doc found more damage. Furnace is dead and a water pipe burst. We're assigned to either the hospital or a new clinic opening across town."

"Couldn't tell from the outside when we retrieved my SUV." Angela took out her phone. "I got a text from Doc too. I'm to call the hospital HR department when we get back."

"Yeah, me too." Parker slipped his phone back into his suit coat pocket.

"You need to go back early?" Bass asked, looking in the rearview mirror.

"No, Dad. We've got the rest of the week." Angela leaned forward and patted her Dad's shoulder. "We're here to help you and Mom."

Linnea turned slightly in her seat. "Thanks, honey. Remember Fiona believed in being prepared. She had a directive set up with the social worker at the assisted living facility. They're packing her things up and cleaning out the apartment."

"I think maybe a potluck family dinner is in order," Bass offered. "Parker gets to meet more of the family. You get to help with cooking which I know you and your Mom enjoy doing together. I also get to use my new barbecue."

Linnea laughed. "Just don't try to cook half a cow on it. Your last attempt damn near sent the prior grill up in flames."

Bass shot Linnea a look. Angela knew that look. The wounded male ego one. She pressed her lips together, trying to keep the grin threatening to form suppressed. Both of her brothers practiced the look until they could almost mimic it perfectly. Blessings abounded that Parker wasn't like that. At least not about his cooking.

Angela settled back against the seat closer to Parker. He looped his arm around her shoulders, getting as close to her as he could without undoing his seatbelt. Both of them could use the time off. Resting and relaxing sounded wonderful. Bless Fiona for gifting all of them with this family time.

Four days later-San Francisco Airport Hotel

Angela looked down at the pregnancy test. The results would show in another forty seconds. She knew the answer already. Cramps, bloating and spotting arrived one right after the other around four that morning. Still, peeing on the strip and waiting for the results made sense. Her sister Lucy had her periods for three months more after she found out she was pregnant.

She took a deep breath, exhaled and turned on the bedside lamp. She raised the test stick to eye level and frowned. A bold blue minus symbol showed. Her nausea was due to her period starting. Angela wiped a tear off her cheek.

Parker sat down next to her. "Why the tears?'

"I'd liked the idea I was going to be a mom. Now I'm not. Silly expectations, I guess." Angela slipped her arm around Parker's waist and hugged him. "Sorry."

"Nothing to be sorry about. I dreamt of two little girls one night. Another about a little boy with your hair and my eyes. Sweetums, we're going to be parents. Just not now. We want to be parents. We'll know when the time is right." Parker hugged her back.

"I'm glad we didn't say anything to Mom and Dad. Izzy is a gem for getting us the test kit on the QT." Angela sighed. "At least we've got a few more hours until we have to be at the airport. More sleep and then food, please."

Parker rose, took the test stick from her, and laid it on the nightstand. "More sleep and food, yes. We can take an extra day too. Do some sightseeing and unwind more."

Angela got back in the bed and covered up. Parker turned off the lamp and got in beside her. She cuddled up to him, enjoying his warmth and presence. Quietly they lay with their arms around each other, enjoying the moment in the semi-dark room.

"I'd rather spend that day with you at home. Your place or mine. I love my family. I love parts of California. Peyton Corners is home. It's where our things are. I wanna go home." Angela turned so she faced Parker. "Does that make sense?'

Parker kissed her and pulled back some. "It does. Angela, I've got something to tell you."

"Okay. What?"

"Remember when I said I thought I was falling in love with you?" Parker cupped her chin.

"Yes." She didn't look away.

"I don't need to think about it anymore." Parker leaned forward until his forehead rested on hers. "I love you, Angela Sewald."

"Know what?" she asked.

"I gave up reading minds. How about you tell me?" Parker combed his fingers through her hair.

"Yes, I'll tell you. I love you, too Parker Jones."

Their lips met, sharing two brief kisses before yawns overtook them. Parker settled her against him, spooning to her, and spread the covers over them. Getting on the plane later together, going home together made sense, felt right and left no doubts in her mind that listening to her heart's desire brought her much joy and happiness. She and Parker had a lot to talk about and figure out once they got back.

CHAPTER TWENTY-NINE

Peyton Corners, Two Weeks Later

Angela slowed as she started down her driveway's incline. Still no calls from Parker. He'd said he'd call on his way home this morning. A week of hit-and-miss texts and short calls had to mean something was wrong. Doug had done the same thing. So had a few other guys. One-night stands, short-lived affairs, and her stupid mistake in marrying the braying ass Doug. Where had this gone wrong? Or what unspoken message had she misread?

She took a deep breath, slowly exhaled and refocused her thoughts. Parker apologized in his last two calls, even sent her several texts during the day before he slept and a few as he worked. Neither of them had much free time in the last two weeks. She'd pulled two double shifts herself and worked two weeks straight without a day off. Lots of colds, flu, and spring births kept the emergency room hopping. Doc Stilwell's retirement had caught the clinic by surprise. None of them blamed him. Twenty-five years practicing medicine left little time for relaxation and recreation. She hoped Doc and his new bride found bliss in their new home in Hawaii.

She braked as her front flowerbed came into view. A section of her tulips and daffodils was missing. Had the neighbor's kids raided her garden again? Flowers for their mom. The new couple and their three children had moved in right after the snowstorm. Spending it holed up in a hotel room had been a blessing for them. Television and room service for three days kept the rambunctious triplets occupied while their parents read and relaxed. Now if they could stop helping themselves to the joint flowers they planted with her, there might be a chance to enjoy them. The triplets had already waded through the wildflower patch separating the two properties.

She looked up as she continued down the drive toward the house. She squinted, shook her head and sighed. Who was on her front porch? Had her neighbor come to apologize again? Angela grinned the closer she got. There was no mistaking who it was. Parker slumped in Fiona's rocker. He looked like he was asleep. Poor man. He'd worked two twelve-hour shifts with barely eight hours between to eat and sleep. The new clinic he was helping out at was forty-five minutes away. She bet he'd come straight from work. Wait—where was his truck?

Angela parked and got out. She hated to wake him. Did he need a ride home? Would he accept her invitation to stay? She missed his cuddles as they slept. Missed his intermittent bouts of snoring. Even his fake denials he didn't snore. She closed the door with a quiet click. As she started up the steps, her gaze roved over Parker, taking in his tousled hair, the dark beard line along his cheeks, and a couple of soft snores. Her smile widened as she got to his hands. In his right one, he clutched several of her tulips and daffodils. In his left he held. . .she couldn't quite make out what it was.

She moved up alongside the rocker, leaned down and whispered, "Time to wake up, Parker. I love you."

Parker stirred and snored more. Angela pressed her lips together, suppressing her mirth. He was out. How long had he been waiting? She wished he'd told her he was coming over. She would have given him a key to get in. But when in the last two weeks had their paths crossed, other than to wave across the emergency room on two of the busiest nights? She leaned closer, brushed her lips across his cheek and repeated, "Parker, time to wake up. I love you."

Parker blinked, tried to stifle his yawn and looked up. Angela stood in front of him, grinning. Damn, he'd closed his eyes for a moment trying to fight off his sleepiness. Mitch had dropped him off after they'd dropped his truck at the dealership for work. Loaning Mitch his truck for the day made sense. His mom needed help moving furniture. Parker yawned again, blinked and straightened. He clutched the box in his left hand tighter. Would Angela say yes? Or was he imagining the two soft 'I love you' he heard?

His gut clenched as she pointed at him. "You know, you could have asked before helping yourself to my flowers."

"Yeah, but they're so pretty, darling. Just like you." He scooted to the edge of the rocker. "Please forgive me."

He stood, squatted down on one knee, laying the crumpled bouquet on the porch close to Angela's feet. "It's hard for this country gent to resist such pretty things like them and you."

"Oh, I might forgive you." Angela started to squat down.

"Hold on darling. I got something that might help my apology." He looked up as he opened the box, holding it forward, he continued. "Angela Sewald, you got my heart. You're my joy. You add a whole lot of love and sunshine to my world. Spend the rest of your life with me, please."

Angela gasped, dropped down on her knees beside Parker, cupping his face with both hands as tears started. She kissed Parker twice and nodded. "Yes, Parker Jones, I'll marry you and spend the rest of our lives together. I love you."

Parker slipped the ring on her finger, kissed her finger and stood. He took her hands in his. "I love you, too. Here's to us."

As they entered the house, Angela knew she'd come full circle. Shared good and bad times with Parker. Learned what made a good relationship and even set the foundation for their loving friendship turned into relationship. Maybe there was a bit of truth to something Doc Stilwell had told them at the last Christmas party. Love finds you when you least expect it. It sure had for her and Parker. They'd each found their heart's desire.

THE END

Don't miss out!

Visit the website below and you can sign up to receive emails whenever Solara Gordon publishes a new book. There's no charge and no obligation.

https://books2read.com/r/B-A-RAUJ-YOQDB

BOOKS 2 READ

Connecting independent readers to independent writers.

About the Author

Solara loves and lives with her partner of 21 years in the Metro DC area. What started out as a bi-coastal romance soon settled on one coast.

A vivid imagination keeps her busy creating her next fascinating romance. She enjoys creating unique characters and watching their journeys unfold. "Love freely given multiplies and will return endlessly" is a key aspect of her stories. Add in alternative lifestyles and her love for the paranormal, and the uncommon becomes the norm in many of her stories.

Her day job in the financial services industry pays the bills while she pens her erotic tales.

Read more at https://solaragordon.com/.

www.ingramcontent.com/pod-product-compliance
Lightning Source LLC
Chambersburg PA
CBHW051644260626
47170CB00004B/1332